The Key:
Book One of the Sophie Lee Saga

The Sophie Lee Saga, Volume 1

Stormi Lewis

Published by C.S. Press, 2021.

STORMI LEWIS

This is a work of fiction. Similarities to real people, places, or events are entirely coincidental.

THE KEY: BOOK ONE OF THE SOPHIE LEE SAGA

First edition. October 1, 2021.
Second Edition. January, 7, 2026.

Copyright © 2021 Stormi Lewis.

Written by Stormi Lewis.

No part of this work may be used for AI training or reproduced in any manner whatsoever without written permission, except in the case of brief quotations embodied in critical reviews and articles.

For information, contact Stormi Lewis:
cspresspublishing@gmail.com

This work is 100% organic. No part of it was created by AI.

THE KEY

Discover us online:

https://linktr.ee/chasingstormi

STORMI LEWIS

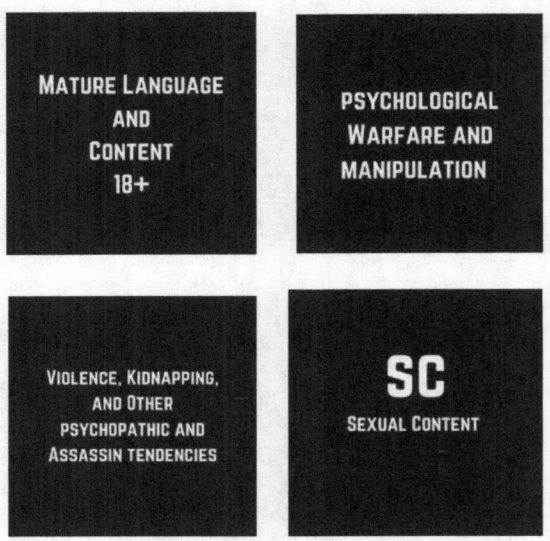

Full list of Trigger Warnings is listed at
https://linktr.ee/chasingstormi

THE KEY

Praise for
The Key

"The Borne Identity meets Atomic Blonde... that's the story of The Key in a nutshell! I love a kick-ass female lead and Sofie Lee is definitely that!"
- Stephen Galgon, Author of The Circle series

"There is not a dull moment in this book, each page contains twists, turns and tidbits about each character. A nicely woven web of mystery and action that moves seamlessly from present day to plot-changing memories. I can't wait to learn more about Sophie and her family in the next books in the saga! Easy and fun to read, I felt like I was a part of the story."
- Good Read Review

"You want romance? You got it! A solid mystery? You got it! A twisty thriller with LOTS of action? YOU GOT IT! If you want a quick and fun read-pick this one up! I'll be looking out for #2."
- Good Read Review

"Lewis choreographed the fight scenes brilliantly, and Sophie's memories are written like she's an audience member watching her younger self. The ending will leave you reeling for more! What did they find?! I can't wait to see what book two will bring to the table!"
- Santana Sanders, Author

"I was connected with the characters so much that at a certain point I wasn't sure if I was rooting for the right side! This is not my usual type of genre, but badass assassins always lure me. I was so please with Sophie's character, it was pretty intriguing!... The story read like a movie, there was a ton of action and suspense. Finding out the secrets kept me glued to the story!"
- Amazon Review

STORMI LEWIS

To Shyera McCollough Thomas, who convinced me to go back to my roots, helped me find my way. Shyera convinced me that this story was worth sharing with the world and kept me going on my weakest of days.

To my parents, who put up with me throughout the entire process, and let me talk their ear off per usual on a daily basis. To my dad, who took the extra time to help me edit this book, and to my mother, who also put in valuable feedback.

To Mario, for challenging me to step outside of my comfort zone, talking me into writing my first saga, and for giving me a noble character to write about.

To my beta readers, that gave me valuable feedback to make this book the best version of itself for you.

Last, to my Storm Chasers, who never stop conquering their personal storms while supporting my passions and personal growth. I would not be here without you.

THE KEY

One

Her hand stretched forward, turned the handle, and pushed open the door. She covered her eyes as light quickly filled the room. In front of her sat a little girl around the age of seven with pale skin as bright as the moon and curly red hair that cascaded down her back. The little girl sat cross-legged on the floor surrounded by books, including the *Anne of Green Gables* novel she clenched in her hands. A smile crept across her lips. Just then, a tall, thin man with short brown hair snuck up behind her and covered her eyes.

"Peanut," he whispered. "It's time to get moving."

"Just a few more pages," whined the little girl, without moving a muscle.

"But the world has great things for you today," he said with bright hope. "Books will get you far, but living life to the fullest will get you further."

She lowered the book to give him an annoyed look, but he just laughed.

"Come on," he said, smiling and holding out his hand. "I'll make it worth your while."

The little girl lowered her book with resignation, but took his hand with a smile.

Then the man looked right at her, eyes full of alarm and with great urgency as he yelled, "Peanut...RUN!"

She sat up immediately, heart racing and gasping for breath. She knew better than to ignore his warning. She quickly grabbed the backpack beside her, flung it on her back, and raced for the fire escape. She just needed a little rest. She was so tired. But stopping meant dying, and that wasn't an option. She took a deep breath, grabbed the railings, and slid down the fire escape before landing gracefully on her feet and running down the black street and into the night.

"Why do we keep coming to these parties?" James asked with a mixture of annoyance and resignation. It was yet another mansion in Virginia, owned by someone Tina knew, in the middle of nowhere. The house was crammed with half naked twenty something year old's inside and out, and various empty to full red plastic cups of alcohol strewn everywhere. No one could move, let alone hear themselves think with the pop music that blared from the sound system nearby. James estimated that people in New York could probably hear it, but no one had bothered to call the cops yet.

THE KEY

"Because you love them so dang much," replied his best friend, Ben, laughing as he took another sip of his beer.

James glared at his friend before laughing and rolling his eyes to the ceiling.

"We probably wouldn't have to go to so many if you would just mate already and get Tina off both our backs," Ben said, nudging James in the ribs.

"I love that girl to pieces, but her goal to get me matched and married is totally unnecessary," James said as he went to take a sip of his own beer before putting it down in disgust. "I think I'm going to get some air." He got up and wandered out onto the private balcony, but it was full of people. In desperate need of some solitude, James headed down the stairs and walked toward the tree line of the backyard forest. He always loved the woods. They reminded him of home and helped block out the fact that Tina had spent the last couple of hours introducing him to countless women that did nothing for him. Maybe some distance would allow his swirling head and what felt like an empty heart to clear. He headed closer to the woods.

This new crew was definitely persistent, she thought to herself as she zigzagged through the forest. Too bad they wouldn't take a night off. She could use the rest to recharge her batteries. The night was on her side, and the forest thick of trees. She could maneuver anywhere, but the forest was a delightful change of pace. The east coast was proving to be pleasing. But pop music playing broke the silence in the distance. What the heck? She thought nothing was out this far, but she was learning that there were random houses miles apart out here. All the others had been dead to the world as she passed them. Without even realizing it, her feet headed towards the music. There was enough distance. It wouldn't hurt to check it out. It might be a suitable cover. Plus, the curiosity was too much to ignore.

It took a while, but she finally reached the house, making so much noise. Young people seemed to fill the house inside and out, laughing, dancing, playing games, and having a good time. She slowed her pace down and crept like a ninja up to the edge of the tree line. Her heart ached while she watched hundreds of men and woman enjoying life without a care in the world. That was supposed to be her life, too. Until the fate of the world was put in her hands without asking for permission. They had no clue what was really going on in the world, and that was how it was supposed to be. She drew the short straw in life, but she also knew they forced her because she could do what was needed. She took a step closer, and a twig snapped under her shoe. She froze immediately.

"Hello?" she heard a male voice ask with curiosity. She held her breath, willing with all her might that he would drop it and walk away.

"Is someone there?" he asked.

Then a sound much more disturbing was heard way behind her. The sound of a gun preparing to be fired. Crap! She'd gotten distracted and now someone was going to pay for her mistake. She picked up her foot gracefully and slid down the tree with her back to it to allow her eyes to adjust to the darkness once more. She closed her eyes and heard twigs snapping as the team closed in. They were still far enough away she could draw them away. She took a deep breath and sprinted forward before zagging to the left and trying to lead them further into the forest.

James started walking towards the noise he had heard. He knew he wasn't alone, but surely it was just an innocent deer out for a midnight stroll. When suddenly, a slim black figure shot up from behind a tree and sprinted like the wind deeper into the forest. "Or not," he said to himself, cautious and curious at the same time. Surely it wasn't some drunk idiot that had strayed from the party that was going to get themselves lost. Not running like that. Something wasn't right. He didn't like it at all. "Well, I guess I'm going for a jog," he said to himself, took a deep breath, and tried to keep up with the figure in front of him. Damn, they were fast! At least he had his running shoes on.

Seriously?! Someone was on her tail, but it wasn't with the team. Who the heck was following her? Ugh! She didn't have time for this! She halted and slid behind a tree and waited. It wasn't long before the stranger reached her. He slowed his run down and tried to slow down his breathing. "Dang it!" he cursed under his breath, and slowly started moving towards her hiding spot.

In a swift movement, she reached out and grabbed him, pushing his body up against the tree and holding her hand over his mouth. He was surprised, but didn't move. She looked around the tree, cocked her head to listen, and waited a full minute before assessing what she had to deal with. She turned to find the deepest blue eyes she had ever seen, and her heart skipped a beat. For a split second, she completely forgot where she was and what she was doing. She held a finger to her lips as she slowly removed her hand from his incredibly warm lips. He nodded slowly. She reluctantly took a step back. He was about 5'9", athletically built with a slight tan. His light brown hair was short and spiked on the top. A smile crept on his lips as he stared into her eyes. Whoa, she thought to herself.

"Why are you running?" he whispered softly.

She put her hands on his shoulder and looked around the tree again before returning to slowly slide him down the tree. She couldn't run with him in tow. She would have to take them out. She looked around at her options. There weren't many.

She slid the backpack off her back and handed it to him. She pointed to his chest and then to where he was already sitting. Apparently, the stern look on her face encouraged him to nod again, and he pulled her backpack to his chest and waited. She tilted her head in amusement as a smile reached the corner of her mouth before she took off, running back in the direction from where they came.

James clasped the bag to his chest and tried to digest what he had just seen. The first woman to actually take his breath away at first sight. Her bright blue eyes seemed to look directly into his soul. Though her short, chin length black hair was messy, and her face a little dirty, she was the most beautiful thing he had ever seen. She was thin, but athletically built, and pale as the moon's light, with black clothing that clung nicely to her curves. He did not know why she was running, or who was after her, but he found himself instantly drawn to protect her at all costs. How could that be when she hadn't even said a word? How could a complete stranger have such an effect on him? He had no clue, but he had to try and find out more.

Once she reached a spot that was far enough away, she quickly climbed up the tree and waited in the branches, slowing her breathing down. She could knock them out, but that just meant they would chase her once they woke up again. Although that was usually her first choice, it might be time to defend herself. Either option meant it confirmed that she was there putting others in danger, but she couldn't run with the man who insisted on following her and was currently hiding behind a tree waiting for her return. So much for getting away quietly.

A heavyset man holding a gun with a silencer and dressed in all black ops attire, crept closer to her. Why did he have a silencer? Wasn't the order to take her in alive? Well, that definitely helped to decide.

She waited until he was right underneath her before jumping onto his shoulders and quickly snapping his neck. She picked up the gun and dashed forward to her next position of attack.

She closed her eyes to listen better. Five distinct footstep patterns headed her way. Well, at least there was a manageable number this time. They were approaching in a staggered line formation, giving her enough time to take each one out individually. Not their usual M/O, but everything about this team had been different from the rest. However, this wasn't the time to analyze their strategy.

She quietly slid her back down the tree and waited for a tall blonde man to walk past her before she took the kill shot. She quickly checked his neck for a pulse, despite knowing there wouldn't be one, and zig zagged to her left. An average brunette woman of athletic build was headed her way. She'd never seen her before. None of them, actually. This was definitely a different crew, and they weren't exactly moving quietly through the forest. It was almost like they wanted her to take them out. What the heck was going on? But before she could think anymore, she felt the barrel of the silencer on the back of her head.

"Drop it," whispered a male with a Russian accent.

She dropped the gun she held in her hand and put her hands up.

"I hope you're ready to die tonight, because I'm done chasing you, Bitch," the man said, panting down the back of her neck.

"But I thought we were having so much fun," she said flatly.

"Where is it?" he yelled, pushing the barrel deeper into her skull.

"I think I left it in my other outfit," she said sarcastically.

"Give it to me!" he shouted, jamming the gun into what felt like her eye sockets.

"You know, the last team was a lot more fun," she said, trying to buy some time while she caught her breath. It was going to have to be quiet and quick.

"I'm losing my patience!" he yelled, lifting the gun off her skull just enough to allow her to spin around, grab it, point it at his chest, and pull the trigger. He was bigger than expected and made more noise falling than she desired. A shot grazed by her eye. She quickly ducked and took off running. The brunette was in hot pursuit, but when she turned the corner, she ran right into what felt like a brick wall, and stumbled backwards, trying to catch her footing.

THE KEY

"UGH!" James breathed out as he stumbled backward to catch his own footing. By the time he found it, she had grabbed his hand and was yanking him behind her. Luckily, the backpack was already on his back, because they were weaving and dodging through the forest faster than he could truly keep up when they suddenly came to a halt.

"Go that way," she said, shoving him to the left of her, and she took off to the right before he could ask any questions. But she didn't get far before she heard the brunette yell, "STOP! Or I'll shoot." She couldn't catch a break if her life depended on it! Once again, she held her hands up in the air and turned around.

"Where is it, my love?" the brunette asked, with a voice smooth as jazz and a crooked smile on her lips.

"You know, everyone keeps asking me, but I just can't seem to remember...." she said, matching her opponent's tone.

"Now, no one wants to hurt you, Love," said the brunette, adding more sweetness to her tone.

"That's funny, considering you are all using silencers and you've already shot at me once tonight," she said, raising her eyebrows as the corner of her lips curled up.

"Here," said the brunette, putting the gun on the ground. "Better?"

"Not for you," she said, smiling a little wider.

"Listen," coaxed the brunette. "We're all a little tired, so why don't you just give it to me and we can call it a day?"

"Well, technically it's night," she said, tilting her head as she watched the brunette slowly walk towards her.

"I know you're tired. You've been running for so long. Just give us what we want. You can even put it in my hand and no harm will come to you," the brunette said, smiling as she held out her hand.

"Yeah, just not feeling it," she said more flatly.

"Come on now," the brunette said, nearly right in front of her when they both heard the twig snap and the brunette quickly had her in a headlock.

"Let her go!" James said, aiming the gun at them both.

"This doesn't concern you, Handsome," said the brunette sweetly.

"Well, seeing as you're holding my friend in a headlock, I'm going to have to disagree," he said sweetly and grinning from ear to ear. It was hypnotic.

"Your friend just needs to give me what I want, Honey, and then we can all go home," the brunette cooed.

"She can't give it to you because I have it," said James, trying desperately to ignore the glaring look coming from the woman he was anxiously trying to save.

"Well, doesn't that change things," said the brunette.

"Not really," she said before elbowing the brunette in the stomach and quickly dislocating her shoulder connected to the arm that had been around her neck. The brunette stumbled backwards and quickly found her footing before lunging right at her.

James tried to focus his eyes in order to wing the brunette, but they were moving too quick to get a clear shot. Then, out of nowhere, a shot buzzed by his shoulder. He immediately spun around and took aim. An average built blonde man was dodging around a tree and taking shots at all of them, so James ran to the tree closest to him and returned fire. After a couple of shots, James was able to take him out. When he turned around, the brunette had her pinned by the throat up against a tree. He immediately took the shot. The brunette released her grip and fell to her knees before falling forward on her face. James ran up to her as she rubbed her sore throat.

"Are you okay?" he asked urgently. She nodded while massaging her reddened throat. "Come on. We've got to get out of here." He went to grab her elbow to help her up, and she jumped back instinctively, her eyes wide like a deer looking into headlights. "Hey," he whispered, raising his hands in the air. "I'm the good guy." She dropped her eyes to the ground. "But since I'm guessing there are more dead bodies in this forest, I'm thinking this probably isn't the best place to be hanging out," James whispered softly.

She looked up at him and nodded while slowly getting to her feet. She held out her hand, and he shook his head. "I've got the bag," he said. "The road's just up ahead. We can follow it back," and without waiting for her to disagree, he started walking towards the road.

They walked in silence for a few minutes before James asked hopefully, "So, do you have a name?" keeping his eyes straight ahead, but she made no response. After a few minutes of walking in silence, he tried again. "What's in the bag?"

"Supplies," she replied flatly.

"Don't suppose you're going to tell me who's after you or what they want, huh?" James responded.

"Bad guys and no," she said, with a hint of humor in her voice. Hope strongly swelled in his chest.

"Is it in the backpack? Cause I was hoping I actually had it," he said with a boyish grin.

"Nope," she said, returning his smile.

"Damn," he replied as they reached the road. "House should be less than a mile that way," he said, nodding his head to the left. She nodded yes and followed in suit.

She heard the engine rev up before she saw the black van gunning in their direction. She quickly shoved him to safety before turning around and getting blinded by headlights. She instinctively jumped into the air and felt her feet push off the hood. Her body slammed against the windshield, cracking it. She rolled across the top of the van and eventually landed on the road behind it. Darkness filled her head.

Unable to open her eyes, she listened to the wheels speed off into the distance. She felt hair being brushed away from her face as a frantic male voice whispered in her ear, "You're going to be okay. Stay with me! I've got you."

She was exhausted. Maybe if she just rested for a second. She was so tired….

She was in and out of consciousness. James was pretty sure she had a concussion, and a few broken bones, for starters. His first thought was to take her to the hospital, but when he mentioned he was taking her there, she begged desperately not to go. He guessed it had to do with the people trying to kill her in the woods. The only other place he could think of was his parent's house, but it was a few states away.

Tina had made it the safest place to be if anything happened, and his dad's friend, Dr. Stephens, could look her over. If it was anything too serious that required a hospital, he would have to come up with a Plan B. For now, he would have to keep chugging caffeine, chew on caffeinated gum, and take minimal bathroom breaks until they arrived safely. After all, she had just saved his life at least twice. It was the least he could do. He also wasn't ready to part ways just yet, but he was sure it had to do with making sure she was okay. Didn't it?....

She opened her eyes partially to see rapid passing of lights late in the night. She was in a moving car, headed to who knew where, when a warm soft hand gently grabbed hers. "We'll be there soon," whispered a male voice with a hint of panic. She needed more sleep. She closed her eyes and drifted off again.

"S-o-p-h-i-e..." sang a woman's voice. "It's time to wake up and play a game! Can you figure out where you are?..."

Sophie slowly opened her eyes, and immediately every inch of her body ached. She quickly closed her eyes to make the pain go away, with no success. She tried to focus on more pleasant things, like the soft, warm bed she currently laid in.

"Get up, Peanut," whispered a male voice in the distance.

She had absolutely no desire to, but Sophie forced her eyes open all the same. She turned her head slowly to the left and saw the sun creeping into the curtains, with the sounds of waves breaking against the rocks. She was on the coast somewhere.

Wincing with some pain, Sophie turned her head slowly to the right to find a young man sleeping uncomfortably in the chair next to her, holding her hand. It was warm and soft, and felt like it oddly belonged.

Sophie studied him in the sunlight that was filling the room. He had very distinguished facial features, with short, light brown hair and wild spikes on top. His lips were full and a light shade of pink. He was in flannel pajama bottoms and a grey t-shirt that did nothing to hide his bulging muscles. Athletic for sure. He seemed to know her, but she couldn't think of his name to save her life. Come to think of it...she couldn't think of hers either. Panic set in.

Sophie carefully pulled her hand out from underneath his and assessed her own body. There was a long bandage on her right arm and left leg, and her ribs seemed to be taped, but it still hurt to breathe. What the heck happened? She closed her eyes to remember, but all she could see were bright lights coming right at her, forcing her to open them abruptly.

Maybe looking around would jog her memory? When she removed the covers, it relieved her to see she was at least dressed in a t-shirt and boxers, with her sports bra and underwear in place. The wooden floor was freezing under her bare feet. Sophie slowly stood up to quietly wander around the room.

On the nightstand next to her laid some books, a lamp, and a silver necklace with a smaller silver heart inside the larger one. She instinctively picked it up and watched it shine in the sunlight before putting it back on. The walls were bare except for one that was covered with pictures. There were various pictures of the man that slept in the chair with other people. She was guessing they were his friends and family. It looked like a girl and another boy, mostly, along with an older couple that Sophie assumed were his parents. She didn't recognize the younger couple, but the older man seemed familiar to her. She didn't see herself. She wondered how long they had known each other. Surely long enough. He had obviously slept by her side all night.

There were several trophies scattered throughout the room. Educational and athletic achievements. Two caps from graduations, books, and a desk in the corner. She lightly traced one of the golden trophies on his desk.

"What are you doing out of bed?" James asked with concern, forcing her to jump and knock the trophy off the desk. He rushed over to stop her from picking it up off the floor. She stared at the floor in embarrassment. "How are you feeling?" he asked, picking up the trophy and placing it back on the desk. Sophie shrugged and winced immediately.

"That's what I thought," he said, frowning. "Back to bed, Missy. I can bring you whatever you need." James pointed towards the bed with all the authority he could muster, forcing her to giggle and grab her ribs immediately. Although hearing her giggle enlightened his heart, he instantly felt guilty for causing her pain.

"I'm so sorry!" he said, rushing over to her. Sophie held up her hand and shook her head no. After a few quick breaths, she straightened up and smiled. James' heart skipped a beat. She was incredibly stubborn and drop dead gorgeous in his t-shirt and boxers.

"Are you hungry?" he asked, trying to ignore his overwhelming desire to kiss her. Sophie smiled and licked her lips. "You're killing me,

Smalls," James said under his breath as he took her hand and gently led her downstairs. The kitchen was bright, with its white kitchen cabinets and stainless steel appliances. The island and counter tops were a white marbled granite, with light yellow curtains on the windows. The floor had antique cement tiles, and was obviously designed to welcome the sun that came through the glass French doors and windows throughout the room. A large wooden table waited patiently to be used in the dining room. Sophie sat on one stool while James went to the other side to pull out supplies. "How about eggs, bacon, pancakes, and fruit?" he asked. Sophie's mouth dropped open. What army was he planning on feeding?

"What? Not enough?" he teased. She rolled her eyes. James picked up a large knife, and Sophie tensed up. He placed it on the counter after seeing her reaction and put his hands up, showing her he meant no harm. "Hey," James whispered. "I can't imagine what you've been through, but you're safe here. You have my word." Then he saw the look of confusion sweep over her face. He waited a second. "Do you remember what happened the other night?" James asked cautiously. Sophie looked at the floor, closed her eyes, and after a long pause, shook her head no.

"Do you remember your name?" James asked patiently. Sophie's eyes grew wide, and she started backing away with a slight look of terror in her eyes. Who was he if he didn't already know her? She began looking around frantically for an exit. "Whoa," James said softly, and moved around the island, but that just made Sophie retreat further away from him. He froze. "Okay," James said, a bit panicked. "My name is James," he said softly, locking his eyes to hers. "I found you the other night in the woods." Sophie went to look away to find a

THE KEY

quick exit, but his voice sounded familiar and she didn't really want to leave him. He was oddly comforting, which meant something. She just didn't know what.

"Some people were after you. I was trying to help," James drawled. "But one of them hit you with a van and you got hurt." Sophie closed her eyes and once again saw the headlights coming right at her. She jerked them open to find tears forming in her eyes. "I got you to my car, and began to drive you to the hospital," James continued with caution, "but you said you couldn't go. You were in and out of consciousness. So, I brought you to my parent's house and had a family friend look at you instead." He paused, observing her. Sophie looked at all of her bandages, noticing someone professionally wrapped her up. A flashback of the passing lights and James talking to her appeared for a split second and then was gone. "You've been resting for a couple of days. I was worried you would not wake up," he finished, with his eyes looking at the floor, trying not to think about it too much.

Sophie re-evaluated the man before her, who spoke to her with pain and panic in his voice. It seemed odd that a complete stranger would care so much for her safety. She couldn't remember anything before the accident. She was just going to have to trust her instincts, and they told her she was safe and in expert hands. After a moment or two, Sophie slowly took her seat at the island and nodded at James to finish making breakfast.

He didn't move at first. Mostly because he was overwhelmed with relief that she had moved closer to him. It was an odd sensation. He wasn't used to it, but he certainly didn't mind it. He slowly got back to work. Sophie watched him as he moved around the kitchen, cooking. She was pretty sure he didn't know that he had started humming while he cooked, and she found it charming and soothing. She enjoyed watching him buzz around. She could tell he was happy and content.

The front door flung open as Tina and Ben entered, carrying multiple bags. "I love you, but you realize we're only going to be here for a couple of months, right?" asked Ben jokingly.

"I don't comment on your driving, and you don't comment on me being prepared," Tina said smugly.

When she heard the door open, Sophie grabbed the large knife, jumped over the island, and pushed James back against the counter. She was shielding his body with her own while holding the knife up. It caught James off guard, but before he could do anything about it, Tina and Ben came around the corner and dropped their bags.

"Whoa" breathed Tina.

"Bro," said Ben cautiously.

"Hey," James whispered in her ear. "It's okay. These are my best friends. We stay here every summer since I was a little kid." Sophie flashed back to the pictures on his wall and realized these were the two people in all of his photos. She loosened her grip on the knife. James gently wrapped his right arm around her waist and took the knife from her left hand. "And it's not nice to point a knife at our house guests," he said in jest. Sophie looked at the floor in embarrassment, again, while James kept his arm around her stomach and shouted, "Hey gang!"

Tina noticed James' arm around her instantly. He had never been that close to a girl except her, and this wasn't to be taken lightly. "Um...hey," she said, trying to find her thoughts. "I'm Tina," she said, thrusting her hand in Sophie's direction and smiling. Sophie looked at it and shook it timidly. "This is my husband, Ben. Ben, come say hi silly." Ben stepped up cautiously and shook Sophie's hand.

Tina was in her early twenties, stood at 5'4" on a good day with blonde hair just past her shoulders and killer blue eyes to match. Her smile was warm and inviting, and her lips the perfect shade of light pink. Tina may have been short, but there wasn't an inch of fat to be found, for she had a solid athletic build that told everyone she wasn't to be messed with. She wore a blue romper, and white sandal heels that definitely gave the illusion that her legs went on forever. Sophie understood why Ben married her.

Ben, however, stood at 5'8", with short brown hair that was longer on top and looked like it did whatever it wanted. His hazel eyes were bright and innocent, and he had a decent tan going for so early in the summer. Although his demeanor was shy, Ben had his own athletic build. His Avengers t-shirt clung to his muscular arms and chest, and his khaki shorts did nothing to hide his powerhouse legs that carried him.

"Well, we have bacon, eggs, pancakes, and fruit. I bet you're starving!" James said, as if nothing had just happened. "Do you want orange juice?" he asked Sophie. She stuck her tongue out in response. "Okay," James laughed. "Cranberry?" She smiled sheepishly. "Cranberry it is!" he said, reluctantly letting her go and grabbing her a glass.

"So how did you two meet?" Tina started investigating.

"Oh, the other night at the party," said James, not skipping a beat. "She had a bit of an accident, and so I thought it best she come stay with us to recoup."

Tina and Ben's mouths fell open. "What kind of accident?" Tina pried as she took notice of the bandages on Sophie's limbs.

"She kinda got hit by a car. Dr. Stephen says she might have some memory loss, but he hopes she can regain it in a safe environment," James added nonchalantly.

"You poor thing!" exclaimed Tina. "Why isn't she in the hospital?" she exclaimed, throwing her wrath at James.

"Easy Ti," said James with his boyish grin. "Dr. Stephen looked her over thoroughly and said she's just a little banged up. He saw no reason for her to be cooped up in some stuffy hospital where she would know no one. We agreed it would be better for her to be surrounded by amazing people like you, Love," he said thickening his charm, hoping she would stop asking questions. Tina knew his tricks and realized he wanted her to drop it, so she would...for now.

"What's your name, Honey?" she asked, turning her attention back to Sophie. Sophie looked at James with a plea for help.

"We're not sure yet," he interjected, "but I'm sure we'll figure that out, too." James was sure of himself. Sophie was not so sure.

"Well, we can't exactly call her 'Hey you' for the next couple of months. Should we try to guess?" asked Tina, trying to figure out more about this mystery woman.

"I think she looks like a Jessica," Ben chimed in from nowhere. "Jess for short," he said triumphantly. Sophie thought about it, but ended up shaking her head. She didn't feel like a Jess.

"Megan?" Tina asked. Sophie shook her head. That didn't feel right, either.

"Sally?" James asked. Sophie stuck her tongue out in disgust.

"You're terrible at this," Tina teased James.

"That's my mother's name!" James protested.

Sophie got up to get more juice while they debated other

THE KEY

random names. She thought about the voices she heard when she woke up. Surely Peanut wasn't her *ACTUAL* name. Sophie stopped abruptly and turned so quickly that she spilled her fresh glass of juice. Her eyes were lit up with excitement.

"Did you remember something?" James asked cautiously. He'd never seen her so excited before. It was illuminating.

Sophie quickly put her glass down and began searching for a pen and paper. She found something to write on in the living room and scribbled as quickly as she could before racing back to James and handing it to him.

"Sophie," he said, reading the paper out loud. "Sophie?" he asked, looking at her.

She looked at them all and slowly nodded. At least that's what the voice called her this morning. Sophie didn't feel as confident sharing that part, but she felt like the name fit.

"Sophie it is!" Tina said, excited to have some sort of information about this strange woman that seemed to have her best friend's heart. Now, if Sophie could only remember the rest of it. At least it was a good start to Tina's investigation.

Two

After breakfast, James turned to Tina and asked, "Would you mind loaning Sophie something to wear? She had little with her and it's supposed to be quite humid today." Tina squealed with excitement, grabbed Sophie by her arm, and started dragging her up the stairs. James watched Sophie try not to wince from Tina's excitement and noted he would have to be more careful with his suggestions in the future. Ben eyed James suspiciously from across the couch.

"So, how did you really meet?" Ben asked casually.

"I told you," James said flatly, keeping his eyes on the stairs.

"Yeah. I heard. Now, how did you really meet?" Ben asked again.

"I already told you," James repeated, unfazed.

"You know how I always beat you at poker?" Ben asked.

"You do not," James said, reluctantly removing his eyes from

THE KEY

the stairs to look at his friend.

"James, you're the worst liar on the planet. Now, what did you leave out?" Ben asked, tilting his head in speculation.

"Fine, but you can't tell Tina, yet," James said. "She'll go full-on FBI and Sophie needs to heal first."

"You know I hate lying to my wife," Ben whined.

"You just said you 'always win at poker,' remember?" James said sarcastically. "Do you want to know or not?"

"Fine," Ben conceded.

"There was a team of people, I think, that had silencers and were trying to get something from her," James answered, as if it were no big deal.

"Seriously?!" shouted Ben.

"Ssshhh!" James hissed. "Whatever it is, it wasn't in the backpack that she had with her."

"People with guns are after her?" Ben hissed back.

"Relax," James said. "I covered our tracks, and there are several states between us at the moment. Plus, this house is Fort Knox, with your wife's security system. This is the safest place to be until she gets her memory back and we can find out what's going on."

"Seems risky, Buddy," Ben said, with his voice full of uncertainty.

"Well, I couldn't exactly leave her after she had saved my life, now could I?" asked James. He went back to staring at the top of the stairs.

"Then why do you keep staring at the stairs, Bro?" asked Ben, with a gigantic smile on his face. He saw exactly what Tina did, which meant Ben had his work cut out for himself in order to keep his wife's investigation to a minimum.

James forced himself to look at his friend and roll his eyes. "Don't be ridiculous," he added.

"Uh huh," replied Ben in triumph. James went back to staring at the stairs, hoping they would come back soon.

"Hhhmmm," Tina said, surveying her multiple opened suitcases strung across the king-size bed. It was covered in a white comforter with light blue accented pillows and blankets, and a couple of smaller pillows with a starfish on them. The headboard was white and made from cloth to match the comforter. Above the bed was a picture of the sea taken obviously by a professional photographer. The walls were grey, and the windows were covered with thin white curtains. The nightstands and dressers were all made of aged wood that someone had painted the frame a darker grey with antique white for the drawers and side panels. The carpet had a thin cream line that made a simple design throughout the light blue sea of carpet. There were various pictures someone had taken on a beach. The theme was definitely inspired by the water Sophie had heard when she first woke up.

"Definitely a t-shirt, some shorts, and some white sneakers," Tina said to herself. "Let's do the pink one with some jean shorts. That will really bring out your natural colors. Here!" she said, tossing Sophie some clothes. "Do you have make-up?" Tina asked, not skipping a beat. "Not that you need it. You've got great natural skin. I know it can help boost my spirits when I'm not feeling my best. Go on now. You can change in the bathroom. I'll wait here."

Sophie gathered her new outfit and trudged into the bathroom, closing the door. The seaside theme continued into the room. The tile on the floor looked like it was made of pebbles. The bathroom counter had his and her sinks and mirrors to match. The walls were painted a light teal, and pictures held within dark wooden frames shared more beach scenes and close-ups of kids smiling. She immediately identified the smiles coming from Tina, Ben, and James themselves. There were seashells and starfish as simple décor accents and a glass shower lined with blue and grey tile, big enough for two. When she saw her reflection in the mirror, the girl that looked back at her horrified her. Sophie was nothing but a hot mess.

"So, you don't remember ANYTHING?" Tina asked from the other side of the door. Sophie didn't answer. "You don't talk much, do you?" Tina continued, talking more to herself than to Sophie.

She stared at the image in the mirror. Sophie's bruising was more obvious against her pale skin and freckles. There was dried blood stuck in her hair. Her blue eyes had a grey tint to them, with a hint of melancholy and exhaustion. Meeting new people looking like this made her cringe. Sophie found a dark grey washcloth and tried to clean herself up a bit. Her black, straight, chin length hair looked like a rat's nest. Sophie hoped Tina had a brush she could borrow while she was at it. She opened the door once she done and laid James' t-shirt and boxers folded nicely on the bed.

"There you go!" Tina said brightly, already dressed and ready. "Now, let's fix that hair of yours." After brushing Sophie's hair, some makeup, and confirmation from Tina that they were ready to go back downstairs, they left to meet the boys. James opened his mouth a bit in shock, and Ben beamed from ear to ear.

"You look lovely ladies!" shouted Ben, standing up and walking over to kiss his wife on the cheek. James followed, unable to keep his eyes off of Sophie. Ben elbowed him in the ribs.

"Uh, yeah. Everyone looks great." James mustered.

"So, where are you taking us?" Tina said, smiling sweetly at Ben.

The boys looked at each other frantically and back at the girls. "We thought we would just stay in today," said Ben nervously.

"Yeah," James added. "We've been traveling quite a bit to get here."

"Nonsense," demanded Tina. "We're going out."

"Surely, you're exhausted and just want to stay in," James fumbled out.

"What's wrong with you two?" Tina asked suspiciously. "I've been cooped up in a car for days and need to stretch my legs. Now, who's driving?" Sophie watched in awe the power this little blonde 5'4" skinny woman had over these two grown men.

There was no arguing with Tina when she got in this mood. The boys both knew it. James hoped that since the people in the woods were already dead, if there were more, it would be awhile before they got wind of where Sophie was hiding. "Alright," James caved. "Where do you want to go?"

"Let's go to the Plaza!" Tina squealed. "We have to buy Sophie some clothes, anyway." Sophie protested, but lost the battle before it ever began as Tina waved her off. "We'll have lunch and make a day of it!" The boys looked mournfully at each other, but knew it was a lost cause.

"I'll drive," Ben said with as much enthusiasm as he could muster. Tina jumped into the passenger side while James held open the door for Sophie to climb into the black SUV. She spent most of the time marveling at the scenery speeding past her window. James tried not to stare, but it was like watching a child discover the world around them. It was fascinating to watch.

"You lost her, AGAIN?!" yelled a tall skinny pale woman in all black standing in front of a cluster of computer monitors.

"Yes, Ma'am" cowered a 5'11" overweight Russian man in terror. "But she's injured and should be easy to find!" he added quickly.

"I'm over bringing this girl in alive," snarled the lady in black.

"You will do just that, Clarice," boomed a large male voice from the back of the dark room.

Clarice rolled her eyes before turning around. "Of course, Father," she muttered, and left the room cursing under her breath. In the dim light of the room, an elderly male hand slowly tapped his fingers on a gold and black cane.

When they arrived at the Plaza, it was full of people doing their summer shopping. The stores were stacked nearly on top of each other in a strip mall style that never seemed to end. Sophie had seen nothing like it before. She slid her arms around James' left arm and held on while they walked around, and she took it all in.

Tina kept grabbing Sophie's arm and leading her into various stores. She followed reluctantly as Tina shoved clothing and shoes in her direction before dragging her back to the dressing rooms. Each outfit had to be modeled, according to Tina, as the boys did their best to give the appropriate thumbs up or thumbs down.

"I feel a little sorry for her," whispered Ben.

"Me too," whispered James. "But at least we know she's in excellent hands," he said, smiling.

"True," replied Ben with pride.

Each time it came to paying for the new items, Sophie would look at James in alarm. "You need clothes," he would respond, shrugging, handing his card to Ben, and leading Sophie outside to prevent her from hearing the total. Plus, taking her outside meant more alone time with her, which he craved more and more.

"Are you having a good time?" James asked, full of hope. She smiled, causing his heart to skip a beat, and nodded yes. He was overwhelmed with relief. Then, out of nowhere, Sophie grabbed James' hand and dragged him across the street, making sure they didn't get hit by a car. She released him to put both of her hands on the window and smashed her nose to get a better look.

"Would you like some ice cream?" James laughed, enjoying her reaction. Sophie looked at him wide eyed and licked her lips. James felt his pants becoming way too tight and quickly grabbed her hand to pull her into the store before anyone noticed. Sophie looked down at their hands intertwined and felt the electricity and heat that seemed to appear every time they touched. It was fascinating.

"What flavor do you want?" James asked, distracting her from her thoughts. Sophie paced up and down the cases, taking each one carefully into consideration. She bit her bottom lip and raised her eyebrow, deep in thought. James wanted to watch her, but he needed to be able to walk again in public.

After much contemplation, Sophie finally pointed to the chocolate chip cookie dough container. "Nice choice," James said, trying not to sound too aroused. "Two please, and a strawberry and double chocolate." He caught Sophie's curious look. "You can't have ice cream without Tina and Ben," he answered as he paid the cashier in cash. She nodded in agreement. They carefully carried the ice cream across the street to the others.

"We should probably take a break and get lunch," Tina said, snatching the strawberry ice cream out of James' hand.

"Break?!" exclaimed James.

"Yes, wuss," Tina replied, sticking her tongue out at him.

"What are you hungry for?" Ben asked Sophie. "Besides your ice cream," he laughed, watching her devour it. She stopped mid bite and shrugged.

"How about Mario's?" suggested Tina. "It's got a bit of everything."

"Sounds perfect," concluded James.

Ben took Tina's hand and James took Sophie's as they headed to lunch. Tina smiled with pleasure. She was satisfied with the new dynamics, and Sophie was growing on her even though she didn't seem to speak much.

When they walked in, the place was packed. There were red leather booths that lined the walls of the bar and grill, and wooden tables of various sizes that made up the rest of the seating. A wooden bar lined half the room with hunter green leather stools surrounding it. The far wall was a grey stone fireplace with a mantle, and wooden ceiling fans with large faded crystal lights hung above that gave the perfect amount of light and atmosphere. Sports paraphernalia marked the walls, and they blended various celebrity photos taken with what appeared to be the owner in. Country was currently blaring from the jukebox next to the pool table and darts board.

A tall tan man with a grey beard and mustache, small gold hooped earrings, and a blue bandana wrapped around the top of his head greeted them warmly. "Pick a seat! Server will be with you shortly." His smile was infectious. Sophie returned the favor. Mario gave her a quick wink, forcing her to giggle. James quickly escorted her to the furthest booth as possible.

"Hi James!" shouted a bubbly large breasted petite blonde with green eyes. Sophie looked over at James, who couldn't seem to get his eyes to leave the table in front of him. "Where have you been hiding, Handsome?" said the girl wearing an extremely tight black t-shirt, booty jean shorts, and a hunter green apron that matched the décor. She had extremely heavy make-up on with fake eyelashes to match, and large gold hooped earrings too heavy for her ears.

"Staying busy," James muttered, staring at the table.

"Well, lucky for me, I get to be your server!" she exclaimed. "Who's this?" the short blonde asked with a hint of aggravation, as if noticing Sophie for the first time.

James looked at Sophie and beamed from ear to ear. "Wendy, this is Sophie. We would like some menus please, so we can decide what we want," he said, not taking his eyes off Sophie. She blushed in

THE KEY

response. Wendy's mouth dropped open before she handed out the menus, tossing Sophie's in her lap.

"Don't be a cow, Wendy," Tina smiled to counteract her tone. "I'm the one leaving you your tip."

Wendy glared at Tina before quickly pulling herself together. "My apologies," she said sarcastically, before sulking off in defeat. Tina winked at Sophie and she smiled in return.

"Man, she's a sore loser," Tina added to Ben.

"It's your fault for throwing her at James in the first-place," Ben added cautiously and matter-of-factly.

Everyone noticed James still staring at Sophie, but he didn't care. "What are you hungry for?" he asked her gently, still looking into her blue eyes.

"This place really has everything," chimed in Tina.

"We can even order a few things and share," Ben offered. Sophie broke James' stare to take in the menu.

"What's the update?" boomed an elderly male voice from the shadows.

A short, average fit, dark brown headed male studied the computer monitors in front of the room. "Nothing yet, Sir. We checked all local hospitals and police stations, but she hasn't shown up anywhere," he answered.

"That's a disappointing answer, Eddie," the old man replied.

"I've widened the span to several states in all directions. We'll find her, Sir," he finished with determination.

"You'd better," replied the old man. "You know how I handle disappointment."

"Yes, Sir," replied Eddie, staring at the monitors ahead of him.

"Carry on," the old man replied and disappeared back into the shadows. Eddie shivered for a split second and got back to work. His life depended on it.

With their bellies full and bags full of shoes, clothes, and accessories picked out by Tina, Sophie slept on James' shoulder as they headed home. He enjoyed her warmth and natural beauty. He could definitely get used to this.

"I think you wore her out, Ti," Ben whispered, watching his best friend finally share his heart with another woman in the rearview mirror.

"I wore myself out!" giggled Tina. "But that was a blast," she sighed, before drifting off to sleep, too.

Once they arrived at the house, James leaned over and whispered, "Hey sleepy head. We're home." Sophie stirred for a moment. Suddenly, her eyes jolted open, and she used her body to shield James while bracing for impact. "Hey," he whispered softly in her ear. "It's okay. We're home now." She looked at him and quickly lowered her guard, blushing in embarrassment. "I could get used to that," James gently teased, putting a small smile on her lips. He breathed a sigh of relief.

THE KEY

Sophie saw the outside of the house for the first time and fell in love immediately. It looked like a handsomely built two-story log cabin from the outside, although Sophie already knew it was much larger once you got in it. There was a deck that wrapped around the entire base of the house, with a grey stoned base to keep the foundation sturdy. The rooftop was pointed along with two-bedroom windows that matched. The grey stoned base matched the fireplace masonry on the side of the house. It was simple and modern, and the front was so welcoming and inviting. However, Sophie noticed that each glass window and door had an opening above it where a steel cover awaited to be dropped in order to make it a fortress from attack at any moment. They carefully hid it from the unsuspecting guest. Sophie wondered if it was to protect the house from passing storms, or if something else had attacked them at one point. Either way, it felt like home.

They quickly unloaded the car and got inside. "Well," James said hesitantly. "I suppose we should get you set up in a guest room, unless you want to stay in my room, of course," he added, half hopeful.

"She could have the room next to yours," Tina added absent mindedly. James' face dropped a little.

"Let's get these bags upstairs, Love," Ben said, quickly ushering his wife away from the discussion.

"I'll show you," James said, a little heartbroken. What the heck was wrong with him? Sophie followed him upstairs, hoping she could stay as close to him as possible. She didn't know why, but she needed to be.

James set her bags on the queen sized bed. It had a white comforter and dark grey and black accent pillows and blankets. There was a modern wood accent wall behind the bed, with a nightstand on each side made from espresso wood and holding a simple silver lamp. They decorated the room in black and white photos capturing life in the forest, framed in simple black frames. Charcoal grey blackout curtains hung on the glass windows, most likely to block out the bright early morning sun. "The bathroom's through there, and you can use the closet and drawers for your things." There was a long pause before he added, "I'll give you a minute and meet you downstairs." James sulked a bit as he turned to walk away. Sophie grabbed his arm and pulled him into a hug. The heat and electricity between them grew. "Thank you," she whispered before wincing in pain.

"Ribs still hurt?" he whispered, feeling guilty for making her speak. He felt her nod on his shoulder. Neither let go. Sophie closed her eyes and relished in his warm gentleness. It felt so right.

Ben cleared his throat. "We're still a little beat and thought we'd take a quick nap," he whispered, looking at the floor.

"That sounds like an excellent idea," James said, slowly releasing Sophie. "We can all rest up and meet up downstairs to decide what to do for dinner later." Ben kept his head down and left. "Rest up," James said. "I'll come get you in a bit." After a long pause, he headed off to his own room, leaving her to put her things away. She became very drowsy and laid on the bed dosing off immediately.

THE KEY

Three

There was a large wooden door in front of her. She reached out slowly to open it. Before her was a little girl around the age of nine with long red hair waiting patiently on a mat and her hands behind her back. "Most kids my age would be outside playing with their friends," the girl sulked.

"Well, you, unfortunately, are not most kids," replied an older tall woman with chin length curly red hair. "Besides," she added with a smile, "I'm FUN!" The little girl giggled in response. "Now," the woman said, taking stance. She put her left foot forward, carefully balancing on the ball of her foot, and put her right foot directly under her right hip. She held her left hand out at waist level, preparing to block any strikes, and placed her right palm facing up in front of her chest. "Come!" she ordered, signaling with her right hand.

The little girl smiled mischievously and charged the woman. They began to fight, but it was much more like watching a beautifully choreographed dance. Ultimately, the little girl ended up on her back. She frowned in defeat.

"Don't pout, little one," the woman said. "You're getting much better, but you're still leaving your dominate leg exposed. Let's try again."

"This is bananas!" whined the girl. "I'm too small to take you!"

"Bananas?" laughed the woman. "That's a new one!" The woman's face filled with compassion as she reached down to help the little girl up. "You're focusing too much on the size difference and not on the tactics. Size never matters. Tactic always will."

"Why is this so important?" asked the girl, looking up at the woman.

"Because it's my job to keep you safe, and I might not always be available," the woman said, tearing up. She gently brushed the straggling hair away from the little girl's face. "Now," she said, taking stance again. "Come!" The combative dance started once more, but before she could see anymore, Sophie was pulled back with the large wooden door closing in her face. When she opened her eyes, her cheeks and pillow were wet.

"Are you okay?" James asked gently. Sophie nodded yes as she sat up. "Bad dream?" he asked. She thought for a second, then shook her head no.

"A memory, I think," she whispered hoarsely before grabbing her ribs.

"A good one, I hope," he said, stroking her arm. She nodded.

"Let's get you something to drink," he said softly, helping her up and leading her downstairs.

THE KEY

Eddie paced in front of the computer monitors. "Come on Soph," he whispered. "Where ARE you?" The team had been taken out in Virginia. There was no sign of which direction she had traveled. Sophie rarely flew and had been hit by Boris' van. Surely, she couldn't have gotten far. The Carolinas showed no sign of her. The searches in the west didn't prove to be any better. He was just going to have to keep going north. If Eddie didn't find her soon, though, more people were going to die. Including himself. Sophie was good, but Eddie was better. He knew this. Eddie also knew her better than she knew herself, so this should be a breeze. He just needed more time.

Sophie looked with fascination at all the family photos that hung on the wall as they walked downstairs. "Mom likes to remember everything," James laughed as they reached the bottom. "She's the family photographer," he said with pride. Sophie realized that his mother had taken and specially picked all the photos in their rooms, making them even more special to look at. There was a graduation picture of James with Tina and Ben, all wearing different gowns at the very bottom of the stairs. "Let's see what the parents left for us," James said, heading to the kitchen. Sophie continued to take the house in as she followed. It was large and mostly wood. It smelled of the woods. There were pictures everywhere.

"Did you not give the girl a tour of the house?" asked Tina in dismay, as she watched Sophie take the house in. "Good grief! No wonder she feels so lost! Come on, let's go," she directed James.

"I haven't had much time!" he protested in defense.

"Well, do it now!" Tina snapped back. "Nerd," she adding with a laugh.

They wandered through the house. There were four guest bedrooms, his parents' room, his dad's study (that they avoided), a game room, a living room the size of a house itself, various bathrooms, an enormous silver and white kitchen, and a basement that the kids had obviously grown up in, each with its own personality and theme. Outside was a storage shed the size of a barn, with the ocean to the east and the woods to the west. It was classical, modern, and stunning. It was the perfect house.

Sophie learned James was an only child, but grew up with Tina and Ben. They had been childhood friends since around the first grade. His dad was a doctor, and his mother a photographer. Tina worked in IT for the government (no mention of which branch), and apparently had designed the security system for the house. Ben had just finished med school and was thinking about going into pediatric emergency medicine. Sophie soaked it all in like a sponge, but their stomachs rumbled.

"Guess it's time to start cooking," laughed James at their obvious need to eat. "Wanna bet Dad made sure we had some steaks?" he said, as they headed back to the kitchen.

"So, what do you do?" Sophie asked James quietly. Her ribs were still killing her. Everyone stopped and stared at her with their mouths open. "What?" she finally asked.

"We're just not used to hearing your voice, Honey," Tina

quickly recovered.

"Sorry. It still hurts to talk," Sophie said, blushing from embarrassment.

"No worries!" said Ben happily. "There's plenty of time for that." James smiled and winked at her, making her giggle and grab her ribs immediately. He loved the sound, but felt terrible causing her pain.

"How do you like your steak?" James asked, trying not to sound too guilty.

"Medium rare, I think," Sophie whispered.

"What do you want with your steak?" Ben asked.

"Women will take care of the sides while the men handle the meat!" exclaimed Tina, grabbing Sophie's arm and dragging her into the kitchen. "Do you cook?" she asked over her shoulder.

"I don't know," Sophie said, looking at the floor.

"Well, we're about to find out!" Tina said excitedly. James prepared the steaks and quickly got out of Tina's way, with Ben following him to the grill outside.

"Did you get any rest?" Ben asked James, making small talk.

"Some," James shrugged, as he warmed up the grill.

"I like her," Ben said out of nowhere.

"What?" James laughed, not sure where this was going.

"I like her," Ben repeated. "Sophie."

"Me too," said James casually.

"Yeah, I can tell," smirked Ben.

"Stop," said James, laughing. He knew exactly where this was going now.

"You make a good pair. That's all I'm saying," said Ben, smiling.

"Tina approves too."

"Well, as long as Tina approves," James said sarcastically, rolling his eyes and chuckling. "It's not even like that. I'm just helping a friend."

"Are you now?" Ben said, raising an eyebrow. "How long has she been a 'friend'?"

"Well, when you save my life, I kinda gotta share the title, Bro," James said, laughing, and hoping he would drop it. He wasn't sure what he felt or thought when it came to Sophie, let alone could he explain it to someone else.

"I'm just saying, we like her," said Ben casually. "And it's been a while."

"Stop," James said, a lot more sternly. He didn't want to talk about "her". He was enjoying himself for the first time in a long time and he wanted it to last.

"You got it," Ben said, seeming to understand. He grabbed his friend a beer, and they drank and cooked the meat like men should. In silence, appreciating the view.

It turned out Sophie could really cook. She even made a stunning dessert. They ate on the porch, enjoying the cool breeze from the ocean. Once the dishes were cleared, everyone headed to the living room to watch a movie. Tina plopped down next to Ben and snuggled into his side. Sophie sat on the opposite side while James fiddled with the various remotes.

THE KEY

After much debate and a coin toss, the boys picked Hobbs and Shaw. "You'll like this," whispered Tina. "The men are really yummy," she giggled and winked at Sophie.

"Hey!" Ben exclaimed.

"Not as yummy as you, Dear," Tina said, batting her lashes at Ben before reaching in for a kiss. James sat down by Sophie awkwardly and started the movie. After about fifteen minutes, James stretched his arms into the air and put one behind her, careful not to touch her. God, he wanted to touch her. Why was this so hard?

Sophie tried not to laugh out loud. He was incredibly cute when he was awkward. She eyed Tina snuggled into Ben before trying to copy her. Sophie slowly snuggled into James' side. His initial reaction was to tense up. She thought, 'Great, I made it worse.' Before she could move back, the arm behind her pulled her closer, and he melted as Sophie fit perfectly beside him. James exhaled. She found it amusing that he had been holding his breath. Maybe he was worried she wouldn't like the movie.

Sophie was impressed with the fight scenes. They reminded her of her dream. She wondered if she would have another one tonight. The group laughed and hollered at the TV until the very end. It was fun watching this group of people interact with the TV and each other. James continued to hold her close. She could get used to this.

"Don't get too comfortable, Peanut," whispered the male voice in her head. "There's still much to do." Sophie wiggled uncomfortably.

"Are you alright?" James whispered in her ear.

"Yeah, just getting tired," Sophie lied.

"I've got you," James said, giving her a light squeeze. Sophie laid her head on his chest while they watched the end of the movie.

When it was time for bed, Sophie found herself checking all the doors and windows. Everyone watched her with curiosity as she did her inspection and occasionally moved a piece of furniture around.

"You really don't have to do all that, Soph," Ben said. "Tina designed a killer system for the Moore's," he beamed proudly.

"Old habits," Sophie muttered, as she continued until the downstairs was fully secured. James began to wonder how long someone had been after her. He felt guilty for forgetting that part of her. He needed to be more considerate.

"Never hurts to be extra careful," he added reassuringly. "It's getting late and we could all use some rest." Sophie raced up the stairs quickly to Tina and Ben's room.

Tina became concerned watching her. Who had hurt this girl to have given her these alarming habits? Ben went to reassure her she didn't have to, but Tina grabbed him and shook her head no. He looked at her, confused, but followed her order. "Thank you, Sophie," Tina said with an enormous smile. "I feel much safer." Sophie gave her a shy smile and left.

"Why..." was all Ben got out before Tina held up a finger and quietly closed the door. She brought her finger to her lips and waited.

"Because someone has done a number on that girl, and doing this brings her peace," Tina whispered once she thought the coast was clear. "And she cares enough about us to keep us safe too."

"Oh," Ben said, looking at the ground. Then he suddenly remembered the story James told him of the men in the woods. "How awful."

"We need to find out what happened to her," added Tina.

"We can't force it out of her, Love. Her brain's healing and has its own schedule," Ben said.

"Surely there's something we can do for her," Tina said, heartbroken.

Ben took her in his arms. "Be there for her as the truth surfaces."

"I can do that," Tina choked as a tear rolled down her cheek.

Sophie secured the hallway and was finishing up in James' room. He watched her in awe. "I should be doing this for you," he muttered. She paused for a second and shook her head.

"Don't be silly," she said, and got back to it.

"Do you always do this?" James asked, full of curiosity.

Sophie stopped to think. "I guess," she shrugged.

"For how long?" he asked, suddenly alarmed. Clearly long enough to be a habit.

Sophie paused again. "I don't know," she answered, half in wonder herself. "I think always, maybe?" she shrugged.

James' mouth dropped open, and he quickly rushed over to take her in his arms. Sophie began to think her habits weren't normal, based on everyone's reactions. "I guess I'm a little strange," she said, pulling away, embarrassed.

"You're smarter and more prepared," James assured her. "I'd rather have you on my team any day!" Sophie blushed in response.

"I should get some rest," she said, heading to the door.

"Oh...okay," he responded sorrowfully. "Get some rest. I'll see you tomorrow." Sophie gave him a quick smile, nodded, and left. James hoped for her to have pleasant dreams as he got ready for bed, climbed under the covers, and thought of her.

Another wooden door appeared in front of Sophie. She eagerly opened it to see what else she could learn, but she fell into a completely black space.

"I'm worried about her, Jack," a familiar voice spoke. "What if she can't find her way?" she said, full of concern.

"She's smarter and stronger than anyone I know," Jack answered, full of pride.

"She didn't ask for any of this," the woman said, crying.

"Hey, now," Jack said soothingly. "We've given her all the training and tools to beat this. Peanut will save us all," he said convincingly.

"She's too young!" cried the woman.

"Jess," Jack said more sternly, "all we can do is keep up with her training and give her our love. He will not get to take her if you train her otherwise."

"You're right," the woman admitted. "But if we keep giving her desserts, she's going to be too slow and chubby."

"That's my girl," whispered Jack. Sophie heard a kiss followed by several gunshots and dead silence. She covered her mouth and felt sick to her core. She looked frantically around but only saw darkness. A door out of nowhere was yanked open, and someone picked her up

THE KEY

and tossed her over their shoulder as they carried her away. She began kicking and screaming until she heard James' voice yell, "It's okay! You're safe!"

Sophie opened her eyes to see all the horror on their faces. She blushed in embarrassment immediately. She was drenched in sweat, her new lace pj's clinging to her body. It was hard for James not to be aroused.

"Honey, are you okay?" Tina soothed, as she quickly sat on the other side of Sophie, brushing her wet hair from her face.

"Bad dream," Sophie breathed. "I'm really sorry." She felt awful for bothering everyone.

"Nonsense!" exclaimed Tina. "Let's get you in a nice relaxing shower and rinse off."

"Do you mind if I double check your bandages?" Ben asked. Sophie shook her head. He carefully removed all the bandages as a puzzled look appeared on his face. "Looks good, Kid," he said finally with a smile, and Tina led her to the bathroom.

Although this bathroom also had a glass shower, Tina turned on the hot water to let the steam fog the glass up and give Sophie extra privacy. The wooden floor was cool and soothing under her bare feet. The bathroom counter had a single porcelain sink in an espresso wooden base, with a large mirror that was quickly being covered with fog from the steam of the shower. "Hop in," Tina encouraged, as she turned around to give her friend some privacy.

"What's up, Sherlock?" asked James, watching his friend deep in thought.

"When was she hit by that car?" Ben asked.

"Like four days ago," replied James.

"What did Dr. Stephen say when he looked at her?" Ben asked.

"Couple cracked ribs, concussion, large gash on her arm and leg," James shrugged. "Why?"

"Didn't she have bruising this morning?" Ben asked.

"Ben, what's up?" James asked, alarmed.

"Nothing," Ben paused. "She's fully healed."

"That's good, right?" James asked, full of concern.

"Of course," Ben said, lost in thought. *It's just not normal.*

Tina held out a towel for Sophie when she climbed out. She sat her down and began brushing Sophie's hair. "Do you want to talk about it?" Tina asked softly.

"There's not much to tell, really," said Sophie flatly. "I heard a man and woman talking about someone not being ready, but they didn't say for what. It was black, I couldn't see anything. There were some shots, then someone tried to carry me away," she shrugged.

"Do you know who they were talking about?" asked Tina.

"I think it might have been me," Sophie said, barely audible and staring at the floor. "I feel like I really need to remember something, but I just can't yet."

Tina wrapped her arms around Sophie. "'Yet' is the perfect word!" she exclaimed. "And you don't have to do it alone. We're all here for you!"

"Thanks," Sophie said, squeezing Tina's arms. "You'd be a good mom," she said after a moment.

THE KEY

"Awww!" Tina whispered, kissing her on the head. "I knew I liked you!" They both laughed before Tina left to let her get dressed. Someone had brought in James' t-shirt and boxers with clean panties. She was thankful. Sophie quickly got dressed, and took one last look in the mirror. All her bruising was gone, and it hurt less to breathe and move around. Her eyes carried a deeper tint of blue, and her lips were a brighter shade of pink.

"I wish you would remember," Sophie whispered to the image across from her before she turned to walk out the door.

Four

Sophie laughed at the sight in front of her. Blown up mattresses on the floor with pillows, blankets, and stuffed animals as far as the eye could see! She wondered how long she had been in the bathroom.

"The boys have been busy," Tina giggled.

"I see," Sophie laughed back.

"We thought it would be more fun to do tonight as a slumber party style!" exclaimed James proudly.

"Nothing but good dreams here!" added Ben, as he and Tina took to the king sized air mattress. James tucked Sophie into bed, handing her a ratty teddy bear that had seen better days.

"Here's Max," said James proudly. "He's great at keeping bad dreams away." Sophie looked at the bear and realized it was his childhood companion. She was so touched she felt like crying. "And I'm right next to you," James said, pointing to the mattress next to her.

THE KEY

"We're all here, so if you need anything, just let us know," he added softly.

Sophie sat up and threw her arms around him. "Thank you," she whispered. James gently kissed her on the head before tucking her in again.

"Sweet dreams," he whispered. Sophie closed her eyes and drifted off into darkness.

A wooden door appeared once more. She was much more hesitant to open it this time. Sophie looked down and saw Max in her arms. Feeling much more confident, she reached out and opened the door. The little girl sat on a blanket in the middle of the field reading another book while a smaller, dark brown-haired boy ran around her.

"Hurry up Soph!" exclaimed the boy as he continued to circle her. "I want to play!"

"Don't be rude, Edward," she responded flatly. "I'm almost done. You must practice patience."

"I'm trying, but I'm too excited!" the boy exclaimed. He was so tiny, but had the energy of a chihuahua, bouncing around her.

"Well, you will need to calm down, Eddie, because it's time for lunch," said Jess, setting down a large picnic basket.

"We can play some football after we eat," added Jack.

"Man! Your parents are the best!" shouted Eddie.

"Duh," Sophie retorted as she put down her book and began helping her mother pull out the food.

She couldn't hear what they were saying anymore, but Sophie watched them laugh, tease, eat, and play games. She was secretly glad the girls won the games. Her dad picked up the little girl and tossed her over his shoulder. She giggled with pleasure. Suddenly, he was tucking the little girl in bed.

"Thank you for playing with Eddie today, Peanut," Jack said, kissing her on the forehead.

"He has no patience," the little girl huffed and rolled her eyes.

"And that's why you have to look out for him," Jack said, smiling. "That boy's going to get into a lot of trouble before he finds his way, and right now he doesn't have anyone else to show it to him."

"But he never listens," the little girl whined.

"Men and boys never do, because we always want to feel like we're making the decisions and proving ourselves worthy of our loved ones," added her dad, laughing.

"That's why you have to be careful how you talk to them," winked her mother from the doorway. "We'll practice tomorrow in training," teased Jess, coming in for a kiss. Sophie giggled.

"Get some rest, Peanut," her dad whispered. "It's time to get back to work tomorrow."

"Yes, Sir," Sophie replied and shut her eyes tight.

The wooden door closed in front of Sophie. However, she continued to dream that she was snuggling up with James on the couch, falling asleep in his arms. No one came to take her away, and she got a full night's rest.

THE KEY

Sophie woke up to the sun warming her face. She gave herself a good stretch before sitting up. Ben and Tina were missing, and from the smell of it, they were cooking breakfast in the kitchen. James was passed out on the mattress beside her. It was definitely an improvement from the chair, Sophie laughed to herself. She carefully placed Max on his pillow and quietly slipped downstairs.

Tina and Ben were singing with the music coming from Alexa, and dancing around each other as they prepared breakfast. "Morning Soph!" beamed Ben. He was definitely more of a morning person than James.

"Did you sleep alright?" Tina asked in concern.

"Very well, thank you," smiled Sophie.

"Any more dreams?" Tina asked, giving Ben control of breakfast and sitting next to her friend.

"I think I saw my parents," Sophie replied, smiling at the memory. "And some boy named Eddie. We're always kids, but I think he's younger than me."

"A brother?" Ben asked over his shoulder.

"No," Sophie said confidently. "I think, like a neighbor or something. He didn't seem to have anyone, really. They asked me to take care of him, because he's always getting in trouble. But I'm sure he's long gone," she shrugged.

"Well, it's progress," beamed Tina. "Where's James?"

"Passed out cold," laughed Sophie.

"I bet," pipped in Ben. "He stayed awake watching over you all night to make sure you slept alright." Sophie's mouth dropped open. Tina glared at Ben, who was oblivious and kept his back to her while he finished up. Sophie felt terrible.

"Breakfast is served," said Ben, proudly presenting their plates. Then he saw their faces. "What?" he asked, confused.

James woke up to a sun filled empty room with Max by his side. He smiled. From the sound of it, everyone was in the kitchen. Ben must have made his breakfast burritos. He jumped out of bed and raced down to meet the others.

"Hey sleepy head!" greeted Ben.

"Sorry," James replied, sliding in next to Sophie. "Did you sleep alright?" he whispered.

"Yes, thank you," Sophie said, giving him a big smile. His body melted, but his stomach growled, so he turned to eat. "What are we doing today?" he asked between bites.

"The beach!" yelled Tina and Ben in unison.

"Okay then," he laughed and quickly finished his plate.

"Wear this," James said, handing her a hat as they headed out the door. "I don't want you to burn."

"Don't worry, Dad," Tina teased. "She's lathered in sunscreen like nobody's business!"

They stepped out onto the beach, with the warm sand covering their feet straightaway. It rested in a small inlet, between the rocky bluff that overlooked the ocean and the rock-strewn shores. The sky

THE KEY

was bright blue, with fluffy white clouds circling above them, and the sun was warm on their skin. The ocean waves danced along the shore line, teasing to take it over, only to pull back each time. They had their own private paradise as they set up their chairs and towels. James enjoyed growing up with the coast on one side and the woods on the other. It was the best of both worlds. Even with his dad being a doctor, there was always plenty of father-son bonding time.

They teamed up and played a little sand volleyball. The girls won. As it turned out, Sophie had a mean spike and killer serve, despite swearing she had never played before.

"How are you feeling?" James asked when they stopped to rest.

"I'm having a blast," Sophie reassured him with a smile.

"Have you had any more memories?" he asked, observing her.

"Not really," she shrugged. "They come mostly when I'm sleeping, but I'm always a kid."

"It's probably when you're the most relaxed, so your mind wanders freely," added Ben, munching on some chips. "We just need to keep you relaxed," he mumbled with a mouth full of chips.

"Chew and swallow," Tina said in her motherly voice. Sophie giggled at their loving banter. James' heart skipped a beat at the sound.

"I've got an idea!" James whispered, grabbed her hand, and started dragging her to a boat. "We'll be right back!" he shouted over his shoulder.

"Dolphins?" Tina asked.

"Dolphins," Ben confirmed as he put his hands behind his head and was happy for his friend.

James took her hand and dragged Sophie to their private dock that rested at the base of the rocky shoreline. He took the 6-person Bay Breeze blue and white family boat out onto the water with anticipation of her reaction. He was deep in thought and clearly looking for something specific. "What are you looking for?" Sophie asked curiously.

After a second or two, he pointed straight ahead. "There!" James shouted over the engine of the boat. Out of the water jumped a beautiful dolphin. And then another! They started racing beside the boat, a whole pod! "They love to race the boat and chase the waves," he hollered. Sophie raced to the front of the boat for a closer look. It was breath-taking. James cut the engine after dancing with them for a half hour and pulled into a cove. "Can you swim?" he asked.

A vision of the little girl diving into a lake surfaced before her eyes. "Yes," she said it half as a question. He handed her a vest.

"Let's go!" James said, grinning from ear to ear. Sophie took off her shorts and t-shirt, kicked off her shoes, and before he could say another word, she was diving into the water. James' mouth dropped open before he rushed to follow her. When he surfaced, the dolphins surrounded them with great curiosity. He swam closer to Sophie. A dolphin kept swimming under her arm to get petted. "Ornery, aren't they?" James laughed. Sophie giggled. God, he loved that sound. "Is this helping?" he asked, full of hope.

"Yes," she said, grinning from ear to ear. "Thank you."

"Sure thing," James said, swimming closer to her. "Do you

remember anything yet?" he asked cautiously.

"I really like to read," Sophie offered. "And my favorite color is sherbet orange. As for the bigger stuff, it's still blank," she said, discouraged.

James put his hands on her waist. "Lean back and close your eyes. I've got you," he breathed. She gave him a weary look. "Trust me," he assured. Sophie leaned back, closed her eyes, and floated.

The wooden door was in front of her once more, so she reached out and opened it. The little girl ran up and tried to sneak attack her father.

"I see your mother has been teaching you well," Jack laughed as he grabbed her arm and gently pulled her into his lap.

"It's a lot," the little girl exhaled.

"But all important," her father said sternly.

"I know," the little girl said, kissing him on the cheek. "What are you working on?"

Her father gave a vast sigh before stating, "Just work, Peanut."

"You don't seem very happy," she said, concerned.

"Sometimes it's hard to work on something when you know it's going to hurt others," Jack responded, deep in thought.

"Just tell them no," she offered with a smile.

"I wish it were that easy," Jack said with a weary smile.

"Well, you're the smartest man I know! You will figure out something. You always do!" the little girl exclaimed, throwing her arms around him and giving him a bear hug.

"Thank you, Peanut," Jack whispered in her ear.

Sophie closed her eyes and wiped a tear from her cheek. When she opened them, the little girl was back on the mat and waiting for her mother. Jess came in frazzled. "What's wrong?" the little girl asked in concern.

"Huh?" her mother asked, very distracted.

"What's wrong?" the little girl repeated in alarm.

"Oh, nothing," her mother quickly brushed off. "There's just a lot to do, and I worry time is running out."

"But you're not going anywhere, are you?" the little girl asked, with her voice cracking and a tear rolling down her cheek.

"Oh, Peanut," her mother whispered softly as she ran towards her and took her into her arms. "I will never leave you. I will always be right here," she said, pointing to the little girl's heart. "No matter what," Jess added. The little girl hugged her back, quickly realizing her mother had just lied to her.

"There you are!" beamed her father from behind where Sophie was observing, causing her to jump. The little girl ran past her and jumped into his arms. "I have something for you," Jack said, gently setting her down. "You must keep it with you always, do you understand?" he said sternly. The little girl eagerly nodded her head. "Off you go!" Jack said, giving her a love tap on her behind. The little girl giggled as she ran off.

"This should do," her mother said behind where Sophie stood. Jess opened a secret door within the closet. "This is where you need to go and stay when we tell you to. Do you understand?" her mother said sternly. The little girl nodded slowly. "No matter what you hear, you

THE KEY

MUST NOT make a move or sound until someone comes to get you. Am I clear?" her mother emphasized like never before. The little girl's eyes grew wide. "Acknowledge you understand me," her mother insisted. The little girl forced herself to nod. "Good girl," her mother replied. "Now get on the mat." The little girl turned on her heels and walked away in obedience. Sophie heard gunshots behind her and spun around to see who was getting shot. She only saw an older version of herself, dressed all in black, with her hair pulled back, being circled by an overweight boy also dressed in black.

"You're going down teacher's pet!" he spit at her.

"We'll see," Sophie responded flatly. The boy lunged at her and in less than a minute, he was flat on his stomach with his arms behind his back. "Say Uncle," she whispered sweetly into his ear, tugging on his arms until he screamed it loud enough for everyone to hear. Sophie got to her feet and walked away calmly.

The boy scrambled to his feet and tried to attack her from behind. Sophie gracefully allowed him to slide over her shoulder and land on his back. She promptly rolled him over with her foot, putting him right back in his mercy position. She leaned over and whispered in his ear once more with authority. "I don't start fights, but I WILL always finish them. Do you understand?" Sophie said quietly as she tugged on his arms, forcing him to holler out in pain. "I didn't hear you," she said, tugging again.

"Yes!" he screamed in pain.

"Now, play nice with the children," Sophie said sweetly as she climbed off and walked away. Just then, the same version of herself walked past her carrying a stack of books. The girl entered a huge library, spread out her books, and began to study.

A tall man in his early 50s, with a long white beard and mustache and warm blue eyes, approached her. "Sophie, I applaud your dedication, but you still need to have a life outside this library," he stated with concern.

"The library brings me peace, Professor," the girl replied, not taking her eyes off her books.

The man sighed and sat down next to her. "Books are a great escape, and an excellent way to find answers. However, you must still go outside and live in order to learn the much-needed life lessons," he said softly.

"I know," the girl said, deep in thought.

"It's a beautiful day outside. Your immediate assignment is to go enjoy it," the man said sternly. The girl sighed and collected her things before forcing herself outside. But it was dark when she stepped through the door. It was current day Sophie, and she was being drawn to the music playing in the woods. As she walked towards it, time sped up, and the night she first met James played rapidly in front of her. When the headlights came at her, Sophie screamed and sat up immediately. Her feet touched the bottom now, which meant James had directed them towards the shore.

He held her tightly as Sophie shook in his arms. "Easy," James whispered in her ear as he nuzzled wet hair away from her face. "You're safe," he assured as Sophie gasped for air and shook from head to toe. "Breathe," James soothed, gently rubbing her back. He waited patiently for her to calm down.

Once Sophie caught her breath, he pulled away slightly, so they were nose to nose. Her mouth parted. The longing in her eyes was undeniable. Her chest picked up speed as it rose and fell against his own. James' shorts grew tighter as the heat and electricity between them intensified. God, he wanted her, but now wasn't the time. James took a step back to calm his own breathing down. When he looked back up at Sophie and saw the look of hurt and shame on her face, it felt like a knife was jammed in his stomach, constantly twisting.

James grabbed Sophie and pulled her tight against him. As she squirmed to escape, he tightened his grip. "Not here. Not like this," James whispered desperately in her ear. She stopped, sniffling against his shoulder. "Besides," he said, trying to lighten the tension, "Sand and water aren't always user friendly." Sophie gave a half laugh against his shoulder. "That's my girl," he breathed.

She turned her head and placed her cheek on his shoulder. "My dad used to say that," Sophie whispered.

"Oh yeah?" James asked, not willing to let her go or even move.

"Yeah," she whispered. "My parents called me Peanut."

"I like that for a name. It seems fitting," he assured. A few minutes passed before he dared to ask, "Do you remember anything else?"

"The night we met," Sophie said somberly.

"Well, that explains the screaming," James joked. She chuckled, and it relieved him to see her coming back. "Anything else?" he asked.

"Bits and pieces," Sophie responded as a half question. "It was fast and a lot at once. It doesn't really make sense yet."

"I'm sorry," James said immediately. "I didn't know it was going to be so much."

"I know," she said, reassuring him. "It's not a bad thing. It was just a lot."

"Do you know who's after you?" he asked cautiously.

"No," Sophie said flatly. "Or what I have that they want. I still can't remember. I have bits of being little and meeting you. But as for the middle, it's still missing."

"Do you want to go back and maybe rest?" James offered.

"Can you just hold me a little longer," Sophie asked quietly.

"My pleasure," he whispered in her ear, kissed her head, and tightened his grip.

"Hey, how did it....." Tina stopped when she saw Sophie pale, defeated, and exhausted all at once. James shook his head at his friends and stated, "I think we over did it a bit," as he walked Sophie back up towards the house. "Do you want to rest for a bit," he asked her with his hands still on her shoulders. Sophie nodded slowly and wandered back to her room.

"What the heck happened!" exclaimed Tina once she was out of ear shot.

"We were swimming, and she just got bombarded by memories all at once," James said, looking towards the stairs where Sophie had gone.

"That must have been hard on her," whispered Ben.

"I think it was just too much all at once," said James, not moving his eyes.

"Poor thing," whispered Tina, staring at the floor.

"Does she know the people chasing her?" asked Ben, deep in thought.

THE KEY

"I'm sorry, what?" Tina snapped.

"No," James said, paying her no mind. "Just the night we met."

"Someone is after that girl!" Tina hissed.

"Yeah, about that..." Ben started.

Tina sat quietly as she listened to the full story of how Sophie met James. When James had finished, she continued to look past them at the wall behind them. The boys knew they were in deep trouble. It was never a good sign when Tina was this quiet. "Is that everything?" she asked flatly.

"Honey, we just didn't want to upset you," Ben pleaded. "We always planned on telling you once we had more information."

Tina remained quiet. After what seemed like an eternity, she pushed back her chair and stood up. "I will deal with you two later," she said coldly before turning on her heels and heading upstairs.

"Just let her cool off a bit," Ben said with horror and uncertainty in his voice.

Once Tina got to her room, she stopped. Then she went and leaned in the doorway of Sophie's room. Sophie was curled up in the fetal position with her back to Tina, staring out the window in front of her. Tina walked to the bed and climbed in beside Sophie and cocooned her body against hers. She softly combed the hair away from Sophie's face. "I know you don't know me well, but do know this," Tina whispered in her ear. "I will always have your back, and I will fight along-side you, no matter what trouble you're in." Sophie quietly sobbed in Tina's arms and drifted to sleep. No wooden doors appeared. Just nothingness, and a heartbreak for a loss she couldn't remember.

Five

"Hey, sleepyhead," James whispered, brushing the hair off her face. "Are you hungry?" he asked softly. Sophie rubbed the sleep out of her eyes and nodded slowly. "Want to come down for dinner?" Sophie opened her eyes to James, smiling down at her. She stretched and got her bearings.

"Yes," she whispered shyly.

"Are you feeling any better?" James asked cautiously.

"Yes. I'm much more rested," Sophie assured. He held out his hand, and she took it as he helped her get to her feet. Once again, they were nose to nose with the heat and electricity rising between them. James gently brushed a loose strand of hair from her face and lingered on her cheek. Sophie's lips parted as her breathing increased. Just as he leaned in to finally make them his own, Ben popped around the corner.

"Come on, slow pokes! I'm starving!" he exclaimed. James

glared at his friend for ruining the moment, and Sophie giggled as Ben grabbed her hand and dragged her down the stairs to the kitchen.

"Did you get any rest?" Tina asked cautiously.

"Yes, thank you," Sophie replied quietly. She was thankful to have a break from the constant flooding memories.

"Well, let's get some food in you," Tina said in her motherly voice. Ben told her that there was nothing they could do to force Sophie's memories safely to the surface, but if someone was after the girl, they needed to get to the bottom of it. They could all be in danger. "Do you want to talk about it?" Tina whispered in her ear.

"After some food," Sophie agreed. The boys grilled some chicken and fish while the girls prepared the sides and dessert. The boys were still in the doghouse with Tina and unsure of the punishment just yet, but conversation stayed light and upbeat throughout dinner. Once the dishes were cleared, there was an uncomfortable silence that loomed. Sophie knew they needed answers, but there wasn't much to give. They deserved to know what she knew. If someone was after her, they might be after them, too. "So, turns out I'm kind of a badass fighter," Sophie started, trying to lighten the mood.

"Does that mean you're going to teach us some moves?" Ben asked hopefully. Sophie giggled, and everyone relaxed a bit.

"I don't really know where to start," she said honestly.

"The beginning is always good," Tina said reassuringly.

"Well, I've had a lot of memories of being around seven to ten years old with my parents. My mother was always training me to fight, and I'm not sure what exactly my dad did. He was around a lot from what I can tell, but he was working on something that made him uncomfortable at some point," Sophie said, sharing all the puzzle pieces she had been given so far together.

"My mother's name was Jess, and my dad's name was Jack," she said with a smile. "There was a boy named Edward, but I've only seen him once, so I don't really know much about him."

"Do you know what you were being trained for?" Tina asked eagerly.

"No," Sophie answered honestly. "It was important, and time was limited to train for it. They were always in a hurry," she said, shrugging. "But I have remembered nothing to help me with the why or what yet."

"I'm sure it will come when you need it," James said, putting his hand on her thigh and giving her a slight squeeze.

"At one point I was to hide in a secret room," Sophie pushed on. "My mother was very specific that I didn't make a noise or leave until someone came to get me."

"So, something was definitely coming for you even then," Tina added, deep in thought.

"I keep hearing multiple gun shots in the dark, but I never see who gets shot," Sophie added solemnly. "I've only had a couple of memories when I look like a teenager, then I remembered the night I met James." She turned to look at him and met his eyes. He gave her a smile and wink for reassurance.

"A very memorable night indeed," James added softly. The heat from the hand on her leg grew more intense, and the room seemed to empty except for him.

"Do you remember what any of the people looked like from that night?" Tina asked, breaking her thoughts.

"I remembered they were a different crew," Sophie said, still

THE KEY

looking into James' eyes. Then, suddenly, she turned to see Tina for the first time. "They had silencers, which isn't normal when they get close. I know they're not allowed to kill me."

"That's odd," Tina said, clearly processing everything she was being given. "Do you have something they want?"

"Yes," Sophie said, getting excited. "I don't know what, but they also need me."

"Do you know why?" Ben asked, alarmed.

"No, but I think I know whoever is after me, and they want me as a part of the package. I just don't remember who," Sophie said, staring down at the table, defeated. "The middle is still very much missing, so it's hard to know."

"Then how do you know they need you?" Ben asked, confused.

"I feel it," Sophie added softly. "I know it sounds crazy," she added quickly, "but whatever I have that they want isn't the end goal, I don't think. Just a puzzle piece." Sophie turned to James. "Do you still have my backpack?" she asked excitedly.

"Yeah. In my room," he said slowly, not sure where this was going.

"Maybe it's in there!" Sophie said, jumping out of her chair and running upstairs.

"Didn't she say she didn't know what IT was?" asked Ben, completely lost.

"I think she believes she'll know it when she sees it," said Tina, matching Sophie's excitement and racing up the stairs after her. The boys followed closely behind. They entered James' bedroom to see Sophie had dumped the contents onto his bed and was shifting through them; climbing gear, a flashlight, camping meals, a multi-tool knife, matches, a small blanket and pillow, and some very worn out clothing. Nothing stood out as something worth killing for.

"What the heck?" Sophie said in complete frustration.

"Did you have anything else on you?" Tina asked, sitting by her on the bed and examining everything Sophie had in her possession.

"Just this necklace," said Sophie, defeated. "My dad made it for me."

"Do you mind?" Tina asked. Sophie handed it over for her to inspect. It was just a normal silver necklace with hearts on it. Most likely to represent her parents' love for their daughter. Tina handed it back to Sophie. "Well, maybe you're hiding it somewhere," she offered.

"Well, I don't remember where," said Sophie, panicking.

"You told me it wasn't in the backpack that night," James added. "So, my guess is that it's hiding and not supposed to be in their hands, regardless. Even if you can't remember where it is now, it's still safe from whomever is trying to take it from you," he assured her.

"True," Sophie said, staring at the floor. "Well, hopefully I can remember sooner than later. It would just be nice to know," she added.

"We'll figure this out," Tina said, reaching out and squeezing Sophie's hand. "You may have been trained to fight, but I was trained to solve puzzles, and I never give up until it's solved!" Sophie met Tina's eyes and gave her a weary smile.

"There's not a puzzle out there my girl can't solve!" Ben beamed.

"Still in the doghouse," Tina added flatly.

"Yes, Dear," Ben said, sulking.

Sophie looked at them all in confusion, but Tina just winked at her and stood up. "Well, there's nothing to solve tonight, so why don't

THE KEY

we go down and watch a movie?" she asked, eyeing Sophie.

"Sounds good to me," Sophie smiled. She wasn't ready to close her eyes and see a wooden door again just yet. James took her hand and led her downstairs. The boys offered to let Tina pick out the movie without a fight, so she purposely picked some chick flick and sat down a lot less lovingly next to Ben. Sophie had clearly missed something while she was sleeping, but she was too frustrated and tired to sort it out now. She curled up next to James, and he pulled her in close and kissed her on her head while she laid her cheek on his chest to watch the movie.

"Where is she, Edward?" hissed the male elderly voice from the shadows.

"Someone apparently transferred her. I believe up north. I'm close to pin pointing her exact location," Eddie lied.

"You'd better be," said the voice sternly.

"Well, if someone hadn't purposely run her over with a van, she would have been found faster," Eddie replied flatly.

"Watch your tongue, boy," the voice warned.

"Yes, Sir," he replied with no emotion.

"One more week, Edward," the voice pressed.

"Yes Sir," he repeated. Eddie heard the sound of the cane fade into the distance. He knew he owed Sophie, but they were going to have to be even after this. She would get one more week to heal, then Eddie would have to send in the team. Yes, he already knew where she was, but hopefully in a week she will have moved on. Why was she being so careless all of a sudden? Maybe she was hurt worse than he thought. Eddie's job wasn't to keep her safe. It was to bring Sophie in, and it was time he did his job. No matter what their history was. Eddie walked away to clear his head.

James ran his fingers through her hair and scratched her back absentmindedly. Sophie didn't mind. It allowed her to enjoy the movie instead of focusing on her fear of closing her eyes again and dreaming. Her friends couldn't keep sleeping in the room with her just so she could sleep. Besides, maybe Tina would at least let Ben out of the doghouse if they had the night to themselves. Although she wouldn't mind sleeping in the same bed as James.

Once the movie ended, Sophie suggested some additional TV, but after an hour, everyone else was ready for bed. Sophie did her best to focus as she locked the house up to prepare for the night.

"Are you nervous to go to bed?" Tina whispered to her. "Honey, I can stay with you if you want."

"No," Sophie lied. "I guess I'm still awake from taking such a long nap."

"I can stay with you," James offered, hoping not to sound too eager. Sophie's cheeks grew hot along with the rest of her body.

"I'm okay," she mumbled. "Thank you, though." James tried to hide his feelings of disappointment. Everyone headed to their rooms. James turned around and whispered, "Good night," to her. Sophie

THE KEY

stopped to smile at him. "Good night," she replied softly and closed the door behind her.

"You're an idiot," James muttered to himself as he closed his door. Then he stopped and opened it again. He found himself walking towards Sophie's room, but stopped halfway and turned back around to go to his own room. He paced the length of his room ten times before muttering, "This is idiotic. The longer you wait, the better the chance of waking her, and you'll hate yourself if you do," he argued with himself. Tina would be even more mad at him for not letting her sleep. He wasn't even sure Sophie liked him, or if she just felt obligated to stay. It's not like she could go anywhere. Especially not knowing who's after her or why. And James wasn't sure he was ready to have his heart broken. Again. This was all so confusing. Maybe some rest would help him clear his head. Although he knew his head wasn't the problem. They both needed rest. He needed rest and time to figure all of this out. Sophie could very well leave him behind once she remembered. How would he feel? What would he do if she did? James climbed into bed in frustration. "You're an idiot," he mumbled again, closed his eyes, and dreamt of a future with Sophie. Beautiful, smart, and sexy Sophie, without the bad guys chasing her.

"You're an idiot," Sophie muttered to herself and began pacing the length of her bedroom. James offered to stay with her and she said no? What was WRONG with her! Not that she could remember, but she definitely wasn't confident in this area of expertise. Maybe he offered just to be nice, or worse, that he felt obligated. That was probably it. She thought she was obvious in the cove, but he had rejected her. Maybe he didn't find her attractive? She definitely came with plenty of baggage. Baggage that hasn't even fully surfaced. Sophie honestly didn't know if she could handle it all, let alone ask a stranger to. What if staying was only putting them all in danger? Was confessing her feelings going to do either of them any good? She needed to put her focus on the task at hand. Besides, Sophie couldn't tell if he was just being nice, and there was no comfort in asking Tina for help. They were best friends. And if she was wrong, they could laugh at her or, even worse...tell her to leave. Her mother taught her to follow her heart, but she wasn't quite ready for the aftermath if she was wrong. "You're an idiot," Sophie muttered as she crawled into bed, shut her eyes, and dreamt of a future with James. In sunlight and safety.

Six

She woke up to the smell of breakfast cooking in the kitchen. Sophie stretched and relished in the sun's warmth. She was in an amazing mood and skipped down the stairs to find James cooking by himself in the kitchen. "Need any help?" she offered as she reached around him to steal a piece of bacon. He smiled at her playfulness.

"If we're to have anything left for Ben and Tina, I should probably finish," James teased. Sophie giggled in response, and his heart jumped at the sound. Why did she have such an effect on him? This was all unfamiliar territory, and he wasn't sure what to do with it. "Can you get the juice out?" James asked, to distract himself.

"Of course," Sophie said sweetly and got to work.

"Well, you're in a good mood. Did you sleep well?" James asked curiously.

"Oh, I had the best dream!" Sophie exclaimed, distracted by her task at hand.

"Do tell," James said interestedly.

"You were there, and…." Sophie's cheeks turned a rosy red.

"And…" he half pleaded.

"And we spent the day together," she hastily added, full of embarrassment. "It was just nice, is all," Sophie finished, completely flustered. Why did he always make her feel like a silly schoolgirl when she thought about being alone with him?

"Oh," James said, a little disappointed. Sophie felt terrible.

She came up behind him, placed her hand in his, and put her chin on his shoulder. "What are we doing today?" she asked, watching him cook.

"What would you like to do?" he asked, enjoying her touch.

"I don't know, honestly," Sophie said. "Probably shouldn't go too public if someone's still after me," she said, bothered.

"We'll think of something," he assured her, squeezing her hand. Sophie smiled, placed her free hand on the other side of his shoulder and admired his ability to still cook with one hand while still holding hers. It was almost as good as her dream. Almost.

Tina grabbed Ben to stop him from walking into the kitchen. She nodded at their closeness, and Ben smiled. He was happy to see his friend finally moving on. And Sophie was someone to give him a run for his money. "Maybe we should go out and let them have some time together," whispered Tina.

"I'm out of the doghouse?" Ben whispered enthusiastically.

"Let's see how the day goes," Tina whispered back, but her smile gave her away.

"Alright," Ben smiled and winked. "But right now, I'm starving!"

THE KEY

Tina cleared her throat. "Good morning, early birds," she chimed. "What a great day!" Sophie reluctantly stepped back from James to allow him to finish cooking. "Did you sleep alright?" she asked Sophie. Her blushing cheeks were a good sign, but Tina wondered if Sophie was just too shy to tell her how she felt about her friend, or if she was just as clueless as James about her own feelings.

"Yes, thank you," Sophie said shyly.

James served everyone. "We were just talking about what we should do today. Any ideas?" he asked Ben and Tina.

"Actually, Ben and I have some things to take care of in town, so you guys are on your own," Tina said, trying to hide her excitement.

"What?!" James and Sophie exclaimed in unison.

"First of all, breathe," Tina laughed. "Second of all, I have faith that the house will still be standing when we get back," she teased.

"Well, of course," James laughed nervously.

"It's just always fun to have all of us together," added Sophie, without any confidence.

Tina got up, walked around the table, and put her arms around them. "You'll be fine," she assured. "And this isn't up for debate. Come on Ben!"

Sophie looked nervously at James and got up quickly to chase Tina up the stairs. "Let me help you get ready," she offered.

Ben hung back to give his buddy a much-needed pep-talk. "Hey, man," Ben whispered. "You alright?"

"Sure," James shrugged, trying to sound convincing.

Ben tried another tactic. "So, what do you think you will do today?" he asked casually.

James gave up. "Man, I have no clue!" he said, frustrated. "I need help!"

"Okay, relax," chuckled Ben. "We'll think of something. What about a hike in the woods?"

"That's not a bad idea, but it won't take all day. How long are you going to be gone?" James asked in panic.

"Why are you so scared to be alone with her all of a sudden?" Ben poked.

"I'm not," James protested.

"Bro, I say this with love, but your confidence seems to lack the longer she's with us, and I just wonder if you've bothered to ask yourself why?" Ben said gently.

"I don't feel that way," James said defiantly and stubbornly.

"I'm not the only one to notice," Ben pointed out.

"Tina often sees things that aren't always true," James lied. "And I don't think it's a lack of confidence. The girl had people with guns after her. I'm just being cautious."

"Cautious of what?" Ben pushed.

"Just in general," James lied.

"You can lie to yourself, but you can't lie to us," Ben frowned.

"I'm not lying," James muttered.

"Alright then," Ben said, getting up. "The sooner you admit to yourself how you feel, the sooner we can deal with it. I'll be ready when you are." He began to walk away.

"Wait," James said, defeated. "I honestly don't know," he said in hesitation.

Ben sat back down. "I think you know more than you give yourself credit for," he said gently.

"What do you want to hear?" James asked defensively. "That

THE KEY

I've never felt this way before? That I'm nervous around her, because all I do is constantly think of her? Her smile makes my knees go weak, and her giggle makes my heart stop. All I want to do is kiss her, but I'm scared to because I have no idea if she feels the same, and this rejection would be the worst of them all! I can't even keep her safe, and I'm not sure I would survive if she left for some unknown reason!" he hissed before laying his head on his arms.

"Well, it's a start," Ben chuckled. "Now, let's figure out what you're going to do with the girl you're falling in love with." James glared at him, mumbled, and they got to work.

Sophie sat on the bed and wrinkled the blanket in her hands while Tina got ready. "So...when were you going to tell me you were falling in love with my best friend?" Tina asked casually as she put her hair in a ponytail.

Sophie's jaw dropped. Tina allowed her to collect herself before she heard her softly stutter, "I...I...I'm not sure what you mean...."

"It's really quite fine. I approve one hundred percent," Tina winked through the mirror. "Besides," she added casually, "I'm pretty sure he feels the same way."

Sophie thought about her rejection at the cove. "I don't think so," she said, quietly staring at the bed. Tina stopped instantly and rushed to her side.

"I know you haven't known us long," Tina assured, "But I've

known him since he first learned to write his name. I can read him like a book. His problem is he got hurt badly once, and I honestly never saw him heal until you came into our lives." Tina gave Sophie a squeeze.

"Who would hurt him?" Sophie asked in anger.

"That story," Tina sighed, "is not mine to tell. I think he's just worried about getting hurt, again," she eyed Sophie carefully.

"I would never hurt any of you," Sophie assured straightaway. "I'm so scared that if someone is still after me, you all could be in danger. And I could never forgive myself if…." Sophie trailed off as tears ran down her cheeks, and a look of horror crossed her face. Tina embraced her immediately.

"Don't cry, Honey!" Tina begged. "Nothing's going to happen! We're a feisty bunch that can survive anything!" she assured. "And you're a badass at all you do, so I'm not worried at all! Just promise me one thing…." Sophie nodded in her shoulder. "Just promise me if you get the urge to leave us behind to keep us safe, you talk to him before you leave and allow him to decide to stay or go."

Sophie pulled back and looked at her friend. "I think I have been alone for a long time," she whispered softly. "I think they trained me to do it in order to keep everyone safe."

"Well, unfortunately, you're not alone anymore," Tina added sternly. "And he deserves to make that choice for himself. You owe him that much. I'm afraid I can't leave today without you promising."

"I promise," Sophie said, looking Tina straight in the eye.

"Then we're good," Tina smiled.

"Not really," Sophie cringed in embarrassment.

"What do you mean?" Tina asked, suddenly concerned.

"Well," Sophie whispered. "Never mind," she said, shaking her

THE KEY

head desperately.

"Tell me before I burst!" exclaimed Tina.

"I just...." Sophie started. "I don't remember my mom being around past the age of ten, and in all of my memories, I've been alone. Then I met James, and...." her face turned the deepest shade of red Tina had ever seen. "I don't think I've ever been alone with a boy, let alone kissed one!" Sophie whaled, burying her face into a pillow.

Tina had a colossal pain of guilt in her gut. Even if Sophie had her first kiss, or first anything, she couldn't remember them. She's not sure what she would do if she lost all of her firsts with Ben. He was her first to everything. Tina wiped a tear rolling down her cheek. She cursed herself for not realizing how heartbreaking Sophie's life really was. "Do you want to?" Tina asked rubbing her back.

"I don't know," Sophie mumbled into the pillow. "I think so."

"I've learned that our bodies tend to know before we do," chuckled Tina. "As long as it's with someone special, then it's worth it."

Sophie sighed into the pillow. Tina tried a different tactic. "Boys have it much easier than we do," she said frustratedly. Sophie turned her face to look at her friend. "They just don't get how they make our palms sweat, and butterflies jump around in our bellies," Tina added, not skipping a beat. "Their smiles make us weak in the knees. Their touch can make our heart stop. And when they're so close, your body grows hot and electrifying. But the worst is not knowing how THEY feel! It's not like we can read their minds! All you want them to do is just grab you and kiss you back!"

"Yes!" Sophie said, infuriated.

"Oh, and the dreams you have at night!" Tina exclaimed.

"You too?" Sophie asked in shock.

Tina laughed, knowing Sophie was busted. "It's the rollercoaster of falling in love," she shrugged.

"Are you sure?" Sophie asked, biting her lip.

Tina took pity. "Totally, but we're not without our own tricks," she winked at Sophie and began schooling her on the art of flirting.

The girls seemed to still be getting ready, so the boys changed in James' room, then quickly got everything ready for his day with Sophie. "You've got this," Ben said, putting his hand on James' shoulder. He looked like he was going to throw up. "Bro, breathe," Ben said. "You're making me nervous, and you don't want to freak her out."

"You're right," sighed James.

"You are, without a doubt, the kindest, smartest, coolest guy I know. And if she doesn't recognize that, then she's not worth it, man. You know I've never lied to you, so if you can't trust yourself, then trust me," Ben added.

"You sound like Tina," chuckled James.

"I take that as a compliment," beamed Ben, and on cue, the girls emerged from the stairway. James' jaw dropped when he saw Sophie. Tennis shoes and jean shorts showed off her very toned legs, and a t-shirt clung to her curves nicely. Her hair was pulled back, and even though she didn't need it, Tina had given her a little make-up that really brought out her eyes. She was breathtaking. Tina ran down the stairs, lunged at Ben, and kissed him passionately.

"Wow," Ben whispered. "What was that for?"

"For all my firsts," Tina smiled. "Ready?"

"Heck yeah!" he grinned back and took her hand as they walked towards the door.

"Have fun!" Tina shouted over her shoulder, never taking her eyes off Ben.

After they were gone, James turned back to Sophie and cleared his throat. "Did you decide what you wanted to do today?" he tried to ask casually. Sophie smiled shyly, shook her head no, and placed some loose hair behind her ear. James cleared his throat again and shuffled his feet a little. "There's a hiking trail behind the house if you want to check it out," he offered.

"Okay," Sophie said with a smile. His heart stopped.

"Um, okay. After you," he said, holding the door open for her. She smiled at him as she passed. He didn't know if his heart was going to survive an entire day with her, but he was willing to try. James grabbed his backpack and ran to catch up.

"This is pretty," Sophie said, taking in the sights.

"It is," James said, starring at her. She blushed in response.

"So, where's this trail?" Sophie asked, breaking the silence.

"Right over here," James said, pointing the way.

"Well, let's get going!" Sophie exclaimed, grabbing his hand and heading for the trail. It was a smooth dirt trail, mostly. The woods became denser the further they walked.

After a long silence, James cleared his throat again. "So, you're a pretty good runner, if I remember correctly, but do you like to hike?"

"I think so," Sophie said softly. "Are you okay?" she asked throwing him off.

"Yes, why?" James said in sudden alarm.

"Well, you keep clearing your throat. Are you getting sick?" Sophie asked.

"Oh," he blushed. "No. Just a tickle in my throat," he lied, making a mental note to knock it off.

"Let me see," Sophie said, suddenly putting her hands on his face. She felt his forehead before ordering, "Open up."

"I'm fine," James laughed. "Honestly."

"Tongue out," Sophie demanded, and took a thorough look. He was never so glad for using extra mouth wash in his life.

"Alright," Sophie frowned in defeat.

"Don't look so sad that I'm fine," he teased.

"I'm not!" Sophie frowned.

"Come on," James said, grabbing her hand.

"How long have you lived here?" Sophie asked.

"My whole life," he said, smiling. They continued to make small talk until they reached the top of the trail.

"Whoa," she breathed.

"I know," James said, looking at her.

The view from the top was breathtaking. Pine trees covered the hilly base, with an occasional house popping out here and there. The sky was crystal blue with thin white clouds that looked like pulled cotton candy. The sun was mostly up at this point, but still left a sherbet orange and coral hue around it.

After a long pause, Sophie cleared her own throat. "I just wanted to say, thank you...for everything. I can never repay you for all your kindness," she rambled rapidly. "You're a really generous and selfless person, and you should know how special you really are. I think people like you don't get enough credit for how amazing you are, and well, I just wanted you to know, I guess," Sophie finished while kicking a rock on the ground.

James leaned over to kiss her on the cheek, but his sudden movement made her turn her head and their lips met instead. Her eyes opened wide, but soon her body melting into his warm arms. He stepped back, consumed with guilt. "I'm so sorry," James whispered as he tried to get his breath back.

"What?" Sophie asked, full of hurt.

He tried to find the right words. "I just meant that I didn't mean to impose. I just...I just..." he fumbled, realizing he was just making things worse. "I just...oh, screw it!" James exclaimed, taking her face in his hands, pulling her mouth to his, and kissing her properly. He felt Sophie's knees buckle as he held her in his arms. So much for playing it cool. Her mouth was sweet and even better than in his dreams. His tongue feverishly explored with a need like he'd never felt before. He gently pulled away, forcing himself to come up for air while gripping her.

"Wow," Sophie breathed.

"Agreed," James whispered. "Sorry, but I've been wanting to do that since we met, and I just couldn't take it anymore."

"Really?" Sophie asked, stunned.

Second guessing, he started to retreat. "I'm sorry," James said, pulling away.

"Please don't!" Sophie cried, throwing her arms around him. "I hate when you pull away."

Now he was stunned. "I'm sorry. I just never knew how you felt, and I don't want you to feel obligated or whatever."

"I don't at all!" she sobbed, holding onto him even tighter. "I just don't know what to do is all, and I'm really sorry," she sniveled in shame into his shoulder.

"What do you…?" James started, but then realized exactly what she meant. "Oh," he whispered. He felt the heat of her cheeks change colors on his shoulder and felt horrible. He never stopped to think that her hesitation came from lack of experience. "Um, so I have an embarrassing request," James whispered into her ear.

"What?" she sniffed in his shoulder.

"Well," he said slowly. Sophie pulled away with curiosity, just enough to be nose to nose. He was grinning from ear to ear like a boy on Christmas morning. She couldn't help but giggle in response.

"God, I love that sound," James said, starring deep into her eyes.

"What do you request?" Sophie laughed, trying to get the topic off of her.

"Well," he paused. "I'd like to kiss you again."

Sophie grinned so big her cheeks hurt. "You don't have to ask," she said sweetly.

"Good," James said, spinning her around and dipping her. She giggled with glee, then placed her lips on his once more. She ran her fingers through his hair as he slowly raised her up to his mouth, exploring hers to the fullest as he grew light-headed from her sweet taste. "Wow," he breathed when they finally parted.

She placed her forehead against his. "Agreed," Sophie whispered. And just like that, all their nerves washed away as excitement grew between them. Sophie shuttered in his arms.

"Yeah, it gets cold up here. Here," he said, handing her his sweatshirt from his backpack. Sophie obeyed. Her small frame swam in

THE KEY

his clothes, but he loved seeing her in his stuff. "Better?" he asked.

"Much," she said in content as she wrapped herself in its warmth and smell.

"Getting hungry?" James asked. Her stomach growled in response. "I'll take that as a yes," he laughed and offered his hand. She took it eagerly. "Let's get you some lunch."

As they headed back down the hill, Sophie's mind kept circling back to what Tina had told her, or rather didn't tell her, about James' love life. "So, how many girlfriends have you had?" she asked, trying to sound casual.

"What?" he chuckled in surprise.

"Well, you're smart, handsome, polite, and so caring. I assume that list is long," Sophie said uncomfortably.

"Oh," he said with hesitation. "Actually, only one," James answered, keeping his eyes ahead.

"Oh, come on! I have a hard time believing that," Sophie called out in shock.

"Yep. Just one. Got engaged, and she left me standing at the altar. End of story," he said, praying she would drop it.

"Oh," Sophie said softly. "I didn't know."

"I know," he said, squeezing her hand. "And you?"

"Girlfriends? None, that's not my thing," Sophie said, trying to lighten the mood.

"Boyfriends," he chuckled in clarification.

"None," she said matter-of-factly.

"None you remember, I'm sure," James winked, trying not to think of her with other men.

"No, none," Sophie said confidently. "There was a neighbor kid,

Edward, but he was more like a brother. I preferred books over people until I met you," she said shyly. "I'm not sure if I already knew it wasn't in the cards for me, or if I was just always around the wrong people," she shrugged. "I didn't have friends like you do," Sophie said, trying not to sound jealous.

James stopped and turned Sophie to face him and forced her to look him in the eyes. "You do now," he said sternly. "Know that. Believe that. We're always here for you, because we love you. You're never going to be alone again."

"Love me?" she said in shock.

James flustered, not sure what to say. "Well, you are like family," he threw together, even though it wasn't the whole truth. He just wasn't ready to admit it yet.

"Oh, okay," Sophie responded, unsure of what exactly to say.

"Let's hurry and get some food," he said, swiftly changing the subject. "I'm starving!"

"Okay," Sophie said, deep in thought, as he dragged her down the rest of the trail.

James prepared a picnic for the beach. "I'll be right back," Sophie told him. Instead of going upstairs as intended, she found herself walking out the front door.

"They're coming, Peanut," her mother whispered in her ear. "What are you going to do?"

"Fight," Sophie answered, and became familiar with the

THE KEY

parameters of the house, including the rooftops. It was important to know what she had to work with. James was waiting for her at the front door once she got to the front of the house again.

"Everything alright?" he asked cautiously.

"I saw a deer," Sophie lied and kissed him on the cheek as she passed him. "Let's eat!" They laid out the blanket and had lunch while she scouted the beach and memorized all access points. Let them come. She was ready.

Seven

After the picnic, they went inside to clean up. James offered a movie while they waited for the others to return, and Sophie accepted eagerly. He noticed she was deep in thought and tucked a loose strand behind her ear. "Penny for your thoughts," he whispered.

"Huh? Oh, nothing," Sophie answered.

"That was convincing," he teased. "Try again."

"I just have a gut feeling someone's coming, and my gut's never wrong," she frowned.

"What do you want to do?" James asked, trying not to be alarmed.

"Stay," Sophie breathed, taking his face to hers and kissing him passionately. Her sweetness quickly consumed him and he pulled her underneath him as their heat and electricity intensified. She desperately grabbed at his t-shirt to pull it over his head, making him

THE KEY

smile against her lips.

"Hey," he chuckled instantly, followed by, "nothing would make me happier, but we really don't have to do all your firsts in one day."

"Are you sure about that?" Sophie asked with a wicked smile.

"You're killing me, Smalls," James laughed and pulled her up. "There's plenty of time," he said, brushing the hair away from her face.

"Maybe," Sophie muttered.

He pulled her into his lap. "Don't pout," James said, kissing and nibbling on her bottom lip. "I promise that no matter what happens, we will still make time for each other." He couldn't believe the words coming out of his mouth. Even his dreams led to so much more, but he just wanted to savor her and take his time for some unknown reason. He needed it to last. James pulled her close and held her tight. He had no intentions of letting her go. Ever.

She nuzzled her head into his chest and absorbed his warmth. He took a blanket and covered them both up as he started the movie. Sophie closed her eyes and breathed in his sweet sent getting lost in the moment.

"Sophie, it's time," her mother whispered in her ear.

"Peanut, we need you to remember," her dad urged. The wooden door appeared in front of her.

"I'm trying!" Sophie yelled into the darkness.

"Come on, Honey," her mother whispered. "It's time."

Sophie opened the door and saw the little girl approach her

dad sitting at the computer. "What are you working on?" she asked.

"Creating weather," Jack said with a frown.

"Creating weather?" the little girl asked, copying his posture.

He smiled with pride. "Yes, now we can create our own weather," Jack said with a hint of excitement.

"Then what's wrong?" the little girl asked, crawling into his lap.

"Unfortunately, some people want to use it to harm others," Jack frowned.

"So why not make a key that the good guys get to keep so it will stay safe?" she asked.

Jack pulled back in shock that swiftly turned to deep thinking. "Sometimes you're too smart for your own good," he smiled with pride. "Thank you, Peanut," he whispered, squeezing her tightly. "Now go on. I have a key to make," Jack said, winking at her. She giggled and ran off.

Flashes of more training and her dad giving her the necklace played on repeat until Sophie heard kids laughing and running around behind her. She turned to see a younger version of herself in a birthday girl hat and dress. The little girl was talking to another young girl by the pool. Promptly, a young woman, who looked similar to her mother, approached the little girl with a much older man walking with a cane. Sophie couldn't see his face. She couldn't hear what they said to the little girl, but within seconds, the woman pushed her into the pool and held her head under the water. Suddenly, Sophie replaced the little girl and her lungs filled with water. All she could see from the surface was the cane, and the man's legs that stood and did nothing.

THE KEY

"Honey, we're home!" beamed Tina as they came in.

"Shhhh," James hissed, then paused to make sure Sophie was still sound asleep.

"Good day?" Tina whispered with a smile.

"Great day," James whispered, looking down at Sophie. All of a sudden, Sophie started gasping for air. James caught her arms and held them against her just before getting clocked. "Sophie, breathe!" he ordered in her ear. She opened her eyes and gulped for air. "That's my girl," James soothed, rubbing her back. "What the hell happened?"

"Someone was holding my head underwater," Sophie gasped.

"Who?" Tina demanded.

"I don't know. I couldn't see their faces," she answered. "It was my birthday. I think I was five."

James was outraged. "Are you kidding me?!"

"I'm okay," Sophie assured him. "See," she said smiling and gave him a kiss on the lips, calming him instantly, but not making him forget. Tina and Ben looked at each other wide eyed and smiled.

"Do you remember anything else?" Tina asked, returning to the puzzle at hand.

"My dad's a scientist. Something to do with weather," Sophie shrugged. "I saw him give me the necklace again. I think my mother is special ops of some sort."

"Anything else?" Tina urged.

"No. Then I got pushed into the pool," Sophie said, sensing James tense underneath her. "And now I'm starving!" she said, changing the subject. "What's for dinner, Handsome?" she asked James.

"Nice try," he frowned.

"Don't pout," Sophie said, smiling and kissing him, forgetting anyone else was in the room.

Tina pushed Ben into the kitchen. "Well, today seems to have gone well," she whispered.

"That, it did," Ben whispered, pulling her close and laying one on her.

"I meant those two," giggled Tina when they parted.

"Love is in the air," Ben smiled.

James entered with Sophie in hand. "What did you guys do today?"

"More importantly, what did YOU do today?" Tina retorted.

"Hiked and had a picnic on the beach," Sophie shrugged. "Now seriously, what's for dinner?"

Tina defiantly put a pin in it and pulled out the salmon and fresh veggies they had picked up at the market. "You'll have to spill the beans one day," she pouted as they got dinner ready.

After eating, everyone sat down to watch some TV, eventually growing tired and deciding to retire to their rooms. James hung around just outside Sophie's door. "You could come sleep in my bed if you wanted to," he offered with a boyish grin.

"Then we'd never get any sleep," Sophie answered with a wicked smile. James chuckled, but his cheeks gave him away.

"Okay, good night, Honey," he said, kissing her properly before heading to his own room. Sophie closed her door, dancing on cloud nine, and got ready for bed. This was worth staying for. This was worth fighting for.

"Is it worth dying for?" she heard her mother's voice in her head.

"Who said anything about dying?" retorted Sophie. She pulled

THE KEY

on James' boxers and t-shirt. "Bring it," she said before closing her eyes. And, as if on command, the wooden door appeared. Sophie opened it with determination. She watched her mother take down the little girl before her.

"Cocky and confidence are two different things, Sophie Lee," her mother warned.

"I'm not cocky," muttered the little girl as she got back up and took a stance, just like her mother always did.

"Then what do you call it?" her mother asked, knocking her down again.

"Determination," the little girl muttered as she got to her feet yet again. Her mother couldn't help but laugh. The little girl eyed her opponent and tried for a third time, but failed.

"Oh, Sophie. You're so much like me, it's scary," her mother smiled, helping her daughter off the floor. "You wanna know why your dad and I are such a good fit?" The little girl tilted her head at her mother. "He's everything I'm not," she laughed to herself. "He's patient when I'm ready to pounce. He sees the whole picture when I'm too focused on one thing. He calms me when I'm anxious. He loves when I'm ready to fight," Jess said with pride. "But you have both of us in you. And right now, you're channeling me instead of your father to solve your current problem," she said, eyeing her daughter. "So, what are you going to do?"

"Widen the picture," the little girl said, finally taking her mother down.

"That's my girl," her mother laughed. The little girl reached down to help her mother up, but got pulled down into a hug. They both laughed.

"Do you think I will ever find someone to balance me out?" the little girl asked her mother. Instead of answering, her mother turned to Sophie and asked, "Haven't you?" Jess patted the mat next to her. Sophie's eyes grew wide, and she realized that the little girl was gone. Sophie walked over and laid down next to her mother. She carefully reached out to touch her mother's hand and felt surrounded by warmth.

"I don't know," Sophie answered.

"I think you do," her mother said gently.

"But what am I supposed to do now? I feel something bad is coming, but I know I would feel worse if I'm not with him," Sophie said in misery.

"Welcome to love, Peanut," her mother sighed. "Does he help make you feel stronger?"

"Yes," Sophie answered confidently.

"Does he calm you when you're not?" her mother asked.

"Always," Sophie said with a smile.

"Does he help you be a better version of yourself?" her mother asked.

"Yes," Sophie gulped.

"Are you willing to sacrifice yourself for his safety?" her mother whispered.

"Yes," Sophie whispered back.

"Then you have your answer," she whispered.

"You leave me, don't you?" Sophie's voice cracked as she asked.

"Only physically," her mother said squeezing her hand. "We didn't have a choice, but you do."

"I can't leave without asking," Sophie said.

THE KEY

"Then fight," her mother shrugged. "Lord knows I taught you how."

"I miss you both," Sophie said as a tear ran down her cheek.

"I know," her mother said as she squeezed her hand again.

"I needed this," Sophie whispered.

"I know," her mother said gently. "But if you're going to save them, then it's time to get to work." Her mother held out a hand to pull her up, but as she came up, it was the little girl and not herself. It was time to see the whole picture once again.

Sophie watched more training and took mental notes. Her mother was showing her this stuff on repeat for a reason. She was missing something. She watched her dad give the little girl the necklace again.

"What am I missing?" Sophie shouted out.

"You already know," her father responded.

"Well, that's not helpful," retorted Sophie. Then she noticed another door in the background. She walked around her mother, training the little girl to get to it. It wasn't a wooden door. This door was made of steel. She tried to open it, but it was locked. The little girl came to stand next to her and watch. "Why can't I open it?" Sophie asked out loud. The little girl shrugged. "Do you have the key?" Sophie asked her. The little girl shook her head no. "Well, that sucks," said Sophie flatly.

"Maybe you have the key," the little girl commented.

"Not that I know of," Sophie responded. "But I feel like it's important."

"Maybe it's not time yet," the little girl offered.

"But time is always running out. How is it not time yet?" Sophie questioned.

"Sophie Lee," her mother called. "This is no time to be playing around. Come here!"

"Coming, Mother!" the little girl called and ran off. How could this not be important? Then she heard the kids playing behind her. "Oh, great," Sophie muttered before turning around. This time she was just a bystander for her attempted drowning. The faces were still blurred. "Is the man with the cane after me?" she asked.

"Yes," her mother answered.

"Who is he?" she asked.

"Later," her mother warned.

"I should have thought to ask questions earlier," Sophie muttered.

"Answers will come when you need them," her mother laughed. "Now focus, Sophie!" She squinted, but the faces remained blurry. The cane was wooden with a gold top, and the man wore a gold ring with an emblem on it. Then she was pulled back by the wooden door as it slammed in her face.

"Oh, come on!" she yelled at no one in her bedroom. Frustrated to her core, Sophie went to the only place that brought her peace. She quietly climbed into bed next to James and snuggled up to him to steal his warmth.

"You okay?" he asked, half asleep.

"I can't sleep," Sophie mumbled.

"Come here, Baby," he soothed and pulled her closer. They both fell asleep to warmth and bliss.

Eight

James woke up with Sophie in his arms. Although, he couldn't remember how she got there, or when, he knew this was the happiest he had ever been. He could get used to this. James didn't dare breathe or move. He wasn't ready for the moment to end, but Sophie stirred anyway. He patiently waited for her to fully wake.

"Oh, hi," she said shyly once she realized where she was.

"Hi," he said gently and stroked her hair. They laid in silence until their stomachs began to growl. "I guess it's time to get up," James laughed.

"Fine," Sophie pouted. Once out of bed, James grabbed her and kissed her a proper good morning. He felt her melt in his arms. Then he swung her around to his back and carried her to the kitchen, smiling as she giggled the whole way. Ben and Tina were already cooking.

"Good morning, Love Birds," Tina smiled.

"Good morning," James said, bowing. Sophie squirmed to get down, but James just held her tighter.

"Put me down!" she laughed.

"Nope," was his only response.

"Fine," Sophie said defiantly while doing a back walkover, careful not to kick him, and got herself down, catching him off guard.

"Nice!" Ben exclaimed.

"That's fine. I'll remember your trick next time," James shrugged and reached to grab some bacon.

"Something tells me she's got more tricks than you can keep up with, Buddy," laughed Ben.

"It's okay. I've got a lifetime to try," James smiled. Everyone stopped to look at him, but he was too happy to notice and kept eating the food on his plate.

"Just enjoy it," Tina whispered to her as she guided Sophie to the table to join him. "So, how did you sleep?" Tina asked once they were all sitting down.

"Oooo, it was the most annoying thing!" Sophie exclaimed as she recapped the repetition and the new steel door. She left out her encounter with her mother. That was a little too personal.

"Maybe it's so you don't forget how to fight," Ben offered with his mouth full.

"Chew," Tina reminded him.

"Maybe, but I still feel like I'm missing something. Why keep showing me the necklace?" she wondered out loud.

"That new door sounds interesting," James said, deep in thought. "Maybe it's a memory you're not ready to remember. At least, not yet." He felt all their eyes on him. "What?" he laughed uncomfortably.

"Nothing," smiled Sophie as she leaned over and kissed him. "The puzzle is all yours," she winked at Tina.

"Challenge accepted," Tina said with determination. "Now you told your dad to make a key for whatever he was working on, right?"

"Yes," Sophie said.

"Maybe the necklace is the key?" Tina offered.

"I'm not sure how," Sophie said, taking it off to inspect it for the thousandth time.

"That's because we don't have the lock yet," Tina said, deep in thought. Sophie put her necklace back on.

"Well, since things come to you more when you're not forcing it, maybe we should go do something?" James offered.

"Oooo, good point!" exclaimed Tina.

"I think we're running out of things to do at the house," Ben said.

"We had luck at the cove," James said.

"Yeah, too much luck," Tina reminded them.

"I want to try it," Sophie whispered.

"Are you sure?" James asked, concerned.

"Yes," she said.

"You said you liked books," Ben said. "Why not try that?"

"Time is running out," Sophie said. "We'll do it all."

Just then the phone rang, making them all jump. James answered, "Hello?" They all went to the living room to listen. "Oh, hi mom. No, you're not interrupting...How's your vacation...Oh...of course you can have dinner with everyone in the next couple of days. We'd love to see you…yes, mom…Oh! We have an extra mouth…yes…mine…yes…we're excited to see you too…See you then. Love you."

"Your parents are coming home early?" Ben asked.

"Apparently," James shrugged. "We don't have much of a library here, but we can check my mom's desk," he said, getting to the task at hand. He took Sophie's hand and led her upstairs. It impressed Sophie that the room was distinctly divided with his mother's photos and work on one side, and clearly his dad's work on the other.

"Your mother's idea?" she asked.

"My dad's actually," James smiled. "So, they could be together more." Sophie walked around the room, inspecting the photos.

"Breathtaking," she said.

"Yeah, she's fantastic," James said, beaming with pride. "Her books are over here." Sophie fingered the books and landed on *Anne of Green Gables*.

"Oh! This was a favorite of mine when I was a kid!" she squealed. "Do you think she would mind?"

"Of course not," he smiled. Sophie continued to explore the books and the rest of the room. His dad's side was full of medical references and supplies. "Doctor," James confirmed. She continued to explore when a group photo made her stop. A face stuck out to her immediately. But how? That didn't make any sense. Sophie shook her head.

"What kind of doctor did you say your dad was?" she asked.

"I didn't," he laughed. "Infectious disease. Why?"

"That doesn't make any sense," she mumbled.

"What doesn't?" James said, looking at the photo with her.

THE KEY

"What's this photo from?" Sophie asked.

"I don't know," James said. "It's just a work photo. What's going on?"

"I don't know," Sophie said softly as the color continued to drain from her face.

"What do you see?" he asked, staring at the photo, trying to see what she saw. Sophie pointed to the tall, skinny, brown-haired man standing next to his dad. "Who's that?" James asked, confused.

"My dad," Sophie whispered in confusion.

"That's your dad?" he asked. She nodded her confirmation.

"I don't know, Hon," James said, taking her in his arms. "They'll be here in a few days. We'll ask him."

"Okay," she said softly. It was one thing to see him in her dreams. Seeing him in a photograph made him so much more real, though.

"They're both science nerds," James laughed, trying to lighten her mood. "We'll get to the bottom of it. I promise," he stroked her back. "Let's go on that boat ride," he whispered, leading her out of the room. James took one last look at the photo and closed the door.

"Oh! I love that book!" Tina said when they returned. But Sophie was deep in thought. Tina and Ben turned to James with a confused and concerned look on their faces.

"Turns out Dad has a picture of Jack on the wall in his office," James said in a hushed voice. "No clue why."

"Oh," they said in unison.

"Let's get going!" James called out, trying to lighten the mood.

Dolphins chased the boat to the cove. Tina went and sat next to Sophie.

"Hey," Tina said over the sound of the engine.

"Hey," Sophie responded softly.

"How are you doing?" Tina asked.

"A little surreal, to be honest," Sophie said. "It was one thing to see him in my head. Another thing to see him in a photo. It made him real, as stupid as it sounds."

"That's not stupid at all," Tina said, pulling Sophie into a hug. Tina wiped a tear from her own cheek as her heart broke for her friend. They watched the dolphins in silence.

James docked the boat. "Let's eat first. I'm starving," he said, trying to change the mood. They sat on a blanket while Tina, Ben, and James shared about all the trouble they caused growing up. Sophie remembered some of the times that teachers had picked on Edward for being slower, and he came crying to Sophie for help. Apparently, Sophie was great at getting their attention, encouraging them to stop. She remembered going to public school, but being a loner. She spent her free time in the library. By the second grade, she'd read every book they had, so the librarian, Mrs. Porter, would let her be the first to read each new book as it came in. If Sophie liked a book, Mrs. Porter would keep it. The books Sophie didn't care for always got sent back.

Sophie's mother started training her vigorously around age five, most likely after the pool incident. However, despite her rigorous training schedule, there was still plenty of time spent together as a

THE KEY

family. They went to the movies, out to dinner, and spent a lot of time outdoors.

Sophie didn't remember traveling with her parents. Most likely their jobs didn't allow it, but she had a sense that she did when she got older. James was right. Her mind opened up a lot more when hanging out with her new friends. "We should go swimming," Sophie offered. She was determined to open that steel door. "Will you do what you did last time?" she asked James, as Ben and Tina got in the water.

"I don't know, Babe," James said, full of concern.

"Please!" Sophie begged. "You'll have me if I need to be pulled back."

"I'm not very comfortable with this," he stated sternly. "But if it means that much to you, we will try it one more time. But only once," James warned.

Sophie kissed him gently, making all his reservations disappear. "No fair," he mumbled against her lips, making her smile. They held hands and walked into the water. He held onto her as she leaned back. Tina began to protest, but James just held up his hand to silence her. Her friends circled her and held her as she floated and closed her eyes.

Like clockwork, the wooden door appeared. Sophie eagerly opened it. It was time to get to work. The little girl watched her as she came in. She was by herself. "Where is everyone?" Sophie asked. The little girl shrugged. Sophie saw the steel door across the room. She made a beeline for it, but when she tried to open it, the door was still locked.

"I don't think you're supposed to open it yet," the little girl whispered.

"But time is running out. The man with the cane is coming for me, and I need to open this stupid door!" Sophie yelled in frustration.

"He's not allowed to hurt you," the little girl almost sang.

"What?" Sophie asked in confusion.

"He's not allowed to hurt you," the little girl said more flatly and matter-of-factly. "He wants you to join him."

"The pool incident says otherwise," mumbled Sophie.

The girl sighed and rolled her eyes. "A test," she said flatly again.

"Don't get an attitude with me, Missy," Sophie said, sticking out her tongue. They both laughed. "Well, this isn't helpful," Sophie mumbled, putting her hands on her hips.

"Who said I was done," retorted the little girl as she took Sophie's hand and led her away from the steel door.

This training was different. The little girl stood next to her as she watched a teenage version of herself have training with various teachers. A Buddhist taught her to meditate, a Japanese instructor focused on Aikido and Jiu Jitsu, a Korean man taught her Hapkido, she learned Krav Maga in Israel, Muay Thai in Thailand, and countless others, but her mother was nowhere to be found.

"Where's mother?" Sophie whispered.

The little girl put her finger to her lips. "You must pay attention!" she hissed at her. "They want you to remember."

"Who?" Sophie hissed back, but she already knew the answer.

"You need to remember our training," the little girl whispered softly. "To save them...to save him. Whole picture," she said, smiling.

Sophie stopped asking questions and focused. She closed her eyes to center herself. When she opened them, she was suddenly

THE KEY

blocking hits and attacks. Her body gracefully dancing with each opponent, as her body woke up from its long slumber. Every lesson Sophie ever had was suddenly rushing back to her. Finally, the attacks stopped coming and Sophie stood by the little girl, catching her breath.

"Feel better?" the little girl asked.

"Actually, yes," Sophie confessed.

Then, out of nowhere, rapid gunfire came from behind the steel door, followed by screaming and more gunshots. Sophie pushed the little girl behind her to keep her safe. Something was on the other side, abruptly banging to be let out. Sophie felt the little girl tremble behind her. Blood started oozing out from under the door and engulfed the floor. They kept backing up to avoid it.

"Go!" the little girl screamed, tugging on Sophie's hand.

"I can't leave you," Sophie said, unsure of what was exactly taking place.

The little girl got in front of Sophie. "GO!" she yelled as she pushed her through the wooden door that slammed and locked behind her.

Sophie opened her eyes as her friends held her safely with looks of concern. She took a deep breath in and let it out. "I'm okay," she said as her feet found the ground beneath her.

"Are you sure?" James asked, eyeing her suspiciously.

"Yes," she chuckled lightly and gave him a gentle kiss.

"Well?" Tina asked eagerly.

"I think this was more to remember all my training," Sophie said as she retold everything she witnessed. "But whatever is behind that steel door is ugly, and it wants out," she said with a shudder. James put a towel around her and held her tight.

"But no parents this time?" Tina asked.

"No," Sophie said. "Just my mini me."

"And she said the pool was a test?" Ben asked in shock.

"Yeah, that made little sense to me either," Sophie stated.

"Well, whatever is behind the door, it is definitely some sort of trauma," Ben stated in his doctor voice. "It sounds like your body's trying to prepare you to receive it, but you still don't feel ready."

"Clearly you survived whatever it is, because you're still here," Tina said in her cheerleader voice and elbowing Ben. "And you've got us this time as an added bonus!" she cheered, giving Sophie a bear hug.

"That I do," Sophie laughed, trying to ignore the uneasy feeling in the pit of her stomach. She may not be ready for whatever was behind the steel door, but she took comfort in knowing she was more than ready to take on keeping her friends safe.

"Let's get back before it gets too late," James offered, looking at the sky. Everyone agreed and packed up their things.

James grabbed her hand. "Are you sure you're okay? You don't have to lie to me, ya know." Sophie took his face in her hands, kissed him gently, and put her forehead to his.

"I know," she whispered with a smile. Then they walked hand in hand to the boat.

"Edward, prepare the team!" ordered Clarice. She stood 5'11" without heels. Her hair was thin, fine, and a shade of ash brown that didn't flatter against her pale moonlight skin. She looked anorexic if

THE KEY

you hadn't witnessed her eat. She had an infectious smile that drew you in and blue eyes that reflected barely any life. Her bark was loud, and if she was in the mood, her bite killed. She was rude, demanding, and always put herself first. Eddie assumed it came from growing up with the old man.

"Yes ma'am," Eddie replied. It wasn't a full week, but there was nothing more he could do. Sophie was on her own.

"I want her back in one piece!" threatened the old man from the shadows.

"Yes, Father," mumbled Clarice as she rolled her eyes. Despite her desire to take the girl out for good, he would have Clarice's head, even though Sophie was a nuisance from the day she was born. If only she hadn't been interrupted all those years ago. Clarice smiled at the thought of Sophie floating face down in the water.

"Stop wasting time!" her father ordered, interrupting her thoughts.

"Good luck, Sophie," she whispered wickedly. "We're coming for you."

Nine

"Do you need to lie down?" James asked.

"Stop fussing," Sophie said, smiling. "I do need food," she giggled. Her laugh was music to his ears.

"Yes ma'am," James laughed and got to work.

After dinner, they nestled in for another movie. There were so many Sophie hadn't seen. She tried to relax in James' arms, but the image of blood oozing from under the door kept resurfacing. Someone had clearly been murdered. Sophie wondered if it was her parents and instantly became nauseous and shivered.

"Here," James said, pulling a blanket over them both.

"Thank you," Sophie smiled and kissed him on the cheek. She couldn't save whoever had been murdered back then, but she had clearly gone to a lot of lengths to make sure it didn't happen again. It couldn't. She would die before she let anything happen to her friends.

THE KEY

Sophie knew the man with the cane was coming, and he would regret the day he did.

"You alright?" James whispered, kissing her on the head.

"Of course, why?" she lied.

"You don't look like you're with us anymore," James frowned, knowing she was lying.

"Just wondering if I slept in your room tonight, if we would get any sleep," Sophie smiled wickedly.

"One way to find out," he responded to her challenge.

"Hmmm," Sophie sighed.

Two can play this game, he thought. James wondered if she would ever get to the point where she wouldn't lie to him to spare his feelings. Either way, he was willing to spend the rest of his life finding out. This much he knew. On cue, Sophie snuggled closer as they continued to watch the movie.

Sophie slept in her own room that night. Apparently, she didn't think James could behave long enough to get any sleep. She was probably right. James was lying in bed with his hands behind his head and thinking about Sophie when he heard a light knock on the door. "Come in," he said with a smile on his lips, but it was Tina who entered his room instead. "Oh, hey," he said, a little thrown off. "What's up Ti?"

"I'm worried," Tina started off slowly.

"Why? What's wrong with Sophie?" he asked, sitting up in alarm.

"She's fine," Tina reassured him while sitting on the edge of his bed. "I'm worried about you," she whispered.

"Me? Why?" he asked, confused. "I'm fine."

"Listen," she breathed. "I'm coming from a good place. Honestly.

I'm so glad to see you happy again after all this time, but…"

"Get to the point, Tina," he warned.

"We still don't have a clue who's after Sophie, and they will come with guns," she said, not looking at him.

"I've got my own," James said defensively.

"I'm well aware of your James Bond skills," Tina snapped back. "But how far are you willing to go to be with her?" she said, starring straight into his soul.

"As far as I have to," he said, calmly starring back.

"Are you sure?" Tina asked, not flinching. "She's made a lifetime of sacrifices. Is she worth it?" she asked, staring him down.

"Yes," James said, glaring back at her.

"Okay," Tina shrugged. "As long as we're both on the same page," she said, getting up.

"We?" he asked. "This is not your fight."

"It's not yours either," she said matter-of-factly.

"I mean it. If it's heated and we have to leave, you and Ben have to tap out and stay safe!" James insisted.

"Yeah, not happening," Tina said, putting her hands on her hips defiantly.

"I'm serious," James stressed. "You both have jobs and lives! You can't live on the run!"

"You let us worry about what we can and can't do, Mister," Tina

THE KEY

warned, glaring at him.

"Ben!" James hollered, glaring back at her.

"Nice try, but we've already had this discussion. She's family now, and we keep our family safe. Together!" Tina retorted back.

"What the...?" Ben asked, coming into the bedroom to see Tina and James at a standstill with their arms crossed. "Oh," he said, rolling his eyes.

"Will you tell your wife," James started, but Ben held up his hand.

"I will tell her nothing because I agree one hundred percent, and there's nothing you can say or do about it," Ben stated. Tina stuck her tongue out at James.

"Real mature," he growled.

"What's going on?" Sophie asked as she came around the corner.

"Nothing!" everyone shouted. Ben dragged Tina out of the bedroom. "Good luck," he said, giving Sophie a weary smile as he pushed a muttering Tina into their bedroom. James was grumbling and pacing angrily across the bedroom floor.

"So," Sophie said cautiously. "What did I miss?"

"Pure stubbornness," he snapped.

"Which side?" Sophie asked, but retreated at his sizzling glare in response. "Okay...." she said, looking around the room. Sophie grabbed the white handkerchief off the dresser and waved it while she held her other hand up in surrender. "Wanna talk about it?" she asked softly.

He slumped his shoulders, consumed with guilt. "No," he mumbled.

"Well, whatever it is, I'm sure she means well," Sophie shrugged.

"She does," he sighed.

There was a long pause. "It's not because of me, is it?" she asked, suddenly alarmed.

"No," James lied, immediately understanding her need to lie to spare him. He made a mental note to change that.

"Okay," Sophie said hesitantly.

"I could use a pleasant distraction," he said devilishly, sauntering towards her, taking her face into his hands, and kissing her passionately. He felt her body melt against his.

"No fair," Sophie whispered when they parted.

"Who said anything about being fair," James said, showing off his boyish grin.

"Oh, I'm in trouble," she laughed as he picked her up and gently placed her on the bed. "You sure you don't want to talk?" Sophie asked nervously.

"Nope," James said, grinning from ear to ear as he leaned down to kiss her. The heat between them rose as the electricity ignited their blood. "I like you in my clothes," he teased, tugging on his t-shirt she was wearing. A look of fear came to her eyes. "I think we'll keep them on you tonight," James said, winking at her. Sophie gave a quick sigh of relief. He let out a small chuckle.

"What?" she asked.

"I love how cute you are," he laughed, remembering how nervous he was his first time. Sophie froze. There was that "L" word again. It kept coming up, but did he really mean it? He pressed his mouth against hers, making her forget everything. There was a sudden need. A need for him, and his need for her. Their hands explored as they became intoxicated by each other's sweetness, yet he remained a gentleman and kept his promise that their clothes would remain on.

Sophie began tugging his shirt up, and he knew if they didn't stop, they would both be goners. Instead, he rolled her on top and pinned her against him as they caught their breath.

"Ugh!" she growled in frustration.

"I know," he laughed, holding her tighter. "Trust me!"

"Then why not!" she yelled in frustration.

"Because your first time should be really special and not in a house full of people, for starters," James sighed. Sophie suddenly felt guilty. It wasn't because he didn't want to. He needed it to be special, even though everything with him was special to her. He obviously knew what that should be, and it was as important to him as much as being with him was to her.

"Okay," she said, smiling up at him, making a mental note to let him take the lead on this. She'd take what she could get. Sophie slid down his side to snuggle up against him. "This is good too," she assured.

"Yes, yes, it is," he said, smiling as he kissed the top of her head and played with her hair.

"Good night," she sighed.

"Sweet dreams," he whispered as she closed her eyes and drifted to sleep.

Instantly, the door was in front of her. "Well, if I'm going to be frustrated, I might as well work some of it off," Sophie said sarcastically to no one. She opened the door and was blinded by a white light. It took a second, but once her eyes adjusted, she saw the little girl sitting in a white chair. An average man in a lab coat was checking her vitals. He kept his back to Sophie, so she couldn't see his face. It smelled overwhelmingly like a hospital.

"How's my favorite patient?" he asked her.

"You say that to all your patients," the little girl said, rolling her eyes.

"Yeah, but you're the only one that I mean it with," he said with a smile.

"Okay, I guess," the little girl shrugged.

"Just okay?" he asked with interest.

"Sally knocked my books out of my hand, so I told her to knock it off. But then she tripped me on purpose to make me fall, so I punched her in the face and broke her nose," the little girl shrugged. "I warned her, though," she emphasized.

"Oh my," he laughed and got some syringes ready. "What happened then?" he asked, intrigued.

"I got suspended again. Mother's really mad, but Dad said I did the right thing. Well, not the breaking her nose part, but the protecting myself part," she clarified.

"Well, I agree with your dad," he said bluntly. "Just don't tell your mom," he whispered. The little girl giggled. "Ready?" he asked.

"How many?" the little girl whined, looking at the tray.

"Only twelve," he said, trying to sound positive.

"Everyone's always giving me shots," the little girl whined.

THE KEY

"Dad, you, Dr. Cox. I don't like them. They make me feel funny!" she protested.

"We have to make sure you stay healthy," he assured.

"But I'm not sick!" she pouted.

"I know," he said, taking pity. "We're making sure of that. I know this can't be easy for you, but we do it because you're designed to handle anything that's thrown at you. One day, you will make us all safe. I know you didn't ask for this, but you're special. And sometimes we have to do things we don't want to for the greater good. Do you understand?"

"Yes," the girl huffed. "It's still not fair."

"No," he agreed. "And it's a thankless job, but we'll know the truth. That's all that matters."

She stuck out her arm. "I think I should get a cape," the girl said after the first stick.

"I agree," he laughed and stuck her again.

"Tell me about your son," she asked for distraction.

"Well, he's as stubborn as you are, but I'm very proud of him," he said, sticking her again. "I think you would like him."

"He's handsome like you," the girl said, wincing as she took another injection. "He has your smile," she added. "Superheroes never get to live happily ever after with anyone, do they?" she asked, getting another stick.

"No," he said mournfully. "Not usually. It's safer that way."

"It's lonely that way," the girl said, full of sorrow.

"Maybe you can have a sidekick some day," he offered.

"A dog would be cool," the girl said randomly, making him chuckle.

"I'll remember that," he said with a smile, sticking her again.

"I will miss you," she whispered.

"We still have time," he said, pausing his injections. "But you're going to have to stop getting suspended," he added sternly.

"Yeah, I keep hearing that," the girl shrugged. "It's not my fault though!" she protested. "I never start fights, but I do finish them," she said, smiling triumphantly.

"Well, you need to find another way," he said firmly. "Let's talk about options." The conversation faded and she couldn't hear anything anymore.

"Come to bed," James said, suddenly pulling on her hand. There was no steel door to be found.

"That was weird," she muttered to herself as he led her to his bed, they climbed in, and she forgot once more everything she'd seen. All she saw was bliss and happiness with the man she was head over heels for.

Ten

Sophie and James woke up entangled with each other. She started to get out of bed when he suddenly pulled her back on top of him. "Not yet," he whined. Her laughter was extra magical this morning.

"We'll have to get up eventually," she giggled. "I require food." Her tummy gurgled in response.

"Alright, alright," James said, rolling on top of her and kissing her gently. "Can't have my girl starving to death after all," he said, winking at her before pulling her out of bed.

"Your girl, huh?" she teased.

"Of course!" he said, grinning from ear to ear. "If you'll have me, that is," James said, holding his hand out while holding his breath for her response.

"I like the sound of that," Sophie finally said.

'Thank God!' he thought before responding, "Me too." He tossed her on his back and enjoyed her giggling all the way to the kitchen.

"Can I have cereal today?" Sophie asked quietly.

"Honey, you can have whatever you want!" James laughed, and showed her the options. She settled for frosted mini wheats, his favorite, so they had a bowl together.

"Good morning," Ben beamed as he entered the kitchen. Tina barely made eye contact with James when she entered. Sophie watched James' demeanor change completely. "Knock it off, you two," Ben warned. No one said a word. "Are your parents coming in today?" Ben asked, trying to break the ice.

"Yeah, I think so," James said with little emotion. Ben looked helplessly at Sophie.

"What are they like?" Sophie threw out.

"My mom's a little over the top, and my dad's more laid back. I can't wait for you to meet them. They're going to love you," he winked and said assuringly.

"They're both really sweet," Tina added quietly.

"Alright, enough," said Sophie out of nowhere. Everyone stopped to look at her. "I can't take this weird dynamic, you two having going on," she blurted out. "It's driving me insane! So, whatever's going on between you two needs to be resolved now. I don't care what pride or stubbornness you have to swallow, just take care of it! Got it?" When she stopped, she noticed everyone's mouths were open.

"Yeah!" Ben added, getting up from the table and taking Sophie's hand. "And we're not coming back until you do!" he said, dragging Sophie out. "Great job, kid!" Ben whispered, smiling at Sophie.

"I don't know what they're fighting about, but it seems like it's pure stubbornness on both sides," she said, putting her hands on her

THE KEY

hips and rolling her eyes.

"You have no idea," Ben laughed, sitting on the couch and patting the cushion next to him. Sophie obeyed.

"It's not over me, is it?" she asked again.

"No, Soph," Ben assured. "This has everything to do with their need to be right," he laughed, shaking his head. "They'll be out before too long."

"How do you know?" Sophie asked curiously.

"Not my first rodeo," Ben laughed as he picked up the remote and turned on the TV. Shortly thereafter, as Ben had predicted, James and Tina emerged.

"Well?" Sophie asked eagerly.

"We agreed to disagree," James shrugged. Well, it was something which was better than nothing in Sophie's book.

"What's the plan, Stan?" Ben asked with his usual ornery smile.

"Today, we clean the house for our gracious hosts," Tina said in her motherly tone.

"That's not a bad idea," James added. Everyone headed upstairs to get some clothes on.

"Hey," James said, grabbing Sophie's hand and pulling her to him. "Thank you," he smiled and kissed her gently. "I'm sorry we were fighting. It's just," he paused, "they're my family, too, and I always want the best for them." He kissed her again.

"Well, I'm glad you agreed to disagree at least," Sophie smiled. "You both mean well, but you're both stubborn as mules," she laughed.

"I knew it was bothering you, so I selfishly needed it resolved." She kissed him back. "Now, let's get to work!"

"The team is closing in, Sir," Eddie informed. "They should be there by nightfall." A pit in his stomach grew, but he didn't know why.

"Excellent," was the only response.

"I would have thought you'd be more excited," chimed in Clarice, coming in to stand next to Eddie.

"She's not here yet," her father answered flatly. "Your teams haven't exactly proven to be successful," he added for an extra sting.

"Well, if you didn't require her to be alive," she retorted back. Clarice always knew when to back off in order to keep herself alive. She may be blood, but that didn't mean she wasn't expendable. He'd proven that.

"You know why," was his only reply.

"They're armed to take down all of New York. I'm sure they'll get Sophie this time," Eddie offered with little belief in his own statement.

"They'd better, or I will deal with you both, as a result," the old man warned. Eddie swallowed hard. Clarice tried not to show any fear.

"You first," she whispered in Eddie's ear. He rolled his eyes. Clarice was all bark and not much bite, from what he'd gathered. Her father was a different story. Once, the old man made Eddie watch as he had another man's skin pulled off his body, just because he didn't care for the color.

"Keep me posted," the old man barked. "And remember, Edward, I gave you this job for a reason. I can take it away just as easily."

THE KEY

"Yes, Sir," Eddie nodded. The pit in his stomach grew. Sophie was being brought in to do great things. Why did he find himself rooting for her escape when it meant his life might end as a result? He shook his head and walked away.

They had cleaned, showered, and had the laundry caught up when James' parents pulled up. Sophie, Ben, and James were on the couch, and Tina was in the kitchen grabbing drinks.

"Children, we're home!" his mom sang as she walked in. She was average height, slender, and wore glasses that matched her short blonde hair that was turning slightly grey at 53. "Well, hello," she smiled warmly when her bright green eyes met Sophie. "I'm Sally. You must be our new guest," she said, not missing a beat.

"I'm Sophie," she said shyly, sticking out her hand.

"Oh, none of that here," Sally said, bypassing her hand and grabbing Sophie for a bear hug.

"Easy, mom," James said, looking apologetically at Sophie.

"Oh hush, Jamie. You never bring new friends to the house. Let me welcome her the way I want," Sally sighed.

"This is why," James muttered and rolled his eyes.

"Roger, hurry up!" Sally yelled. "You must come meet Sophie!" Roger walked in with his arms full of groceries. He stood around 6'3", and still maintained a muscular build, even at 52. His beard and mustache were turning white amongst his rich, deep brown hair, and his bright blue eyes sparkled with a hint of mischief.

"Let me take that," James offered, taking a bag from his dad and reaching for another, when his dad suddenly saw Sophie, turned pale, and nearly dropped everything. "Whoa!" James hollered, trying to catch everything before it hit the ground. "Dad, you alright?" he asked once everything was situated. Roger looked at his son as if seeing him for the first time.

"Jamie, sorry about that. I guess I'm getting clumsy in my old age," he said, rushing for the kitchen. Sophie froze at the sound of Roger's voice and grew pale herself.

"Soph, what's wrong?" Ben asked in alarm once everyone was in the kitchen.

"I know that voice," she whispered.

"James' dad?" he asked, confused.

"Yes," Sophie said, barely audible.

"Do you remember how?" Ben asked cautiously.

"He used to give me some sort of shots," Sophie whispered.

"Well, he is a doctor, but he does infectious diseases," Ben said, confused. "Were you sick?"

"No," Sophie said firmly.

Ben took her in his own arms and gave her a much needed hug. "We'll get to the bottom of this...of everything. I promise," he tried to assure her, but her gut told her otherwise.

Ben and Sophie entered the kitchen and James was right by her side. "So, where did you two meet?" his mom asked while she unloaded the bags on the island. His dad kept his distance and chatted with Tina on the other side of the room. He had a slight frown in response to whatever she was saying.

"At a party," James interjected quickly and put his arm around

THE KEY

Sophie's waist.

"Oh, how lovely," Sally said, trying not to bring too much attention to her son's sudden display of affection with this stranger. "Where are you from, Dear?"

"How was your vacation, Mom?" James asked, clearly changing the subject. His mother played along.

"Oh, the usual. Your father did his investigations, and I got some great photos. The food was amazing, and the sights were to die for. You kids will definitely have to come next time. You, too, Sophie," Sally said, winking. Sophie smiled.

"I like her," Sally whispered to James, who winked back at her.

"So, Dad," James called out casually. "I was in the office showing Sophie some of mom's work, and I was trying to remember where that picture on the wall behind your desk was taken at. What was that for, again? I'm drawing a blank."

"I'm not sure," Roger said vaguely. "Those are all old photos. I can't remember myself," he lied.

James eyed him suspiciously. "It's the one with all the guys standing together in lab coats," he pushed.

"That doesn't narrow it down, unfortunately. I'm sorry, Son," Roger shrugged.

"I can go get it," James offered.

"Doesn't mean I will remember," his dad laughed. "But I do have some steaks to grill. Sophie, how do you like yours?" he asked, giving her a brief smile.

"Medium rare," Sophie answered, eyeing him herself. He was clearly lying and wanted it dropped. James went to say something else, but Sophie grabbed his hand and pulled him back to her. "Thank you," she said sweetly. Then nodded to James to go to the living room while everyone else prepped for dinner. "We'll be right back," Sophie smiled and pulled him into the other room.

"Well, that was strange," his mother stated bluntly.

"Agreed," Tina confirmed.

"That's ridiculous!" James exclaimed once they were in the living room.

"Shhh!" Sophie hissed. "Listen, I honestly don't think he can say," Sophie whispered.

"What? Why not?" James asked, confused.

"My dad could never talk about his work," Sophie recalled. "Maybe your dad can't either, if they were working together."

"What would they be working on together?" he asked. "You said your dad was a scientist, and my dad is an infectious disease doctor?"

"I don't know," she breathed. "But I remember your dad."

"You remember him?" James asked, more confused. "How?"

"When he spoke. I remembered his voice," Sophie said, starring at the floor, trying to pull the memory back forward. "He used to give me shots when I was little. He was nice and gave me advice," she shrugged.

"Gave you shots?" James asked, shaking his head in disbelief. "Like a patient?"

"Yes," Sophie answered.

"Were you sick?" he asked, alarmed.

"I don't remember," Sophie lied. She did not know why she got so many injections. Her mini me said she was never sick. There was no sense in getting James any more riled up over the unknown. "Let me

THE KEY

see if I can get him to talk to me, okay?"

"Okay," he mumbled in disagreement.

"Thank you," Sophie said, kissing him on the cheek.

"Nope," James said, grabbing her and kissing her on the mouth. He felt her knees buckle as he claimed her mouth. He smiled against her lips. "You're welcome," he murmured gently. Sophie walked away, laughing and shaking her head. But it didn't mean he couldn't still help.

Everyone helped put dinner on the table. Once they were all settled, James casually stated, "Oh, Dad, before I forget, Dr. Stephens stopped by. He said to call him as soon as you got back."

"Oh?" Roger said, trying not to sound alarmed. "I will have to give him a call after dinner." Clearly, someone was hurt at some point, and James was letting him know without alarming his mother. The main missing piece remained...what was Jack's daughter doing in his house with his son? Surely the battle had not ended yet? 'Why would she be so careless?' he wondered.

Sophie looked at James. Obviously, he wasn't going to wait patiently for her to get his father alone. James patted her leg and gave a reassuring smile. Tina sat back and observed all parties. She knew all of James' tricks, but was thrown off by his father's resistance. Dr. Moore never held back when it came to his son. Small talk continued throughout dinner.

Roger leaned over to his wife. "I'm going to give John a quick call," he said, kissing her on the cheek. "I'll meet you on the patio for dessert," he hollered over his shoulder as he headed up to his office.

"So, which one of you is going to tell me what's going on?" his mother asked as soon as her husband was out of earshot. Everyone looked at each other. "Don't make me call on you," Sally warned in her mom voice.

"It's kind of a long story, Mrs. Moore," Ben spoke up.

"Well, it's a good thing I've got time," Sally smiled as she handed out the dessert and nodded towards the patio. Each one took turns giving an edited version of the last couple of weeks. Sally listened carefully to the stories they shared and patiently waited for them to finish. She looked at Sophie and patted the cushion next to her. Sophie got up and sat down next to James' mother, who immediately pulled Sophie into her arms. "You poor thing! I can't imagine how you must feel right now, but know this," Sally said sternly. "You are a part of this family now, and we will get to the bottom of this!"

"Thank you," Sophie said softly, feeling a bit overwhelmed.

"And shame on you three for not telling me," Sally lectured, looking disapprovingly at the rest while she hugged Sophie.

"You were on vacation!" James protested.

"You know better," Sally retorted.

"Did you know my dad?" Sophie asked with hope.

"I'm afraid not, Dear," Sally said somberly. "Roger keeps his work very private, but I never met a Jack at the functions we went to. I would have remembered. I love that name," she said, smiling at Sophie.

"So, you didn't take the photo?" James asked.

"No, I was in Africa around then," Sally said, deep in thought. Just then, they heard Roger coming out. "We will get to the bottom of this," Sally whispered in Sophie's ear. Sophie gave her a weak smile in return. Her gut was going into overdrive. Whatever was coming would not end well. That much she was sure of. "What did John have to say?" his mother asked casually, interrupting Sophie's thoughts.

"Oh, nothing much," Roger said, eyeing Sophie carefully. He had

THE KEY

lost all the color in his face. "He mentioned Sophie had some headaches, and I should probably examine her tonight." Roger looked at his son, who smiled back triumphantly, unknowingly playing with a fire that could take them all out.

"Dessert first," his wife intervened. There wasn't much that scared her husband like this. Several years ago, he worked on a project that gave him the same look. Sally wondered if it had to do with Sophie's dad, but right now she needed to help give her husband time to think. Roger eyed her suspiciously, but followed along. To buy him some time, Sally shared about some of her photography assignments. Sophie listened intently with wide eyes full of wonder. "In fact, we should take a current picture of you kids! Let me go get my camera!" Sally exclaimed.

"It's late, and I'm sure everyone's tired, Hon," Roger said in a panic.

"Oh, I'd love that, Mrs. Moore!" exclaimed Tina.

"Let's take a look at you, Sophie," Roger said as a last resort.

"Just let us take a quick picture first," James protested.

"She needs to be looked at now," Roger warned in a tone like never before.

James opened his mouth to say something when his mother warned, "Jamie," in a tone which everyone knew he was meant to drop it immediately. Sophie gently kissed James on the cheek.

"It's okay," she whispered, knowing exactly why she couldn't be in the photo, and turned to follow his dad to his office.

Everyone watched in silence as she left the room. "Mom, I can't," James said in sudden panic.

"You can, and you will," Sally said firmly. "Now, tell me more

131

about the girl that has stolen my son's heart," she said, patting the cushion next to her once more and smiling. James reluctantly sat down next to her while Tina broke the ice by sharing her favorite things about Sophie. Everyone kept their ears on any movement from the office upstairs.

Eleven

Roger closed the door behind them. "Hello again, Sophie," he smiled weakly.

"Hello, Dr. Moore," she said quietly. He froze for a bit.

"I heard you were in an accident," he said cautiously.

"If you call being run over by a van an 'accident', then yes," Sophie said bluntly.

"Why are you here?" Roger asked softly.

"Your son found me and brought me here," Sophie said honestly.

"Why did he find you?" he asked, crossing his arms.

"You mean how?" Sophie asked, confused.

"No, I mean why," Roger said firmly.

"I don't know," she said truthfully. "I just remember being in the woods and hearing loud music. It distracted me, and I went towards it."

"Distracted you from what?" Roger asked harshly.

"I don't remember," Sophie emphasized. "There are still too many gaps," she said, staring at the floor.

"But you remember me?" Roger asked, confused.

"When I heard your voice," Sophie said, looking back at him. "What were the shots for?" she asked eagerly.

"You remember those?" he asked cautiously.

"Some, yes. What were they for?" Sophie pressed.

"Do you remember your parents?" Roger asked more delicately.

"Only as a kid. Now, answer the question," Sophie said more firmly.

"How far back do your memories go?" he asked sympathetically.

"Answer my question first," Sophie demanded, crossing her own arms.

"Just as stubborn as an adult, I see," Roger laughed, uncrossing his arms and leaning against his desk. "Preventative shots to keep you healthy," he said vaguely. "How far back?" he repeated.

"Around ten," Sophie said, uncrossing her arms. "How do you know my dad?" she asked gently.

"He came to me when you were younger. He was working on a project, and he asked me to help keep you healthy," Roger said, starring at the floor.

"I wasn't sick," Sophie said matter-of-factly.

"That was the point," Roger shrugged.

"Who's Dr. Cox?" she asked.

"I honestly don't know," he said. "Never met him personally. I

THE KEY

just know he studies genetics, and you had to see her too."

"That doesn't make any sense," Sophie said, confused.

"All I know is that your father was preparing you to handle anything thrown at you, because you were special and meant to survive," Roger said, smiling weakly.

"Survive what?" Sophie asked impatiently.

"I don't know," Roger half lied. "How much of your memory is missing?" he asked, concerned.

"I don't know," Sophie said, frustrated. "Between ten and now, mostly." She shuffled her feet on the floor.

"Well, I am glad to see you're doing alright," Roger said, changing the subject. "How long are you staying?" he tried to ask casually.

"I don't know," Sophie said slowly. Her gut was killing her. "Why?"

"Well, you travel a lot, and you've already been here for a while," Roger shrugged.

"You don't like me here, do you?" Sophie asked, being coy.

"No," Roger said slowly. "I just thought you would be ready to move on," he added carefully.

"It's not safe, is it?" Sophie poked.

"No," Roger finally admitted.

"Where's my dad?" Sophie asked impatiently.

"I don't know," Roger lied, looking at the floor.

"Where's my dad?" Sophie asked, raising her voice. She heard footsteps on the stairs.

"Sophie, calm down," Roger said, walking towards her.

"Where's my dad, Roger?" Sophie almost screamed. James was

the first to enter.

"Sophie, calm down!" Roger yelled back, but it was too late. The room was spinning into darkness as she fell to her knees. But instead of the wooden door, it was the steel door in front of her and it was cracked open. She heard James calling and begging her to come back, but she couldn't. It was finally time. She got to her feet and pushed the door open.

On the other side was a simple, small house. It seemed empty, but very familiar. The living room had a very homey feel to it. There were pictures of Sophie with her parents scattered throughout the room, and bookcases filled with books everywhere. A lumpy brown couch sat against one wall with a recliner to match beside it, while they placed a much older TV in the corner.

Sophie saw the staircase and went upstairs. She found what she guessed to be her own room, also full of books and stuffed animals. A picture of her with her parents sat on the nightstand in a handmade frame. Painted on her walls were motivational sayings and butterflies. Unlike James' room, there were no trophies or pictures of friends. Just books. A little pained by that fact, she left to wander down the hall. The room next to hers was an office. She was guessing her dad's. It contained more books and family photos, and a couple of computers. There were papers and notebooks everywhere, but the pages were oddly all blank. Sophie moved on and found her parent's bedroom next.

It was a simple room with more family photos, but fewer books. They painted love quotes on their light grey walls. There was black and white accented décor throughout. Sophie found herself in their giant walk-in closet. Her mother's side was mostly full of black

THE KEY

clothing, and the rest was full of color. Her dad's side contained mostly suits with a few casual clothing items on the end. She picked up a t-shirt and took a big whiff. The familiar smell of her dad came rushing back. Sophie reached for one of her mother's tops, but froze at the sounds of voices downstairs. A sharp pain stabbed her in the stomach. She wrapped her arms around herself, took a deep breath, and headed downstairs.

She walked slowly and cautiously. Whatever was behind this door was ugly. That much she knew. Her guard was fully up and ready. When she reached the kitchen, she saw the little girl having lunch with her mother and father. The room was full of happiness and light. They were laughing and sharing jokes. Sophie had never seen them so happy, when out of nowhere she screamed out and was doubled over in pain. Once she caught her breath, she looked up and saw only the little girl had turned around and was staring at her. She held her tiny finger to her lips while shaking her head "no". Then she turned back around and was laughing with her parents once more. When suddenly, the little girl pointed towards the window and all laughter stopped. Both parents watched her, then looked at each other in alarm.

"It's time," her mother said gravely. "Take her," she ordered. "I'll hold them off as long as I can." Her dad opened his mouth to protest, but there was nothing more they could do. "Sophie, Honey," Jess said, getting down to her daughter's level, "it's time for you to go into the closet. Do NOT come out until someone comes to get you. Do you understand?" Jess said sternly. The little girl began to cry, but nodded for her mother. Jess pulled the little girl into a tight squeeze. "I will always be with you. No matter what! But right now, I need you to be brave for Mommy," Jess said more softly, with tears in her eyes. "I love you, Peanut," she whispered in her ear. "Now, go with your father!" she ordered as she grabbed guns secured under the table and counter, and took the safety off. "Go!" Jess ordered one last time.

Her dad picked up the little girl and ran to the hall closet. "I need you to try and remember everything we've taught you," Jack said urgently as he placed her on the ground. "And don't forget this," he said, putting the necklace around the little girl's neck. "Do NOT come out until someone comes and gets you. No matter what. Promise me!" Jack shouted.

"I promise," the little girl cried. Jack got to her level and clung to her tightly. "I will always love you, Peanut," he whispered in her ear, fighting back his own tears. "No one is smarter, braver, or more capable than you. Well, except for your mother," he chuckled. "Now go, Honey," Jack urged.

"You're not coming?" the little girl asked in panic.

"No, Peanut," Jack said, trying to sound reassuring. "I have to go help your mother. Now, go," he said more softly as he pulled out the gun from the back of his pants and prepared it for firing. Jack nodded gently in the closet's direction. The little girl reluctantly turned and crawled into the safe room hidden in the back of the closet. Sophie watched while her dad closed the door and pushed something heavy in front of it before heading in the kitchen's direction.

She closed her eyes in pain and grabbed her stomach. She took another deep breath, but when Sophie opened her eyes, she had become the little girl hiding in the safe room. Immediately, she heard the gunfire. Sophie went to climb out, but the door was locked and blocked. All she could do was sit and wait. She listened eagerly, but no one was talking. There was only shooting.

THE KEY

"Jack!" she heard her mother scream, followed by more shots. After what seemed like an eternity, Sophie heard her mother gasp, "You will never have her…"

"We'll see," said an elderly voice, followed by a single gunshot. "Find the girl," he ordered.

Sophie heard footsteps running all over the house, but it was the echo of a cane that caught her ear. She put her hands over her mouth and held her breath. Sophie heard the closet door open as he walked in. The cane thumped against the floor until it stopped nearly directly in front of her face. She heard the scraping of hangers being pushed around on the rod.

"Sir," a deep voice said, out of breath. "We've torn the house apart. She's nowhere to be found."

"Well, that's a disappointment," the old man said monotonously.

"She must be with someone else, Sir," the deep voice added with a tremor.

"Then I suggest you find out who if you would like to see tomorrow," the elderly voice stated with a warning.

"Yes, Sir," the deep voice said with determination. Finally, they left, shortly followed by silence. Sophie's stomach growled as hunger kicked in. There was no food to be found in the safe room, just loneliness and darkness. Just when Sophie was sure she was going to die, trapped in this horrific memory, she heard different footsteps that entered the closet. Something scrapped against the floor as it was moved aside, then the tiny opening flooded with light as a shadow figure crouched before her.

"Hey, Sophie," the figure whispered. "Your parents sent me to get you." Sophie stayed silent. "It's not safe here anymore. We need to go," the figure said, gently wrapping her in a blanket, picking her up, and carrying her out while holding her head down. "Don't look, Peanut," he whispered, as he carried her quickly through the kitchen and out the backdoor. But she did....

Sophie saw her dad laying on his stomach with multiple gunshot wounds and blood everywhere. Her mother laid next to him, face up, with just as many wounds and the kill shot in her forehead. The last shot Sophie heard. Tears streamed down her cheeks, but she made no sound as they carried her into the night. Sophie closed her eyes and silently grieved as the house disappeared before her.

"Sophie," she heard James pleading for her to come back.

"Roger," his mother pleaded. "Just tell them what you know. Where's the poor girl's father?"

"Dead," Sophie said drained. "They both are. I remember," she said, struggling to find her voice.

"Sophie!" James exclaimed as he pulled her into his arms. She opened her eyes fully and found herself surrounded by her friends.

"I can't be in photos with you," Sophie said, getting to her feet. "My safety is more guaranteed than yours. Your dad's just trying to keep you safe," she said to James.

Roger pulled Ben and Tina out of the way as he began checking Sophie's vitals. "What did you remember?" he asked, flashing a small light in her eyes.

"The day my parents were murdered," Sophie said wearily.

Everyone froze.

"Sophie," Roger whispered with his voice full of pain.

"Not your fault, Doc," she said flatly.

THE KEY

"It's not safe," Roger said. "You've been here too long."

"I know," Sophie said, putting her hand on his shoulder.

"They'll be coming for you," Roger warned. Sophie held up her hands to silence everyone and closed her eyes to listen.

When she opened them, they were wild with alarm. "They're already here," she said matter-of-factly. "Get everyone in the safe room," she ordered him. Roger nodded, grabbed his wife, and began pushing everyone to the saferoom.

"You heard the lady," Roger ordered.

"What's going on?" Tina and his mother demanded in unison.

"The people with guns have come to take me," Sophie said, pushing everyone out of the office. "I'm sorry," she said, looking everyone in the eye. "Now go!" she ordered.

"Hell no!" James exclaimed, running to his room.

"Agreed!" yelled Tina, racing into her bedroom.

Sophie watched them in horror. "We don't have time for this!" she yelled at them. "There's at least three vans coming, and I'm pretty sure they're full!"

"How do you know?" Ben asked, confused.

"Can't you hear them?" Sophie asked. But no one heard anything at all.

"Ready!" James said, coming out fully armed.

"Here," Tina said, handing them each an earcom from the backpack on her back. "Use these to communicate. I'll be watching the cameras to give you a heads up," she said with authority. Tina grabbed Ben and dragged him to safety.

"Take your family to the safe room!" Sophie ordered James.

"I love you, but no," he said defiantly. "You will not be able to handle that many people alone."

His father and mother froze. They knew what it meant and took for their son to finally say those words again. Sophie was too panicked to hear them.

"I can't have you all getting hurt because of me!" she yelled at James.

"I'm not leaving you!" he yelled back and kissed her quickly on the mouth.

"Be careful," his mother surrendered.

"Be safe, Son," his father warned as they hurried to the safe room.

"Ugh!" Sophie yelled in frustration. James smiled in triumph. "Kill the lights and stay inside," she ordered. "I'll get as many outside before I come meet you."

"You're cute when you lose," James winked and went to kill the lights. If they made it through this, she would have to talk to him about his stubbornness during times like this. Sophie quickly got out the front door and took off towards the shed.

Twelve

She heard the metal shutters fall, covering the door and windows, putting the house on lockdown as a hissing sound hurried around the house. An invisible electronic parameter moved quickly around the house. A smile crept across Sophie's lips. She would have to make sure never to underestimate Tina again.

The vans stopped at the tree line of the drive. "I count twenty-four total," Sophie whispered.

"Good. So, twelve each?" James teased.

"You're not helping," Sophie grumbled.

"Children, knock it off," Tina interrupted in her motherly voice. "We have work to do."

Sophie took to the woods. "Where's your weapon?" Ben asked.

"What!" James said in alarm.

"I don't need one," Sophie smiled wickedly and quickly climbed a tree. "Now, be quiet please, so I can listen," she whispered and closed her eyes. "They're spreading out wide to flank the front and sides of the house. They know the ocean is to your back, but watch it all the same. No surprises," Sophie whispered.

"On it," Tina responded from the safe room with several computer monitors at her disposal.

Sophie was not a fan of killing, but she had five people waiting in the house to survive this. There were way too many to play nice. She didn't have to wait long before a stout Puerto Rican man was underneath her. Sophie leapt from the branches like a cat, gracefully landing on his shoulders, and snapped his neck before landing on the balls of her feet and taking off to the next one. "One," she whispered with a smile.

"Oh, we're keeping score now?" James teased, trying not to be worried about her fighting alone.

"Maybe," Sophie said, smiling. She knew they were worried. Those watching her would definitely look at her differently when all was said and done, but there were way too many to not need the extra eyes. Something kept telling her to watch the water, too. But she couldn't think about all of that right now. First, she had to make her friends safe. That meant taking out as many as possible, as quickly as possible. After all, they were in danger because of her to begin with! If they never wanted to see her again, Sophie would accept that.

"Stand up," a female French accent ordered.

She really needed to get focused! Sophie held her hands up in the air and stood up leisurely. "Turn around, slowly," the French woman ordered. Sophie obeyed. The French woman was around 5'9", athletically built, had short blonde curly hair, and was dressed in tight

THE KEY

black clothing.

"Sophie?" she heard James' voice full of concern in her ear.

"They're really pulling you all globally these days, aren't they?" he heard Sophie respond flatly.

"Only the best for you, Madame," the French blonde responded coolly. "I don't know why. This is so easy," she said, mostly to herself. Sophie's lips curled up on the ends. "Now, walk towards me slowly, and put it in my hands." Sophie walked towards her slowly, as requested.

"Probably because I'm difficult," Sophie said, shrugging once she reached her. Before the French woman could even think about responding, Sophie had her gun and was pointing it at her chest. "Two," Sophie said before taking the kill shot.

"Sophie!" James yelled in her ear.

"Babe, I'm going to need you to focus," she said assuringly as she took off again. "We're in a kill or be killed situation, so we need to focus. Neither of us can do that if you're distracted by what I'm doing," Sophie said in a calm, motherly voice.

"Bro, she's KILLING it!" yelled Ben.

"Yeah, we've been watching, and she's a real badass," confirmed Tina with a hint of pride in her voice.

"See," Sophie said. "So, I need you to focus, because you have to keep your family safe. Now, they tend to send the weakest first, but don't underestimate anyone. Okay?"

"Okay," James said reluctantly.

"Tina, watch the water. It's a perfect ambush entry," Sophie ordered.

"On it," Tina responded. "Watch your right!" she added

urgently, and out of nowhere came a thick athletic arm swinging to take Sophie out. She ducked just in time to dodge it.

"Well, a hello to you, too," Sophie said, annoyed. "What? No gun?" she asked sarcastically.

"No need," said the Russian giant, who towered at least 6'6". He had blonde spikey hair, wore a black t-shirt that was struggling to cover his bulging muscles, and black cargo pants with steel-toed boots.

"Oh, goodie," Sophie said flatly.

"Where is it?" the giant asked.

"No clue," she responded honestly.

"Give it to me!" he ordered.

"Can't," Sophie shrugged.

"Then I take!" the giant yelled.

"Bring it," Sophie said, putting her fists up and taking a deep breath.

"Whole picture," her mother whispered in her ear.

"I remember," Sophie whispered to no one.

The giant swung, so she dodged and did a sweep kick. It didn't make him fall, but he stumbled backwards. Sophie observed the giant carefully. He was solid, and would take some wearing down first. She needed to pace herself. Three more joined them. This was definitely going to be a long night. Sophie assessed the situation promptly and waited for their first move.

Although she checked the water regularly, Tina couldn't believe what was happening in front of her. It didn't look like a fight at all, but rather a beautifully choreographed dance. She had never seen someone so fast and graceful before. No wonder Sophie had been training since she was ten. Whoever was after her wasn't messing

THE KEY

around, but this girl was taking on three goons and a freaking giant! Tina definitely didn't have to worry about Sophie in a fight, but she worried about Sophie's head and heart, and the toll all of this had to be taking on her. Tina promised herself that she would do her best to help Sophie with as much as she could. Sophie definitely would have to teach them some moves before their next encounter, though, because Tina wouldn't always be able to be behind a monitor. Ben needed to stay safe, too.

James listened intently to his earcom while he stared at the sealed windows around him. He could tell from her breathing that Sophie was trying to pace herself. She clearly was fighting more than one person right now, and she was taking the occasional punch. It was killing James not to have eyes on her while having to sit on the sidelines. But he needed to show Sophie he had faith in her. Even if he didn't care for the current situation.

Sophie took a few shots in order to give better ones. Something her mom taught her. She wondered for a split second if her mother would be proud of how far she had come. The tiny German and the average Spaniard were already down, but the giant remained tough, despite growing more tired by the second. Now was her moment. He swung one more time as expected, allowing her to dodge, run up the side of a tree, push off, grab his head and twist. Sophie fell forward with him and landed on top.

"Holy crap!" she heard Ben yell in her ear.

"Three through six," Sophie said, catching her breath.

"That's my girl," James said, relieved. "Only eighteen more to go."

"Not helpful," Sophie said, trying to slow down her breathing.

She heard him chuckle in her ear, and it was enough to re-energize her.

"Do they always send this many?" Tina asked with concern.

"No," Sophie responded shortly. Whoever desired her wanted to make sure she actually came this time. That was obvious. Sophie was trying to pace herself, but this was getting ridiculous. James watched the windows, and Tina watched the water. They could tell Sophie was getting tired, but she continued to count each victory. No one was sure if it was for their benefit, or her own, but they cheered Sophie on all the same.

They never came all at once. Sophie was pretty sure they were instructed to wear her down first, and it was working. She needed to be smart as she continued to pick them off one by one. It surprised Sophie that everyone was cheering her on. She was taking lives, after all. Maybe they just wanted to stay alive? Either way, it was a welcomed change from being alone.

"You really don't have to take them all, you know," James said, almost pouting. Her giggle was music to his ears.

"Jealous?" Sophie teased.

"You're just having all the fun," he whined.

"Not for long," Tina interrupted. "You're getting six from the water," she said with a hint of concern.

"Finally!" James exclaimed, heading for the back of the house. "Ti, let me out," he ordered, before grabbing the door knob to head out.

"Be careful," Sophie whispered in his ear.

"Focus babe," James whispered back, and slid out the side door. She smiled with pride and got back to work.

"You're looking a little tired there, Sophie," said a male shadow figure leaning up against a tree with a thick French accent.

THE KEY

"Well, you know," Sophie shrugged, trying to pull as much energy into her muscles that she could muster.

"You could just give me what I want and come with me. We might even spare your friends," he said coolly.

"And what fun would that be?" Sophie asked sweetly.

"Loads! Just think of the possibilities!" he shouted, remaining in the shadows.

"No thanks," Sophie said with a smile.

"Are you sure? You are destined for great things," he taunted.

"Oh, well, in that case," Sophie said sweetly. "Maybe you should come and tell me all about it."

He sighed and shook his head. "Remember, I tried," the shadow said, shrugging and disappearing deeper into the shadows as someone attacked from the back and both sides. Sophie defended herself immediately, but there was something about him she really didn't like.

"Track him, Tina," Sophie said, growling as she ducked a swing.

"Already looking," Tina responded with great determination and focus.

James holstered his gun. The more he could take out without it, the better he thought, especially since he didn't have a silencer. He didn't want to make things more difficult for Sophie than they already were.

There wasn't much coverage between the house and the water, but he needed to keep them from getting inside. "Group brawl it is,"

James whispered to himself, and walked out towards the water with his hands up. "Hey, fellas," he yelled over the roar of the waves. "Nice night for a stroll, huh?"

"What are you doing!" he heard Sophie yell in his ear.

"Focus, babe," he assured. "I've got this." The men in front of him were very confused and looked at each other. James used it to his advantage and started his own dance. After a bit, Sophie heard, "One," and a smile crossed her lips.

"Let the games begin," Sophie whispered as she used the gun in her hand to take out someone charging from behind. "Nine," she said out loud.

"Five," she heard James grunt after a while. "And you had a head start," he sulked. Her giggle fueled his desire to win. "Six," he finally said. "Anymore coming?" he asked Tina.

"No, but you need to go left. There's some almost to the house, and Sophie's too far out," Tina reported.

"On it," James said, taking off.

"Meet you there," Sophie breathed.

Although James hadn't fought in a while, and definitely not this many at once, it was like riding a bike. They both continued to count out loud, so they knew how many were left.

"And who do we have here?" asked the male French shadow. Sophie froze. She knew the voice, but couldn't place it. She just knew she didn't like it.

"Who wants to know?" she heard James reply, and took off in his direction.

"Careful," she said in his ear. "He's really dangerous."

"Are you important to our Sophie?" the shadow inquired.

THE KEY

"All life is important," James shrugged. "Minus yours, of course," he added with a smile.

"This should be interesting," the shadow replied smugly before disappearing once more.

"Tina!" Sophie yelled as she picked up speed to get to him.

"On it," Tina assured, but he was nearly impossible to track. It was as if he knew exactly where all the cameras were. Frustration brewed in Tina's core. No one could escape her system. Dodging cameras or not. She had put everything she had into the system to make sure of just that, and yet, this French lurch was trying her patience.

James was too busy fighting the last of the goons off to see where the shadow had taken off to. Sophie caught up to help. They used each other to help take out the rest. It was like they had trained together all their lives as they continued the dance. Everyone watched them in awe.

Sophie took James' hand as she ran up a tree and round kicked a tall, athletic black haired man who spun and fell face first. She then swung James, to do his own round kick, to knock out another tall athletic brown haired woman who fell backwards and never got back up. When they needed to catch their breath, they stood back to back and reassessed the situation before dancing once more. They were a powerhouse duo that couldn't be stopped.

"Look at him, Roger," his wife whispered. Roger nodded in silence. Sophie and James were never meant to meet. He had made sure of it. Yet fate had a different intention all along. Roger had helped to design the greatest weapon of all, but it would be that weapon that would give his son life again. He wondered if Jack knew all along, or if he would be just as blown away as Roger was.

"Twenty-nine," Sophie said, wildly annoyed.

"Tina?" James asked.

"I'm sorry," she said, completely infuriated. "I lost him," she added with a hint of hostility through her clenched teeth.

"I don't think so," Sophie warned.

"You mean he's watching?" Ben asked, concerned.

"I guess that's all of them," they heard her reply loudly. "Let's get back to the house." James took her hand and began tracing in her palm. He seemed upset and uncomfortable. She'd never seen him so distant. Sophie felt her stomach drop completely, and she suddenly needed to throw up.

Her head whipped around wildly as she looked everywhere for the French shadow, but Sophie knew deep down she wouldn't see him until he wanted to be seen. No one was safe. Not until she took the French shadow out.

Thirteen

They walked into the house, and James dropped Sophie's hand immediately. His mother ran over and pulled her son into her arms, mouthing a soft, "Thank you" to Sophie, who nodded in response.

"Thank you for saving us," Roger said, taking Sophie's hands in his. She had turned out so much better than expected. "Your parents would be proud."

"You're welcome," Sophie said, smiling weakly. "But I had quite a bit of help." She winked at Tina, who smiled back. "We're not out of the woods just yet, though," Sophie said grimly. "A clean-up crew will come for the bodies," she warned Roger. "It's important no one is here. You might need to go back on vacation for a while. Keep your heads down and don't talk to anyone while you are away." Roger nodded in agreement.

Sophie slowly turned to James. "I made a promise to ask you

directly when I felt it was time to leave, to see if you wanted to come with me. Understand, we'll be on the run for a while, and you will have to say goodbye to everyone now. It will not be safe for them if you talk to them, so I understand if you don't want to walk away from your life," she finished, holding her breath while waiting for his response.

"It's okay, Son," his father said as his mother nodded encouragingly.

After what seemed like an eternity, James looked Sophie in the eyes and replied, "No."

"What!" everyone shouted at once.

"No," he replied coldly. "Being with you puts my loved ones in danger. I don't even really know you. You're just a stranger I found in the middle of the road, and you can't replace my loved ones just like that." Everyone was shocked, but it was Ben that glared at his best friend.

"Have you lost your damn mind?" Ben shouted. Sophie backed away a bit from James' bitter words. Her ears were on fire. How could she be so foolish?

"You can be an idiot if you want," Ben demanded, "But you don't speak for us all, and Tina and I are going with her!"

"Go ahead," James shrugged. "But weren't you just in my room the other night, Tina? Going on about how you stand by your family and all that crap, or are you just talk, buddy old pal?" James said glaring straight at her. Tina grinded her teeth and glared back as she assessed her friend. "So, you're going to be a dick to me, too, now?" she warned her friend. His parents stood by helplessly.

"Make your choice!" James barked at Tina and Ben.

"Sophie!" Ben yelled back.

THE KEY

"Why are you being like this?" his mother pleaded.

Tina studied James before determining what needed to be done. She slowly faced her husband. "Ben," Tina said softly while pulling him back. "James has made his choice, and we have to support him."

"You're both mental!" Ben yelled, crossing his arms.

"Sometimes," Tina said in her motherly voice. "Sometimes you have to do things you hate to keep your family safe. We have to do that now and go with James," she said, choosing her words carefully. "I'm sorry Sophie. You're on your own," Tina said, tearing up as she said goodbye to her friend from a distance.

"This is ridiculous!" Ben shouted.

"I'll be gone in a few," Sophie said, staring at the floor before running up the stairs in tears. She packed as quickly as she could, shoving what she could carry into her backpack. She wiped away the falling tears and sniffled as she went. Sophie couldn't really blame him. Everything James said was true. It didn't make it any less painful, though. She ran out of the room and nearly knocked Tina off her feet.

"I will take care of whatever you leave behind," Tina said, looking at the floor.

"Take it all," Sophie whispered. "There's nothing I want to remember from here anyway," she blurted out, going around Tina and racing down the stairs.

"Goodbye, Ben," Sophie said, looking at James, who refused to make eye contact with her. She flung open the front door and was gone before anyone had a chance to respond.

"I can't stay here," James reported angrily to his parents.

"Where will you go so late at night?" his mother asked in

desperation.

"Anywhere but here," James said, taking off to go upstairs and pack. He tried to be selective in his packing. He had no desire to come back any time soon. His family was in danger, and that made him sick to his core.

"You sure you handled that the best way?" Tina asked suddenly behind him. "She took it very badly."

"It had to be done," James said, focused on his packing.

"Understood," Tina said flatly. "Where are we going?"

"Wherever they have a room," he responded.

"I'll go pack," Tina sighed and turned to go to her room.

"Thanks," James said more softly.

"Anything for family," Tina shrugged and went to go pack.

Ben paced in the living room while James' parents whispered back and forth. He couldn't ever remember being this mad before, let alone being this furious with James. He didn't even notice Roger leaving and returning with a separate backpack.

"Ben," Roger said cautiously. "I need you to take this with you." "Why? What's in it?" Ben asked, stopping and looking at him with confusion.

"Jack always made it a point to be prepared when it came to his daughter," Roger shrugged. "I guess it wore off. Give this to James. It's just some extra supplies, food, etc. But maybe it will help him find his heart again."

Ben was utterly confused, but put the bag on his back. It was undeniably heavy and full. "I'm not sure there's much hope, Dr. Moore. First Helen, and now this," he said, shaking his head.

"You know he's stubborn," Sally assured. "But take care of him

THE KEY

all the same," she said, kissing him on the cheek.

"I'll try," Ben muttered, shaking his head in disbelief. James and Tina came down with less luggage than expected. "Where's all your stuff?" Ben asked Tina.

"I thought I would keep it light for a bit," Tina shrugged. "You don't mind, Mrs. Moore, do you?" she asked politely.

"Of course, not dear," Sally smiled. "We're right behind you," she winked. "We forgot to get the bags from the car, anyway."

"Be careful, Son," Roger said, hugging him a little too tightly.

"Return the favor," James replied. His father winked at him and smiled.

"We love you with all of our hearts," Sally said, holding back tears.

"I love you too, Mom," James said, hugging her tightly. "I'm sorry."

"I know," she whispered back. The kids piled into the SUV while Roger held his wife on the porch, waving goodbye.

"God's speed," Roger whispered.

"Let's go, Roger," Sally ordered. They got in their own car and drove away, never looking back. Ignoring the twenty-nine bodies that currently surrounded their home.

Fourteen

Sophie ran until her feet couldn't carry her anymore. She had no clue where she was, but she didn't care.

One person couldn't possibly track all three parties. She hoped, by leaving first, she bought the rest of them time to get away. But it was incredibly late, and she needed to find a place to get some rest.

There was a house ahead, so Sophie ran, yet again. In the backyard, she found an old abandoned shed. As quickly and quietly as she could, Sophie broke the lock and slipped inside. The shed was small, dusty, and full of forgotten tools. It would do.

Sophie pulled out a blanket and laid on the floor, instantly missing the comfort of an actual bed. She looked at her hand, the last place James had touched her. Sophie closed her eyes and cried as she remembered his exact touch. She opened her eyes in alarm and cried even harder. Who knew a loss like this could hurt so badly. Sophie

THE KEY

silently cried herself back to sleep.

James started driving. He had no clue where. He just needed space from that house right now, and all of their memories. Tina was by his side in the passenger seat, silently looking out the window at the passing scenery.

"Are we even going to talk about this?" Ben asked, pouting in the backseat.

"Nope," James said flatly.

"You're being a jerk," Ben growled.

"Ben," Tina warned.

"Mental," Ben muttered to himself, crossing his arms and slouching in the backseat. James finally pulled into a hotel on the plaza.

"One room or two?" Tina asked.

"Two!" Ben shouted. Tina got out of the car to see what was available.

The wooden door appeared before Sophie again. "Of course!" she exclaimed sarcastically, and opened the door. On the other side was a beautiful garden surrounded by trees, with the Eiffel Tower peeking out from the tree line in the distant background. "Paris?" Sophie asked, confused. There was a group of teenagers waiting patiently across from her in a huddle. Suddenly, a gorgeous girl around fifteen, dressed all in black, with stunning bright red shoulder-length hair brushed past Sophie. She was watching the red-headed girl in awe when a taller, very skinny but athletic blonde boy with green eyes popped up beside the girl and put his arm around her shoulders.

"Bonjour, Sophie," said a familiar male French accent.

"Bonjour, Simon," the girl responded flatly. "Now, kindly remove your arm before you lose it, please," she warned.

"Such a tease," Simon said, removing his arm. "When are you going to take my offer and run away with me?" he asked, half pleading.

"Probably after hell freezes over at least twice, and I become bored," the girl answered with no emotion.

"Sophie, my love," Simon cooed, "you know we're the best ones here. I should take these weaklings out of their misery! We can make a life of our own, that will be full of wealth and happiness! Don't you want to be happy?" he asked eagerly.

"I have no desire to be a contract killer," the girl said bluntly, looking him straight in the eye. "Every life should be cherished," she emphasized. "Especially the weak."

"Thinking like that will get you killed one day, my love," Simon said, full of sympathy.

"We'll see," the girl shrugged, flipping her hair in his face, and walking off to join the others.

"You will change your mind, my love," Simon whispered, "and I'll be waiting." The girl tried very hard not to let him see her shiver, but there was something about Simon that just made her skin crawl.

"Gather round students," clapped a tall man with thick, flowing shoulder-length black hair that matched his thick French accent. He was dressed in form-fitting black clothing, that made him look more

THE KEY

like a dance choreographer than any instructor. "Today, we practice in the elements," he said, holding his arms up and twirling around.

"What the heck is he teaching?" current Sophie whispered to herself.

"Sophie and Giselle," the instructor ordered. The girls paired up and bowed to each other before taking stance. Giselle was a little shorter than Sophie, also in all black. Her hair was platinum blonde and pulled back in a ponytail that went past her waist. She looked very fragile standing next to Sophie, but her green eyes were full of determination.

Giselle started towards Sophie, but Sophie did a graceful back handspring, just missing Giselle's attempt to grab her. Current Sophie watched intently, and wondered if this was a dance class after all, but Giselle would not give up so easily. She studied Sophie for a quick second before trying again. Giselle continued to attack, but Sophie escaped without a single touch, using the trees around her as leverage.

"You're still using the same fighting order," Sophie told Giselle. "I know exactly what you're going to do before you do it, because you do the exact same thing over and over. Try switching it up," Sophie offered to Giselle, who was clearly a friend.

"Sophie is correct, Giselle," the instructor confirmed. "You must strategize, and keep your opponent guessing," he said before clapping into the air. The girls stopped immediately, bowed to each other, and bowed to the instructor.

"You'll get it next time," younger Sophie said as she winked at Giselle. *What kind of school was this?*

"Let's try something else," the instructor said, looking around.

"Let's do Giselle and Simon." The girls looked at each other in horror.

"Master, please," Giselle pleaded.

"Giselle, you must practice with different opponents," the instructor ordered.

"Come on, weakling," Simon taunted. "This will end quickly for you." Sophie had a bad feeling suddenly.

"Don't harm her," the younger Sophie warned as he walked past her.

"Relax, my love," Simon smiled wickedly. "I'll simply put her out of her misery."

"Simon," the girl warned, but the instructor clapped his hands and it was game on.

They bowed to the instructor and bowed to each other before finally taking stance. Giselle looked terrified. "You've got this!" younger Sophie yelled to her friend. Simon and Giselle began to dance. Simon typically pinned Giselle against the ground, making her cry out in pain before letting go.

"One more try," the instructor warned. "Use the elements!" Giselle looked wildly around her and began collecting dirt in her hands. They returned to stance. Right before Simon attacked, Giselle threw the dirt in his eyes and did a sweep kick, putting Simon on his butt.

"You bitch!" he yelled, as he wiped the dirt from his eyes. He jumped up and ran towards Giselle, but she used the tree to do a flip over him. The students cheered wildly for Giselle. "Enough!" yelled Simon, with rage oozing from his eyes. They danced a little more before Giselle was in a headlock, with Simon on top of her. His eyes fully dilated, and his face the deepest shade of red.

THE KEY

"Well, done Giselle," the instructor said absent-mindedly, "but Simon still wins this round," he said, clapping his hands. Simon did not move. Younger Sophie's stomach dropped, and she started making her way towards Simon. "Simon," the instructor ordered. "Let her go."

"No!" Simon shouted back. "Enough of this!"

"Simon," younger Sophie said softly, "you've won. Let her go."

"I told you they were too weak!" Simon yelled. "They need to be dealt with!" His voice was cold and collective, his eyes fully black, and he spit from his mouth as he talked.

"Simon," the instructor ordered again, but younger Sophie held her hand up to him.

"Simon," younger Sophie said softly, trying not to let her voice crack. "She has been dealt with. You won, fair and square. Now, please...let her go...for me." She forced herself to look deep into his eyes.

"You will never learn, Sophie, until you lose," Simon said, suddenly calm and cold like ice.

"Simon, NO!..." younger Sophie pleaded as her voice cracked, but it was too late. Simon smiled from ear to ear before quickly snapping Giselle's neck.

"NO!" younger Sophie screamed, running to her friend. The instructor was on Simon, holding him down.

"Guards!" he yelled, while Simon wiggled wildly under his grip. Younger Sophie held Giselle's lifeless body to her own and rocked back and forth sobbing.

"I'm sorry," she cried into her friend's hair. The other students froze in horror. The guards came and dragged the kicking and screaming Simon away.

"Sophie, you must let her go," the instructor whispered softly in her ear.

"No!" Sophie yelled back.

"It's not your fault. You did everything you could," he whispered, gently stroking her hair.

"Not enough," Sophie retorted with pure venom in her voice.

"This is what he wants," the instructor said more sternly. "Will you let him win after all of this? Should Giselle die for nothing?" Sophie glared at the instructor with such hatred in her eyes, but took a deep breath, picked up her friend, and carried her back inside the French doors of a giant building just on the other side of the garden.

"Oh, my gosh," current Sophie whispered to herself. Her dad walked up beside her and put his hand on her shoulder.

"Peanut, I know you're exhausted, but it's time to move. He's coming," he whispered. "You must go. Now."

Sophie sat up with alarm. "Simon," she scowled, grabbed the blanket, shoved it back in her bag, slid out the shed door silently, and took off running once more.

The Mystic Hotel was built in the 90s, but they had redone the rooms to reflect a more modern touch with grey, black, and white décor. Each room had a king-size bed with a white comforter and enough pillows on it to smother a tiny army to death. There was a small desk coming from the wall, with a computer chair and a lamp set up in the corner of each room. It was simple, and cheaper than other

THE KEY

hotels in the area. Once in their adjoining rooms, Tina began checking the entire room with her hands. "What the heck are you doing?" Ben asked, already extremely irritated by this bunch.

"You know me," Tina said. "Always have to keep my hands busy at times like these," she shrugged and continued to feel every inch of the room with her hands.

"Ben, I know you're upset," James started.

"You have no *IDEA* how upset I am with you right now," Ben growled. "Do you know how many people she just killed in order to keep us safe, and we just abandoned her at the drop of a hat?!"

"Ben," James tried again, "sometimes, you have to do what's right even if no one else can see it," he said, looking at the floor. "People just aren't what they seem to be," he said, sighing.

"You're clearly not," Ben said, grabbing his bags and heading for the second room.

"Let him cool off," Tina said as she continued to feel the room. "He can't see the whole picture right now."

"He's never been so mad at me," James said, looking at the opposite room.

"Ben liked her. Like the sister he never had," Tina said sorrowfully as she put a hand on James' shoulder. "But you did what you had to. He'll see that soon enough."

"I hope so," James said gloomily.

"Get some rest," Tina said, kissing him on the cheek. "Tomorrow's a new day, and frankly, I'm exhausted." She walked into the other room and closed the door. Once she was done feeling everything in their room as well, she put her pj's on and climbed into bed. "Ben, Honey," Tina begged. "Come get some rest."

"I don't know that I can," Ben said honestly, looking out the window. "She saved our lives, and we just left her. Alone. By herself."

"I know," Tina said, climbing out of bed and going to the window to console her husband. "But we watched the girl take out all those people, so you know she can take care of herself."

"Not the point," he said, looking at her miserably. "She can't sleep. She has to run, and she has to be exhausted after all of that."

"Sophie has amazing strength. She will get through this," Tina assured.

"I'm really disappointed in him," Ben whispered and put his head on her chest.

"I know," Tina whispered, running her fingers through his hair. "But he did what he thought was right. He'll find his way. He always does. Now," she said, pulling on his arm. "Please come to bed with your wife. She's exhausted, and can't stand up another second."

"Yes, Dear," Ben mumbled and followed his wife into bed, only to fall fast asleep seconds later.

James laid awake, looking at the hand that held her last. Did he make the right choice? He wondered. James hoped Sophie would understand. He hoped she realized telling her to leave was the hardest thing he had ever done, but he had to. There was no choice. His family was in danger, and he did what he thought would protect them the most. James was sore and exhausted, but when he closed his eyes, all he saw was the hurt in Sophie's eyes, and the tears that had rolled

THE KEY

down her cheeks. He tossed and turned, and felt completely sick inside. After several hours, his body gave in. He slowly drifted off to sleep.

A wooden door stood alone in the darkness that surrounded him. Was this what Sophie was talking about? "Hello," James said warily, but no one answered. He reached forward and turned the knob. Someone suddenly flooded the room with light. Immediately, laughter filled the room. He walked cautiously towards the sound. At a kitchen table sat the man from his dad's photo, and a woman that looked very much like an older version of Sophie.

"James!" the man exclaimed. "Come have a seat with us!" James looked behind him, but no one else was there. He guardedly walked towards the table, pulled out a chair, and sat down in between the couple.

"How do you know my name?" James asked curiously.

"Oh, we've been watching you for quite some time," the woman smiled sweetly.

"It's not every day that someone captures our daughter's heart like you have," the man winked. "Where are my manners! My name is Jack, and this is my wife, Jess," he said, holding his hand out towards the woman.

"I must be completely exhausted," James said to himself, looking at them both.

"We thought this might be an easier way to meet," Jess whispered.

"Meet?" James said. "I'm not dead, too, am I?" he asked in a sudden panic.

"No, dear boy," Jack laughed. "It's just easier to communicate in the subconscious. A trick Dr. Lang taught me long ago," Jack assured.

"And what is it you want from me?" James asked in confusion.

"We just thought you should know that she understands. We all do. We don't want you torturing yourself anymore. You will need your rest for what lies ahead." Jess assured.

"Sophie said you talked in annoying riddles. Now, I get her frustration," James muttered. The couple laughed and looked at each other nervously.

"There are still rules in death, I'm afraid, my dear boy," Jack said, looking around anxiously. "But right now, we need you to relax and get some sleep. We'll take it from here."

"Can you keep her safe?" James asked desperately.

"We do our best," Jess assured. "But you still have a fight a head of you, and you will need all the rest you can get."

"Another fight?" James asked wildly. "I left her! I don't understand."

The couple got up quickly from the table and looked around anxiously again. "It was the right thing," Jack assured hurriedly. "You need to rest now," he said sternly, and touched James on his forehead with his finger. Suddenly, James was being pulled back through the wooden door, and it slammed in his face. He slept the rest of the night without a care in the world. His soul finally at ease.

THE KEY

Fifteen

Sophie ran through the woods the rest of the night, and finally heard the sound she needed. The train. She was already on fumes, but this was the fastest and safest way to gain some ground between them. Once she reached the train, Sophie closed her eyes and took a deep breath. She had to time it just right, or she would miss her chance. She was much weaker now. There wouldn't be a second opportunity for this.

"Go!" she heard her parents yell in her ear. Sophie started racing alongside the train, looking for the opening she needed. She squinted to focus and used the last of her energy to jump and lunge herself at the train. Only one hand could grab the railing of the ladder, forcing her legs to painfully drag beneath her.

"Pull up!" her mother ordered in her head.

"I'm trying!" Sophie yelled through gritted teeth.

"Try harder!" she heard her mother yell. Anger gave her the

last of the fuel she needed to pull herself up, open the car door, and throw herself inside.

"Sleep, Peanut," her father whispered. She didn't argue or respond. She had nothing left to give. She simply closed her eyes and gave in to her exhaustion. There was no wooden door. No James. Just uninterrupted deep sleep in the darkness.

James woke up oddly relaxed and refreshed, all things considering. He stretched in the sunlight. He looked down at the hand that last touched Sophie and fisted it immediately. James had to stay focused. He had to save his family.

James jumped out of bed and got dressed as quickly as he could. Once he was ready, he knocked on the door that separated him from his friends. "Get up," James said through the door. "I need food."

"So, go get some," Ben hollered back, clearly still very upset. Tina opened the door in pj's, and her hair looked like a crow's nest. She'd obviously had a rough night. James stifled his chuckle.

"So, help me," she warned. "If all you're going to do is fight for the rest of the summer," Tina finished with a growl.

"Yes, ma'am," they both answered, looking at the ground.

"Alright then," Tina said triumphantly. "Ben, get dressed. I'm starving."

"Yes, Dear," he mumbled, as he got out of bed. James sat back on his own bed and turned on the TV to watch while he waited patiently. Once everyone was ready, they headed downstairs for

THE KEY

breakfast. Just as the elevator door began to close, an oversized arm burst in, stopping the doors from closing. James, Tina, and Ben stepped further into the elevator to allow more room.

A short, stout man with an obnoxious Hawaiian shirt, and miss matched blue shorts held the door open. His flip-flops were yellow to match his shirt, but Tina was too busy trying not to gag at all the body hair that seemed to flow so freely all over him.

A stunning brunette with long lashes and hair past her waist that flowed back and forth when she walked suddenly entered. The brunette was dressed for a night club despite the fact that it was only nine a.m. Her breast barely stayed contained in her dress. She batted her eyes at James, but neither boy paid her any mind. Tina was pleased.

"So, we're still not talking about this?" Ben asked, standing in the back of the elevator with his arms crossed.

"For the last time," James warned, "I'm doing what I think is best to keep my family safe. Which includes you, Benjamin. So, if you don't like it, you can leave," he finished angrily.

"Enough," Tina growled. "We're staying together. We're not going back to the house, and we're not discussing it anymore!" Tina watched as the stout man's lips curled into a smile. "Sophie's very competent, and can handle herself, Ben," she added more quietly. "She took out almost twenty people all on her own." The man lost his smile, which gave Tina one of her own. "Let's eat," she said smugly. The stout man let the brunette out first. He tried to hold her hand, but she slapped it away. Tina slipped her arms through Ben's as they walked to the buffet.

Once they had gotten their food and found a place to sit, an uncomfortable silence lingered over them. "What are we going to do today?" asked Ben, still pouting.

"I need to get some shopping done," James shrugged.

"Me too," said Tina. "Let's go to dinner and the movies later," she offered. "Some distraction would be nice."

"I agree," said James, shoveling more eggs into his mouth.

"Let me have the car keys," Tina said, holding her hand out. James raised an eyebrow. "It's filthy and needs a bath first," she emphasized.

"You think of everything, don't you?" James asked in shock, while handing over the keys.

"That's why you keep me around," she winked, taking the keys and heading for the front door. The boys finished breakfast and returned to the room in silence. James watched the odd couple from earlier catch the next elevator and go to their own room down the hall.

"What's in the backpack?" James asked, nodding to the bag by Ben's bed once they were back in the room.

"I don't know," Ben shrugged. "Your dad said to give it to you." James walked over, picked it up, and put it on the bed to open it.

"It's heavy," he said, more to himself.

"Try carrying it," Ben retorted. James opened it to find a first aid kit, a mini laptop with a charger, a couple of burner phones, bundles of cash, passports, and other various supplies for someone on the run.

"What exactly did he say when he gave it to you, again?" James asked as casually as possible.

"Just to give it to you, and hopefully it would help you find your heart. Why?" Ben asked, coming to investigate. James grabbed the first

THE KEY

aid kit and closed the bag quickly.

"Here," he said as he tossed the kit to Ben. "You're the doc. You should probably keep track of this," he shrugged.

"This is quite the stock," Ben said, inspecting the contents.

"Well, hopefully we won't need it," James said, distracted. Ben turned on the TV and the boys watched in silence until Tina returned.

"Ready?" she asked when she finally came through the door. She winked at James and grabbed her backpack. James put the new backpack over his shoulder. It was too valuable to leave in the room. None of it was needed. Sophie was long gone, but it didn't hurt to be prepared.

"Let's roll," James said and headed out the door with his friends in tow.

James split off to do some shopping while Ben and Tina headed the opposite direction. James carefully browsed the electronic store for miscellaneous wires, chargers, etc. when the tall, skinny brunette from the elevator backed into him.

"Lo siento!" she said, batting her eyelashes at him.

"You're fine," he said, paying her no mind.

"Oh!" she said in a husky voice. "You speak Español?" she asked, putting her hand on her chest as she stuck it out further in his face. "Only the basics," James said, stepping around her to check out other things. The brunette frowned at his dismissal and chased after him.

"Do you think you could help me?" she asked, leaning into him and batting her lashes at him again.

"The clerk can," James replied flatly, grabbing what he needed. "I'm not tech savvy at all," he lied, trying to get away from her and headed for the counter. "Just these, please," James said, pushing the items toward a lanky brunette boy that couldn't have been older than eighteen. He had thick bug eye specs and was clearly struggling to get any facial hair to grow on his face. The brunette completely distracted him.

"Uh, sure," the clerk stuttered. James turned to the brunette.

"Listen, I'm sure you're really nice and all, but I'm completely over the whole female race right now. I can't stand to look at you guys, let alone be near you, other than my sister," he said flatly. "You'll have much better luck with someone else. Thanks anyway." James threw money on the counter, grabbed his items, and left. The clerk was dumbfounded, and the brunette was pissed.

"I'm available," the clerk offered nervously.

"I'm not," the brunette said, suddenly losing her accent and storming out of the store.

James met up with Ben and Tina outside. "Everything okay?" Tina asked, eyeing the brunette that was clearly pouting outside of the electronics store.

"Nothing that couldn't be handled," James shrugged. "Let's eat." They walked into Mario's and found a seat.

"Just the three of you?" Mario asked, handing out the menus.

"We're back to the tres amigos," Ben answered grimly. It surprised Tina to see the look of concern that crossed Mario's face before quickly disappearing.

THE KEY

"That's too bad," Mario said, looking at James. "You looked good together," he added softly. Ben gave James a nice "I told you so" look in triumph.

"Yeah, well, sometimes it just doesn't work out, and you have to part ways," James said, shrugging, without taking his eyes off his menu.

"Oh?" Mario asked curiously. "Sounds like you could use a drink."

"If it's on you, sure," James smiled wearily back at him.

"Deal," Mario winked, and headed back to the bar. "Damn," he said, muttering to himself. "I always liked that kid." He shook his head and drew a beer for James before handing it to one of the servers to deliver it. "No charge," he said sternly, before the big-breasted blonde bounced away. They all ordered and ate, mostly in silence. Life was just less lively without Sophie in it.

Sophie finally stirred and stretched her sore body in the abandoned train car. She did not know how long she had slept, or where exactly she was, but the sun was going down and she finally felt more like herself. Her cuts and bruises had begun to disappear. She never remembered being so drained. Then again, she didn't remember fighting that many people at once, or much of what happened to her in her teenage years. Sophie did remember Simon, though, and he was a storm that needed to be reckoned with.

Last Sophie knew, they locked Simon up at the university of

whatever in Paris. She remembered his obsessive desire for her, and it made her shiver to her core. He would kill anyone without a single thought. He had proven that already. Simon knew how much she loved Giselle, and he took her life anyway just to prove a point.

Now, Simon was exactly what he had always dreamed of being…a contract killer. Sophie wondered if whoever hired him understood that "alive" might not be a part of Simon's vocabulary, let alone his plan. She looked out the open door of the car as the scenery continued to be trees. No one would check the empty car until it pulled into town. She could jump now, or make sure she got off just before the train pulled into the station. Sophie chose the latter of the two and sat watching the sun slip behind the trees as darkness fell.

This would not be an easy fight. Simon was a time bomb that could go off with no rhyme or reason, but taking him out was her only option. She would have to be strategic, for sure. Plus, she needed to let the man with the cane know she was on her own again, and traveling far away from the Moore's. They would no longer interest him. Sophie was sure they were being watched, just to make sure they weren't playing along with her. Grief consumed her to her core. She looked at the hand that last touched James, fisted it, and closed her eyes as she memorized his last touch.

She had to stop torturing herself. There was no looking back. James made his decision, and it was time for her to focus and make her own. Sophie leaned her head back against the wall and relaxed for the first time since leaving everyone. The battle of her life was coming. She needed to rest when she could. Sophie closed her eyes and drifted off to sleep again.

THE KEY

The wooden door appeared before her. "Only if you're going to show me something helpful," Sophie warned the nothingness that surrounded her.

"Open the door," her mother ordered.

"I'm coming," Sophie sighed and opened the door. The room filled with light. She looked around, trying to figure out where she was. It wasn't the house. It wasn't the training room. It wasn't a previous memory at all. It was just a completely white space. No top or bottom to it. "Hello?" she asked, walking around, not sure what she was walking on since there was no ground. "What the heck is this?" she asked.

"You're not focused," her mother warned.

"Focus on what, exactly?" Sophie retorted sarcastically.

"Watch the attitude," her mother ordered.

"Seriously?" Sophie said to no one. "Ugh. Fine!" she said, sitting cross-legged on what she assumed was the floor. Sophie touched the back of her palms to her knees, and the middle fingers to her thumbs. She breathed in deeply and out deeply. Without a clue about what she was supposed to focus on, exactly, she let her mind wonder freely instead. Memories floated in front of Sophie as if a slideshow was being projected in a presentation room.

She saw herself reading books as a child, and training with her mother, playing games with her father, and everyone laughing as a family. She saw James, Ben, and Tina laughing on the beach, and everyone snuggling together on the couch to watch movies. Sophie saw snippets of both the death of her parents replay before her eyes, and the night she got hit by the van. She saw the last massive battle, and Simon hiding in the shadows.

"Focus!" her mother ordered.

"A little help would be nice!" retorted Sophie, as her annoyance and aggravation grew.

"Peanut," she heard her father cut in. "Don't lose sight of what's going on here."

"Still not helpful!" Sophie yelled back into the nothingness, as her anger increased.

"Peanut," he said more sternly. "Calm down."

"Well, give me something helpful!" she shouted back.

"Sophie Lee, do not talk to us like that," her mother ordered. Sophie sighed heavily and tried to focus. She saw more memories of her playing with her father.

"Stop," her father urged suddenly. Sophie froze. The memory of him giving her the necklace replayed in front of her.

"I have the necklace," Sophie said, annoyed. "I have kept it just like you said."

"I see that," her father said, sitting next to her. "I'm very proud of you for that." Sophie opened her eyes and looked at him.

"What is so dang special about this stupid necklace?" she asked bluntly.

"Remember when you told me to make a key?" Jack asked, looking at her with sympathy.

"Yes, but I have looked at this a thousand times, and I don't see how it could be any kind of key without seeing the lock," Sophie whined in frustration.

THE KEY

Her father looked out into the white nothingness. "So many things don't appear to be what they seem," Jack said. "Just like your James," he added softly.

"He's not mine," Sophie said, looking away.

"Isn't he?" Jack asked. "You are separated and yet you are still willing to die for him. That's no different from your mother and me," he replied gently. "We both know he's more. Look at all he did for you. All he continues to do for you," Jack added.

"Family must be kept safe," Sophie said, looking back at him.

"Yes," her father replied, looking her in the eyes. "We did what we could to keep you safe. I made a key to make the world safe. You keep both safe." Sophie looked down at the necklace again.

"What am I supposed to do now?" she asked him as her eyes began to water.

"First, you must fight Simon. No one is safe with him. You are destined to keep everyone safe," Jack said sternly. "Then you must get back on task."

"And what is that?" Sophie asked, full of desperation. Jack sighed and looked back out into the nothingness, before turning back and kissing her on the forehead.

"Don't lose your way, Peanut," Jack said gravely and disappeared from beside her.

"Oh, come on!" Sophie yelled to no one before opening her eyes and seeing the dusty abandoned train car once more. "I asked for something helpful," she muttered to herself.

"And you got it," her mother retorted back in her ear. Sophie made a face and got back to her plan. First, she must fight Simon. She would have to figure out the rest later. Sophie began drawing on the dusty floor as she made sure to look at the whole picture. There would be no second chances with Simon. The only other option for her was death, and too many people counted on her to live. Sophie tilted her head, looking at the drawing from all angles. Yes. That would do. She looked back out the open door and waited for the scenery to change.

Sixteen

It wasn't long before the scenery changed. The train was pulling into a more residential area. Sophie got up, walked to the open door, took a deep breath, and jumped into the clearing below. She roughly rolled down the hill as the train continued to wiz by.

"Well, that was fun," Sophie muttered to herself as she dusted herself off. But jumping was a lot easier than trying to explain why she was on the train to begin with.

She grabbed her backpack off the ground and placed it securely on her back. She rubbed the necklace for good luck and started hiking towards town. Signs showed she was in Exeter, New Hampshire. Well, at least she was out of Maine so far.

Sophie noticed the town still carried a colonial vibe. Many of the stores had a red brick face. A small white gazebo sat in the middle of the street, directing cars to go around it. She stopped in the Green

Bean to have a quick Mexican dinner. Sophie sat quietly in a red booth, looking out of the window in the back and filled up on their chips and salsa before checking out the rest of the town. There was no harm in doing a bit of sight-seeing, and the more street and security cameras she was caught on, the better.

She wandered up and down the aisles at the Water Street Bookstore, which had been named the largest independent bookstore on the Seacoast. Their selection was admirable. Then she focused on the task at hand. Getting to Vermont. Sophie was sure to stop and buy some chocolates from the Chocolatier. She wondered if her friends had ventured this way. Tina would lose her mind over the chocolate covered cookie dough balls! Then sorrow consumed her again, and she swiftly moved on.

Sophie lucked out and found an elderly man that offered to take her to Vermont if she didn't mind the long ride in his rusty old truck. He had to go for some business, he had stated, and said she could tag along. He proudly stated his name was Bill, and he was 72 years old. His smile was as warm as sunshine, and his blue eyes sparkled with mischief and life. Bill had a slight belly and a white curvy beard and mustache that reminded her of Santa Clause. Although Sophie had always traveled alone in the past, she didn't want to be alone now. "As long as it will get us both there," she said, smiling as she inspected the rusty 1970s red Ford truck.

"Hop on in, then!" Bill laughed. He shared stories of his late wife, kids, and grandkids along the way. He was warm and loving, and he made her giggle often. Sophie imagined that was what a grandfather was supposed to be like. She wondered if she even had one. If she did, she couldn't remember him. She looked out the window and watched the scenery pass by, deep in thought.

"You look like you have a heavy heart, my dear," Bill said, concerned. "What's rattling around in that noggin of yours?" he urged. Sophie sighed heavily.

"Sometimes life just won't stop throwing you curve balls," she said, staring out the window. "Just when life gets good, it's taken away from you."

"Ah, a boy," Bill said, nodding. Sophie laughed in response.

"Why do you say it's a boy?" she asked, laughing.

"When is it not?" he responded with a smile. "We're not the brightest in the bunch, and typically stubborn as hell."

"True," Sophie said, winking at him.

"Well, if he's worthy, he'll come around. And if he's not, well, hell! You dodged a bullet, and he deserves to be kicked to the curb if he doesn't appreciate you!" Bill said sternly.

"That's brilliant advice, Bill," she said, smiling at him. Sophie hastily got him to tell her another story in order to change the subject. Because it wasn't one boy. Currently, it was two. One lethal, and one, well, she had no clue about. There was no need to share her sob story. The more Bill knew, the more danger he would be in, and he was too sweet to have any harm come to him. Sophie hoped Simon didn't cross Bill's path either way. She began looking out the window and laughing with him as they continued on their journey. Sophie had to at least get to New York, but the further, the better.

Bill watched Sophie sleep as the night darkened. He wondered who had hurt her and forced her to run. She seemed so sweet, and he was an excellent judge of character. He never took strangers for rides, but she reminded him of his own granddaughter. Another reason, he agreed.

"Hey, sleepy head," Bill whispered softly as they entered Vermont. "We're here," he said with his warmest smile.

"Sorry, I feel asleep," Sophie said, rubbing her eyes.

"You looked like you needed it," Bill shrugged.

"Thank you," she said with a shy smile, then leaned over and kissed him on the cheek. His face turned a rosy pink.

Bill cleared his throat. "Anywhere in particular you need to be dropped off at?" he asked.

"Here's fine," Sophie smiled. "It will do me some good to stretch my legs."

"On the side of the road? You sure?" Bill asked, full of concern. "I can take you into the first town," he offered eagerly, but the look on her face told him to pull over. "Okay," he said woefully, and pulled the truck over.

"Goodbye, Bill," Sophie said sweetly as she got out of the truck.

"Good luck, Sophie," Bill said with a reassuring smile and a wink. He dragged the truck back onto the road, but when he went to look in the rear-view mirror, she was already gone. "Lord, keep that girl safe," he prayed out loud as he continued on his journey.

THE KEY

Sophie took to the woods, running. She needed to be seen entering Vermont alone, so Simon wouldn't bother tracking down Bill. From what she could tell, the train had added quite a bit of distance between them. It wasn't reason enough to let her guard down. Just enough time to be strategic.

Sophie made sure to be seen by as many cameras as possible without being too obvious. She wanted the man with the cane to see where she was going, even though that usually was not the case. She kept her head down, but not completely hidden, as she made her way to the bus station, bought a ticket with cash, and boarded for New York. Sophie headed to the back of the bus and picked a window seat. She held on tight to the backpack in her lap and looked out the window. No one else sat next to her, so Sophie closed her eyes and rested for most likely the last time.

The wooden door appeared, causing Sophie to sigh heavily before opening it. She was in her mother's training room, but it was empty. She looked around and saw the mat, ready on the floor. Various fighting equipment was organized neatly on a folding table. The century sparring BOB boxing bag sat in the far corner, and punching bags were spread out between the various support columns.

Sophie crossed her arms and waited patiently, but still no one came. "Hello?" she finally asked, but there was no response. "What? No show?" she asked sarcastically.

"You already have everything you need for this fight," her

mother said, stretching as she approached her.

"You sure about that?" Sophie asked with doubt.

"Yes," her mother said, taking stance. "Come," she said signally her daughter.

"I'm not fighting you," Sophie said, confused.

"Well aware, now come!" her mother ordered. Sophie took stance. She felt suddenly very out of practice. She tilted her head to assess her mother, then charged. Within seconds, she was on her back.

"You're not even trying," her mother said with disappointment.

"Says you," Sophie muttered as she got to her feet.

"You're already distracted, and Simon will not be as forgiving," Jess said, dismayed. "Unless, you're just giving up and joining them," her mother shrugged. "I'm sure Giselle will appreciate giving up her life for nothing." Anger stimulated from Sophie's core. "So, what's it going to be, Peanut?" her mother taunted. Sophie took stance as her anger grew. "Try focusing that anger where it belongs," her mother advised before they danced once more.

"What's his weakness?" her mother asked, leaning back to dodge Sophie's punch.

"Time bomb," Sophie breathed, throwing another punch. "Psychopathic arrogance," she grunted, blocking her mother's attack. "Obsession," she said, snarling as she attempted a swift kick.

"Strengths," her mother shouted as she jumped to miss Sophie's kick.

"Smart," Sophie grunted as she barely missed her mother's strike. "Animalistic strength," she hissed as she made a strike back. "Complete lack of emotion," she grumbled as she flipped out of her mother's reach. "Laser focus," Sophie breathed out as she took a quick second to catch her breath.

"Your strengths?" her mother asked, waiting for her daughter to catch her breath.

"Smarter," Sophie said with a wicked smile before lunging at her mother again. "Faster," she grunted, doing a jump kick. "Whole picture," she shouted as she did a swipe kick. "Prettier," Sophie added just for fun, and winked at her mother. "Designed to save all life," she said, nearly hitting her mother square on her jawline.

"Weaknesses?" her mother asked with pride.

"Too laser focused," Sophie said, remembering her mother's lesson about finding balance as she ducked just in time to miss Jess' swing. "Out of practice," Sophie said honestly, jumping to miss her mother's swipe kick. "Emotional," she said and watched her mother stop in mid-swing.

"Why do you consider that a weakness?" Jess asked, putting her hands on her hips to catch her breath.

"Emotions get in the way," Sophie shrugged. "And it was a lot easier to fight for the innocent when I didn't have an emotional tie to them," she said, looking at the floor.

"Like your friends?" Jess asked softly.

"Yeah," Sophie said, shuffling her feet on the mat.

"Peanut, every innocent has a name. They are a child, a sibling, a grandchild, a someone to multiple people around the world," Jess said, sitting on the mat and patting the floor next to her. Sophie went and sat cross-legged in front of her mother. "You're quite lucky to have met people that give you a reason to fight. You just have to remember that our emotions aren't there to weaken us. They're there to fuel us so we can do what needs to be done," she paused, looking carefully at her daughter. "I guess I missed a lesson," Jess said in defeat.

"You just ran out of time," Sophie said, tearing up.

"Oh, Peanut," her mother said, sweeping her daughter into her arms. "I'm so sorry you have to do any of this, let alone doing it by yourself," Jess cried. "But you were chosen because we knew you could," she said proudly. "Look how far you have come!" Jess exclaimed. Sophie enjoyed the warmth of her mother's touch and inhaled her usual scent. These moments were rare, and she wanted to remember this to the fullest.

"No matter what happens," her mother warned, "each death will be fuel for your fire to go on. Each magical moment will remind you what you fight for. Every love will make you fight harder, and every heartbreak will only make you that much stronger." Her mother pulled away to look into her daughter's eyes. "They are not ghosts that haunt you and make you weak. They are the silent army that carries you to victory."

Just then, Giselle sat down with them and lightly stroked Sophie's hair. "Go get that asshole for me," Giselle said with her usual weak smile as she winked at Sophie.

"I promise," whispered Sophie, with sorrow and determination.

"Sleep now, Peanut," her mother whispered. "You need your rest," she said, gently using her finger to push her daughter into dreamland. For the rest of the trip to New York, Sophie saw only happy memories as her body silently prepared for her next battle.

Simon. It was time to fight for her life and the lives of her friends and family.

THE KEY

"Wake up, Peanut," her father whispered. "You're here." Sophie rubbed her eyes and slowly found her focus. It was time to prepare for family. She threw the backpack on her back and headed to the front of the bus. Sophie made sure to be seen as she headed to where she would take her stand. She secretly hoped it wouldn't be her last. Sophie took off quickly, making sure to be seen occasionally.

"Come find me," she whispered to no one.

Seventeen

Sophie arrived in Brooklyn and found the old abandoned power plant she needed. From the outside, it didn't look like much, a six story plain brick building that was showing its age by its faded exterior and clouded windows. Inside was where the magic was.

The power plant was huge, with tall ceilings. There were catwalks along the exterior walls, leaving the center completely open from the cement floor to the ceiling, where metal cross beams and pipes were housed. It was a beautiful collage of copper, browns, and greys, but the thick layer of white dust covering all the surfaces gave away the fact that it hadn't been used in a long time. She had been here before and remembered the layout. This would be an advantage for her.

Sophie hid the backpack out of site and made sure her necklace was secure. She went to the middle of the floor, sat cross-legged with

THE KEY

her eyes closed, and waited for Simon's arrival. Sophie needed to conserve all of her strength for this fight. Simon was stronger and took any advantage to get the upper hand. He had no soul and didn't care who he hurt, as long as he won, but his weakness was only seeing what he wanted. She needed to be wise enough to see the whole picture if she was going to survive.

Simon purposely waited until nightfall, knowing darkness was his saving grace. They both knew that. While she waited, Sophie kept her breathing calm and focused on the task at hand. Finally, she heard the shuffling of footsteps come up from behind her. Only, there were two sets and not one. Apparently, Simon had brought someone to help him win.

"Bonjour, Sophie," she heard Simone's sickening sweet voice call to her.

"Bonjour, Simon," she said flatly.

She heard the ripping of tape come off someone's skin. "Sophie?" Bill said, weak and confused. Sophie's eyes shot open in alarm instantly.

"Focus," she heard her mother's voice call to her urgently.

"I thought I would let your friend see who you really are," Simon said, taunting her.

"A ride and a friend are two different things," Sophie said, trying to keep her emotions in tack. "You would know that if you had any friends to begin with," she retorted.

"Sophie?" Bill said, very confused about what was taking place. Sophie got to her feet and turned to face both of them.

"He was simply a mode of transportation, Simon," Sophie said as flat as possible. "There's no need to drag the poor man into any of this." Bill looked hurt, scared, and confused. Her heart broke for him, but Simon couldn't see how much Bill meant to her, even in the short time they had spent together. Now, his life was in danger because of her. Sophie's heart was beating into her throat and she found it hard to breathe.

"Pauvres Sophie," Simon said, faking empathy. "Your heart still gets you in trouble, doesn't it?" he mocked. "You still feel for the weak, instead of taking your place with the strong."

"What do you want, Simon?" Sophie asked, changing the subject.

"I want you to come join me, my love," he said with sudden excitement in his voice.

"Did hell freeze over at least twice, and I became bored without realizing it?" she asked, tilting her head, showing nothing but annoyance.

"Maybe," Simon said with a wicked smile.

"I'm afraid not," Sophie said, putting her hands on her hips and looking bored.

"But, Sophie! The possibilities, my love!" Simon said, clearly having their life planned out completely already.

"Aren't you supposed to just bring me in?" she asked slyly, with a wicked smile of her own.

"That man's an idiot," Simon scuffed. "He has no IDEA of your potential!" he said, raising his voice.

"Oh, and you do?" Sophie asked sarcastically.

"If only you knew what I knew!" Simon exclaimed. Sophie's heart stopped. *Did he know? Did he know more than she did?*

"Don't let him play with you," her mother warned in her ear

THE KEY

and Sophie breathed out, trying not to show her relief.

"That man wants me pretty badly," Sophie said, changing tactics. "Are you sure you can beat him?" she asked with sudden interest.

"Oh, my love!" Simon said with excitement. "Together, NO ONE could stop us!" he shouted. Sophie pretended to contemplate her options.

"If I go with you, will you let the old man go?" she asked, trying not to sound too eager.

"Him?" Simon asked, throwing his head in Bill's direction. "He's seen our faces. We can't risk it," he said matter-of-factly.

"Simon, the man's in his 70s and about to go senile. Who's going to believe him, anyway?" Sophie asked bluntly. "Besides, I'm tired of leaving so many dead bodies behind," she shrugged. Sophie tried to ignore the immense fear coming from Bill's eyes as his body shook.

"I don't know…" Simon said, looking Bill up and down. "What if you change your mind again? I might have to teach you another lesson," he said, focusing on Bill and not paying attention to the reddening of Sophie's face as anger built quickly from her core.

"Put that anger where it belongs," her mother whispered softly, with a hint of concern. Sophie did her best to blow all the heat out of her nose without being noticed and remembered Giselle asking her to kick Simon's ass. She'd given her word, and she didn't take doing so lightly.

"Simon, if you're going to just keep teasing me, then we might as well part ways now," Sophie said, showing a bit of her annoyance. "I'm already bored with this conversation," she shrugged and turned to walk away.

"Wait!" Simon said eagerly. "How do I know you speak the truth?"

"I guess you're going to have to trust me," Sophie said pointblank. "But right now, you're just wasting my time," she said, walking away once again.

"Fine!" Simon shouted. Sophie grinned before turning around.

"Then leave the man, and let's go," she ordered, praying very hard that he would just leave Bill and come with her, but he didn't. He continued to look from Sophie to Bill and back to Sophie again. "Well?"

Sophie asked impatiently, trying to will Simon to come to her.

"Okay," Simon shrugged, but just before he walked away from Bill, he slowly put his arm around his shoulder, and with no hesitation, snapped Bill's neck. No sound came from Sophie's mouth as Bill's lifeless body fell to the ground before her. His knees hit the ground first, and as if in slow motion, Bill fell forward. His head landed on the floor facing Sophie, with his eyes open and full of terror.

Fury swiftly spread all over her body, even to her fingertips. Sophie's eyes were wide, and her face grew redder by the second. "It's no good to leave loose ends, my love," Simon said flatly, walking towards her. No care for the life he had just taken. It was just a check on his list of things to do, and it didn't bother him in the slightest.

"Sophie Lee, control your anger," her mother pleaded inside her head.

"No," Sophie hissed to no one through her grinding teeth. "Enough!" she breathed through her clenched jaw. Simon wasn't paying any attention to her, but rather admiring his handy work behind him before turning around to see Sophie suddenly in stance.

THE KEY

"What?" he asked, very confused.

"You will take no more lives," Sophie growled.

"Oh, you can't be mad about him?" Simon said flatly. "He was just transportation," Simon said, haunting Sophie with the last words Bill heard from her. She remained in stance and let the anger course through her body, fueling her need to make the world right once more. "Are you serious?" Simon laughed at her. Sophie simply remained silent and signaled for him to come for her. "Oh, Sophie," he said, shaking his head in dismay. "I was hoping I wouldn't have to kill you, but if that's what you want, then so be it," Simon shrugged and took stance. "Just like the old days," he laughed wickedly. Giselle's smiling face flashed before her, and she saw Simon kill Giselle in front of her once more. Sophie was so hot, she felt like she was going to explode!

He would try to wear her down first. She needed to make sure that didn't happen. They assessed each other for a split second before Simon charged her. Sophie blocked three of his punches before kicking Simon in the stomach and pushing him back to give herself some space. They took stance as they caught their breath. Simon smiled mischievously before coming at her again. Sophie spun while continuing to block his hits and swipe kicking him, but Simon jumped and easily cleared her leg.

"Out of practice, I see," he taunted her as he quickly caught his breath.

"If you say so," Sophie smiled back at him with hatred fueling her fire. She resumed spinning rapidly in both directions as she continued to block his swings. She allowed one to get through, and Simon quickly grabbed her by the neck, pushing her back up against a pillar. Sophie took her left leg and pushed him back with her foot in his gut to gain some space.

They briefly caught their breath. Then Sophie lunged at him, but Simon grabbed her hand and flipped her onto her back while twisting her wrist, causing Sophie to yell out in pain. Simon climbed on top of her, and Sophie used her free leg to kick him square in the jaw, knocking him back. She continued to kick Simon's stomach until he finally let her hand free. Then she scooted back to push herself up to her feet again, her wrist already sprained. Simon got to his feet and didn't hesitate before coming at her again.

Sophie pushed with her legs and growled in pain as she did a few back flips to gain some extra ground. Her wrist was going to be broken before they were finished. She began to quickly account for that. Her legs were her strong suit. It was time to use them. Sophie paused to catch her breath, then did a series of jump kicks before jumping onto his shoulders to stick Simon's head between her legs and squeeze as hard as she could. Simon turned his head and bite her thigh hard enough to break her skin. They rolled away from each other and got to their feet. Both were breathing heavily, but still had a way to go before someone would win.

Simon's eyes narrowed, and he quickly came for her, throwing everything he had at her. Sophie blocked what she could, but took some hits in between. She was wearing down faster than Simon, and they both knew it. Sophie put her arm around his neck and swung promptly onto his back to buy her some time. Simon backed up immediately and repeatedly jammed her against the column behind her. Sophie let go and fell to the ground.

"Guess you're not as strong as I remember," Simon sneered, preparing for victory as he walked around Sophie's limp body.

THE KEY

Sophie was growing tired. Too tired. Too quickly. Her fury for Giselle and Bill had been used up. She had nothing left to give. Her breathing slowed, and she closed her eyes as life began to leave her. Suddenly, a bright light shined into Sophie's face. "Get up, babe," she heard James' voice in the far distance.

"I don't think I can," Sophie wheezed with some broken ribs.

"That's funny," James said, bending down in front of her with that smile that made her knees go weak. "Because I know you can," James said, winking at her. "Now, get up," he said more sternly. She hesitated to collect her bearings. "Get up!" James ordered. "I need you to fight for me," he demanded. "And us," James said, pointing to a group of people behind him. Coming into focus stood her mother, her father, Bill, Giselle, James' parents, with Tina and Ben in front. "You've never quit anything before in your life," James said. "Are you going to quit on us so easily?" he asked. "On you and me?" he added, taking Sophie's hand to his heart. His warmth flooded through her body, providing energy and strength like she had never felt before.

"No," Sophie whispered to James as she took his energy and let it consume her body. Love coursed through her heart and spread quickly through her entire being.

"What?" Simon asked, confused to hear from her at all. He knew her wrist was ready to break. He'd cracked several of her ribs, and blood oozed from various places on her face. Her nose was bleeding, her hair was matted with blood, and bruising was speedily taking over her body. Sophie was losing, and Simon relished in her weakness.

But Sophie no longer felt pain, only warmth and love. She was designed to protect, and she was going to fight for her loved ones.

Despite her broken ribs, she took a couple of deep breaths before pushing herself to her feet once more. Simon looked at her, half impressed, and half excited that she wasn't going to end his enjoyment so soon.

"That's my girl," she heard James whisper in pride. She didn't know if she was just hallucinating, or if any of this was real, but it was exactly what she needed. Sophie let love fuel her to her core. For this was stronger than the anger she had started with. She found herself oddly calm and seeing nothing but the whole picture. Nothing but the task at hand. Nothing but the love she had for her friends and family. Nothing but taking Simon's head.

Sophie took stance for the last time, eyed Simon and saw him clearer than she had ever seen him before, smiled her wicked smile, and signaled him to come.

Simon tilted his head as the corner of his lips curled up into a smile. "Very well," he said, taking stance, eager to get started. He charged her immediately. Sophie spun and blocked all of his strikes again. *Where did this fresh burst of energy come from?* Simon wondered.

Sophie kneed Simon in the groin and started a new jump kick series, pushing him back. She ran past him, ran up the column, and with all her force, hit him square on the jawline. He stumbled back in the opposite direction. Sophie landed gracefully on the balls of her feet, using her good hand to balance while holding her now broken wrist in the air. She looked up at him with fierce determination, like he'd never seen.

"You Bitch!" Simon shouted, as his eyes became dilated. His face reddened, and saliva poured from his mouth as he yelled. His own face was bloodied and bruised to match hers. Sophie smiled like the Cheshire cat and waited for him to make the first move.

Anger blinded Simon, and he ran towards her with pure rage. Sophie stepped back, grabbed him by the back of his shirt, and flung him against the pillar, as if he was as light as a pillow. She heard his back crack when it hit the cement and watched his limp body slide down to the floor. Sophie took stance and waited for Simon to find his footing before coming for her again.

He yelled from his gut and came swinging at her with everything he had. Sophie blocked his attacks with her injured arm and jabbed him high and low with her good hand and elbow. He staggered back to catch his breath. "You think you're better than me!" Simon spat at her. Sophie just smiled and patiently waited. He was weakening quickly, but she still needed him to be broken before she would show him mercy and take his life. No more would he hurt her loved ones or anyone else. One of them wasn't leaving this power plant, and Sophie would do everything she could to make sure it was him.

"You will not leave here!" Simon yelled, spitting at her like a rabid dog.

"We'll see," Sophie shrugged with a smile. Anger exploded through Simon as he charged her. Sophie laid on her back and pushed him into the air with both of her feet before pushing off her hands to land in a standing position. She quickly took stance and waited for Simon to get his footing. He immediately charged her again. Simon pulled out the gun from the back of his pants as he ran towards her.

"You've already lost," Sophie whispered as she grabbed the gun before he could shoot, spun around, and held it at his chest.

"You can't pull the trigger," Simon laughed as he knocked the gun out of her hands. It slid across the floor. He socked her in the stomach and forced her to fall back a few steps. Without hesitation, Sophie began swinging and kicking him back toward where the gun had fallen. Simon fell to the ground and abruptly rolled to his left, barely missing a fatal kick.

Simon saw a loose pipe and grabbed it. He scrambled to his feet, and began wildly swinging at Sophie, pushing her back against a wall. Sophie turned, ran towards the wall, ran up it, and flipped over Simon's head, clearing him by a couple of feet. She landed on balls of her feet with her good arm balancing her, and her broken arm held up in the air. Sophie promptly located the gun and stared Simon in the eyes. She smiled and challenged him to come at her for the last time. Simon lost it and charged her with blind fury.

Sophie ran at him head on, but at the last second dodged to the right. She slid to her knees, passing him, while grabbing the gun. She stuck the gun under her injured arm, closed her eyes to listen for his heartbeat, and pulled the trigger. Taking the kill shot through his back and piercing his heart.

Simon gasped for air as his momentum propelled him forward a few steps before stopping. Falling to his knees and wavering as he struggled to breathe. Blood oozed from his mouth as he began to slowly drown in his own blood. Sophie fought to slow down her breathing. She opened her eyes, got to her feet, and faced Simon, who was on his knees with his back to her. Sophie could hear the life gradually escaping his body. She took the bullets out of the gun and slowly walked to him.

"Nicely done," Simon said, gurgling blood from his mouth.

THE KEY

"Thank you," Sophie whispered softly.

"I guess you're the stronger one after all," he spouted. Sophie didn't respond. "Au revoir, Sophie," Simon said as he took his last breath. His body fell forward and his face hit the cement floor. Sophie waited for confirmation as the last of his life escaped him.

"Au revoir, Simon," she whispered as she wiped the gun for prints before laying it beside him. She went and found her backpack, flung it on her back, and went to Bill's limp body. "I'm so sorry," Sophie cried as she reached out and closed Bill's eyes. She took his wallet, leaving his ID, got to her feet, and left the power plant. Simon's and Bill's bodies behind her.

Sophie was impressed to find a pay phone on the corner of the street. She walked up to it, picked up the receiver, and dialed 911. "Hello, 911," she heard a female voice say on the other end.

"There are two dead bodies in the Jumping Jack Power Plant," Sophie said before dropping the receiver and walking away. The police would get to Bill before the clean-up crew could. He would get the proper burial he deserved, and his loved ones would get to tell him goodbye. Exhausted and numb, Sophie slowly worked her way in the opposite direction. It stunned her how quickly she heard sirens in the distance. "Goodbye, Bill," she whispered, before she disappeared.

Sophie found reasonably sized chunks of wood lying around outside on her way returning to town and cut the bottom of her shirt to make a splint for her wrist after she had reset it. She wasn't sure how long it was going to take to heal. Sophie would just have to hope for the best. She got a wrap for her ribs at a pharmacy. The lady behind the counter looked appalled at Sophie's current condition, but thankfully asked no questions.

"Where's your restroom?" Sophie asked politely in a very fatigued breath.

"In the back," the lady said warily.

"Thank you," Sophie said with a faint smile, and headed back to clean up quickly and wrap her ribs. She got most of the blood off her face and stuck her head in the sink to wash the blood from her hair. Sophie pulled out a brush to make her hair look a little more presentable in public, before giving up and just putting a baseball cap on. She had bought some foundation, and tried to hide the bruising the best that she could.

The evening was getting a lot cooler with the sun long gone, so she pulled out the sweatshirt that James had let her borrow on the hilltop. Sophie let his scent consume her senses. Tears filled her eyes, and she brushed them away swiftly before they fell, streaking the makeup she had just put on.

She looked in the mirror at the poignant creature looking back at her. "That will have to do," Sophie sighed before starting to make it to her next destination. This time, she would not be seen by any cameras. The man with the cane would have to dig very hard to find her. Sophie grabbed the backpack, tossed the rest of her supplies in it, and slung it over her good arm. It was time to get back on task. She rubbed the necklace for good luck before leaving the store and disappearing into the night.

Eighteen

Eddie was relieved but mostly impressed to see that Sophie had beat Clarice's supposed "master team". Although the old man wasn't happy, and Eddie had caught some flak for the after math, he still found himself rooting for Sophie, after all of these years.

Simon had purposely stayed clear, altogether, of the attack on the Moore house, then followed Sophie to New York. Eddie watched her bait him the whole way, making sure to get caught on camera, a tactic she only used when it met her agenda. Simon blindly followed, clearly not knowing Sophie as well as he had claimed.

There was one camera she hadn't accounted for. The one that was put up to watch the Jumping Jack Power Plant intended to stop vandalism on the property. Eddie had watched Sophie limp out to the phone and make a call. It was footage that no one else saw, and he saw to it they never would. He knew helping her would cost him his life in the end, but Sophie and her family had done so much for him. It was impossible not to want to return the favor. Eddie realized that one day he would have to make a choice. At the moment, he wasn't sure which he would choose, but it would be the one that was best for him.

    Eddie was secretly glad that Simon didn't seem to make it. That guy was a true psychopath, which is why the old man loved him, but Simon had his own agenda and would have turned, eventually. Eddie knew his type. His obsession with Sophie was far too great to ever truly be broken, and it made Eddie sick to his core. Sophie looked like she had taken more of a beating from Simon than the twenty-nine people Clarice had sent to the Moore house. There were cameras on the property, but Eddie could not get around the firewall.

    He shifted his feet and tried not to focus on the pain or blood that continued to seep through his shirt. He had received twenty-nine lashes on his back just to prove a point. A lash for each team member that died who the old man couldn't witness for himself. A warning to make sure that Eddie did a better job from now on. However, Clarice was point for the mission, and being his daughter seemed to make no difference. Eddie hadn't heard her cry out much from the room next to his, but that was Clarice. Determined not to let anyone see her emotions. Eddie guessed it came from growing up with the old man.

    "Where is she?" the old man hissed from the shadows.

    "New York," Eddie lied. He knew she was long gone, but there was no footage to prove otherwise.

    "Where the hell is Simon?" the old man yelled his question.

    "I don't know, Sir," Eddie said, trying not to smile. "He has refused to check in since the Moore house."

    "Her friends?" the old man asked, extremely irritated.

THE KEY

"Still in Maine, away from the house," Eddie said flatly. "Team B is still tracking, but they don't do much other than regular vacation stuff. No contact has been made. They seem to be just moving on with their lives," he shrugged, knowing better. No one who met Sophie was able to move on.

"The boy's parents?" the old man growled.

"In London at the moment," Eddie reported. "Also, no contact. Went back to being on vacation with no concern for the children or anything else. Mrs. Moore is back on assignment, and Mr. Moore continues to study up on the latest diseases around the world," Eddie said, shrugging.

"Why is she in New York?" the old man asked no one. "Continue to monitor them all," he demanded. The sound of the cane hitting the cement floor disappeared into the distance. Eddie and his team of techies breathed a sigh of relief. They had survived another day...for now. Eddie wondered how long it would be before Clarice started making appearances again. He was guessing it would be awhile.

It had been a few days since they had seen Sophie. The trio tried to continue on as if they had never met her, but they were quickly seeing how much life Sophie brought to their own. With or without the people with guns chasing her. The odd couple kept their distance but continued to follow them around wherever they went. Tina persisted with her inspections whenever they returned to the hotel and washed the car regularly. Ben accepted her odd behavior, and even though he completely disagreed with James' choices, the boys were back on speaking terms.

The Plaza only held so many activities, and the trio had pretty much done them all. They assumed the bodies were long gone, but no one suggested returning to the house any time soon. Everyone watched the news eagerly, but there was no news about a massive massacre, or any news of a body matching Sophie's description. It was as if they were waiting for something, but no one hinted what, exactly.

"I'd like to go to the library," said Ben, out of nowhere while they ate at the buffet for what seemed like the millionth time already.

"You really do sound like Tina," James teased.

"Hey!" Tina exclaimed. "But not a bad idea. I have a few things to look up myself." So, while the boys finished up, Tina went and washed the car again. She was oddly obsessed about how clean the outside looked.

"Try vacuuming the inside this time," her husband suggested. Tina just rolled her eyes and went out the revolving door. "Everyone grieves differently," Ben shrugged in response to James' curious look. When they left the hotel, their favorite odd couple was arguing in the lobby. The trio left them to it and headed down the street.

Once at the library, they split off in separate directions. Ben headed for the medical research area, per usual. James wandered the shelves of the 2nd floor, and Tina went to the archives. Sophie may not be with them, but it didn't mean the puzzle was going to solve itself. After an hour or two, she was finally able to locate the photo that hangs behind Dr. Moore's desk in his office. A newspaper photographer, Tim Burtynsky, took it. It was an article on local scientists and doctors working together to cure incurable diseases. But

THE KEY

Tina thought Sophie said her dad worked in weather?

With her index finger, Tina carefully went name by name until she found the one she needed...Jack Harris. She knew it was the right one when she saw Sophie's eyes and smile looking back at her. Well, she at least had a name to work with now. Tina started digging further immediately.

After several hours had passed, the boys gave up and found Tina surrounded by stacks of books, newspaper articles, and notebook paper she was feverishly writing on. "Babe," Ben whined. "Let's go get something to eat. James and I are starving!" Tina held up a finger as she finished her thought to finally look up.

"What time is it?" she asked, confused.

"It's almost 2pm, and I got kicked out of my area because my stomach kept growling too loudly," Ben said, rubbing his belly.

"Oh, my!" Tina exclaimed. "Sorry, I lost track of time."

"What are you working on?" James asked curiously.

"Oh, something for work," Tina said, quickly shoving the papers into her backpack. "Come on, Honey," she said grabbing Ben. "Let's get some food in you." James went to take a quick peek at one of the books, but Tina pulled his shirt, dragging him away before he could see the title. They decided some comfort food was needed and headed for Buca Di Beppo Italian restaurant down the street.

"I'm stuffed!" Ben exclaimed.

"You should be!" Tina laughed. "I don't think they have any pasta left to serve anyone else." James laughed at his friends, but his heart remained heavy. "You alright?" she asked gently.

"Of course," James said, giving her a weak smile and walked a head of them both.

"He's definitely missing her," Ben whispered.

"Yeah," Tina concurred. "Let's give him some space tonight."

"Agreed," Ben nodded. They walked hand in hand, heartbroken for their friend, but thankful to have each other.

Tina and Ben decided they were just going to stay in, and James agreed. He laid on his bed, surfing through the channels, finding nothing that interested him. The sun was long gone, and the darkness of the night matched his mood. Despite trying everything he could, Sophie still remained on his mind. James got up to go to the bathroom and threw some cold water on his face. He looked in the mirror, contemplating for the millionth time if he had done the right thing. He tilted his head and studied the reflection that looked back at him. "Took you long enough," James said sarcastically.

"Well, fighting a psychopath and leading a new team on a wild goose chase took longer than expected," Sophie responded sarcastically, with her arms crossed at her chest and leaning against the bathroom door frame. His lips curled up at the corners into a smirk, and he turned around to lean against the bathroom counter, taking her in. She was dirty and exhausted, but as beautiful as the first day he had laid eyes on her. James' heart began to race and beat like it hadn't since the day they parted. "But your message was a nice touch,"

THE KEY

Sophie said, holding up her good hand and wiggling her good five fingers as she smiled her Cheshire smile.

"I thought so," James shrugged with a smile, remembering how he had carefully traced the words "Come Find Me" into her palm before putting on a show for Simon. He couldn't take it anymore and rushed over, pulling Sophie into his arms while pressing his mouth to hers. Immediately, he felt the wooden splint she had placed carefully behind his head, and the wrapped ribs that were under the palm of his hands. "What the hell!" James yelled, pulling back and inspecting her fully.

"Just some battle wounds," Sophie said with a weak smile. "They will heal. It will just take some time."

"I'll get Ben," he said urgently. "He can help." James turned to go get Ben, but Sophie grabbed his hand and pulled him back.

"Tomorrow," she whispered.

"But..." James said, shaking his head in disbelief.

"I've been to hell and back trying to get back to you guys," Sophie said more firmly. "Let me just have one night with you first," she finished, kissing him gently on the lips. Heat spread from his core. He carefully lifted her legs and wrapped them around his waist as he cradled her against the bathroom door. Exploring her mouth with his in a need that just grew stronger by the second.

Sophie took his hair in her good hand, and gently tugged as she leaned her head back and moaned with pleasure. She could feel him growing hard against her. James took his mouth and kissed her neck as her throat vibrated against his lips with her purr of pleasure.

"James?" they both heard Tina ask with a hint of concern in her voice as she knocked on the adjoining door.

James chuckled against Sophie's neck. "Of course," he said, shaking his head as he gently set Sophie back on her feet. "Stay here," he said with his boyish grin that made her weak in the knees. James waited for Sophie to be out of sight before opening the door. He only opened it a crack to hide his erection from his friend.

"What's up?" James said, trying to hide his excitement.

"We just thought we heard you yell something?" Tina said, looking around the room.

"Nope, just the TV," he blamed, looking in its direction. Luckily, he had left it on an action flick.

"Oh," Tina said, not fully convinced. "You sure you're okay?" she asked, looking at her friend, as if trying to read his mind and soul.

"Yeah, just going to watch this movie and probably fall asleep," James said, trying not to sound too rushed. "Stop fussing, Ti, and enjoy your husband tonight," he added with a wink. "You deserve it."

"Okay," Tina said, trying to sneak one last look before turning around to close the door behind her. She heard the lock click from the other side of the door, and the sides of her lips curled up. James never locked his door, which meant one thing. Sophie had finally come back.

"What's up?" Ben asked, lying on the bed and inspecting his wife's demeanor.

"Nothing," Tina said, unable to shake her smile. "He's fine. Just watching a movie, but he did suggest you take advantage of your wife. What do you say?" she asked with a wicked smile.

"I mean, if I have to," Ben chuckled and opened his arms to catch her as she ran and lunged at him on the bed. Ben followed his friend's advice and took advantage of his wife for the first time since they had left the house.

THE KEY

"She knows, doesn't she?" Sophie asked with a chuckle coming out of the bathroom. James noticed she had taken the time to quickly wash up. Her clothes still needed some love.

"Oh yeah," James said, laughing back. "But I'm going to have to make it up to Ben for a while," he said with a sudden frown on his face.

"I think we both will," Sophie said, feeling heartbroken for her friend. She wondered how much Ben would hate them both for doing what they thought was best.

"We'll deal with it tomorrow," James said, shaking his head and focusing on the woman that had stolen his heart from the day they met. "I missed you," he whispered.

"I missed you," Sophie replied softly.

James slowly walked up to her and moved a strand of hair from her face. "You're beautiful," he breathed.

"I'm dirty and a hot mess," Sophie giggled uncomfortably.

"Not to me," James said, pulling her into him and gently kissing her. "I'm sorry I was so mean," he said, full of guilt and putting his forehead to hers gently.

"You didn't mean it," Sophie assured, hoping it was true.

"It still killed me to say and do it," James said, unable to look her in the eyes.

"Hey," Sophie said, gently lifting his head by his chin with her good hand. "It worked," she said with a weak smile. "He bought it hook, line, and sinker."

"I'm still sorry," James said, looking deeply into her eyes for forgiveness.

"I know," Sophie said, giving him what he needed and sealing it with a kiss. Once again, James took her legs and wrapped them around his waist with the lightest touch, and carried her to the bed before slowly laying her in the middle of it. Her heart raced with anticipation, but he stopped to study her with his head tilted and looked her up and down. Sophie's frustration grew the longer he denied her.

"Is something wrong?" she asked, suddenly self-conscious.

"I want you, but I don't want to hurt you," James said honestly.

"You're pretty banged up, Babe," he said, still examining her.

"Oh," Sophie said in disappointment.

"Well, that and your first time can be painful," James said, quickly trying to get her to understand. "I just," he stopped and leaned down to kiss her gently. "I just don't want you to hurt worse than you already do," he said honestly. "I couldn't take that after everything," James said, looking down again.

"I understand," Sophie sighed and tried not to sound as disappointed as she felt.

"Oh, that doesn't mean I'm not going to still devour you," James said with an ornery smile. "Be honest and tell me if I hurt you, though," he added seriously.

"Oh!" Sophie said with anticipation again. "Promise," she eagerly added for good measure.

James carefully straddled her in his grey pj pant bottoms, and white cotton V-neck t-shirt. "Come here," he said gently, as he helped her sit up in front of him. "Are you sure you're okay with this?" he asked her, suddenly full of concern.

THE KEY

"Ask me again, and your body's going to be with Simon's," Sophie said, full of frustration.

"Yes, Ma'am," he chuckled. James gently helped Sophie raise her arms above her head. With the utmost care, he pulled the sweatshirt over her head and tossed it to the floor. He took her face in his hands and gently kissed her before pulling the black long-sleeved t-shirt that clung to every inch of her upper body, up over her head. It was covered in dust, sweat, and blood. Sophie winced, causing James to pause instantly, but she promptly nodded her head 'yes', encouraging him to continue. James swiftly pulled the shirt off and threw it on the floor, exposing her ribs wrapped in an ace bandage just like the first night she was in his bed. His heart rapidly filled with anger. *What did that asshole do to her?!* But this was not the time to discuss it. Sophie needed this, and so did he.

James looked down at her luscious breasts that were constrained by the black sports bra she wore. They rose up and down with her nervousness and anticipation. "Wow," he whispered before leaning down to kiss the top of each one. Sophie couldn't believe that a plain Jane like herself impressed him at all, but she was glad that he wasn't rejecting her right now.

"Off," Sophie said, tugging on his white cotton t-shirt.

James' smile grew even wider as he responded, "Yes, Ma'am," to her demand. He grabbed the base of his shirt and pulled it over his head and tossed it on the floor amongst the other clothes. James was ripped, every muscle chiseled into his skin as if he were a statue. His skin was bare and tan from the summer sun. Sophie gasped and unknowingly bit her bottom lip. "Is it okay?" he laughed in a half chuckle at her widened blue eyes and plump lip hiding under her teeth. All she could do was nod. "It's all yours," James whispered, looking at her with heat and passion.

Sophie looked at James in shock, but she knew he meant it. He gently took her hands in his, and she hastily pulled the splinted hand away. "It's okay," he encouraged as he took her hand once more and lightly laid them on his chest. They roamed with pure fascination and curiosity. James leaned his head back and took in a sharp breath, enjoying her touch, before looking down at her with his eyes full of need. He grabbed her hair in one hand, as he gently pulled her head back to meet her mouth to his.

Sophie felt him grow even harder against her body as she wrapped her arms around him and devoured his mouth with hers. James reached down and pulled the sports bra up over her head. He tossed it on the floor. His heart broke when Sophie gasped and covered herself up with her arms in shame.

James stopped and looked into her eyes. "Why are you covering yourself up?" he asked, not understanding.

"I don't know," Sophie said, blushing a deeper shade of red.

James leaned in and put his forehead against hers. "You're even more beautiful than I could ever imagine," he assured softly. "I've wanted to be with you from the first day I laid eyes on you," he said, gently brushing the hair from her face.

"Really?" Sophie said in complete disbelief.

James sighed and pulled her into his arms. "Yes," he whispered, slowly laying her down, and rolling her on top of him, trying hard not to jar her injured ribs or wrist. He put his hand on Sophie's head, lightly holding it to his chest, and began slowly stroking her hair. He felt her melt under his touch, and she moved her arms so her breasts

THE KEY

fell softly onto his own chest. "You awoke a heart that I didn't realize had been numb my whole life," James said honestly. "I'm not sure I even knew what love was before I met you," he said as he continued to stroke her hair. "You've had my heart since the first night we met, even if I wasn't ready to admit it," he chuckled. "And being away from you has only made me realize how much I need to have you in my life," he added quietly. Sophie made no noise. He listened to her breathing slow down as her chest rose and fell in beat with his own. "I know that you've been through a lot, but I did just kind of bare my heart and soul to you. A response would help calm my nerves a bit, right about now..." James said, panicking at Sophie's silence. He looked down and saw that she was fast asleep, most likely not hearing a word he said. He sighed a half laugh and continued to stroke her hair. It felt so good to have her in his arms again.

"Sleep tight, Babe," James whispered and kissed the top of her head, as he pulled the covers over them both, continuing to hold her close to him. "There's plenty of time for us," he said with a smile as he turned off the TV with the remote, closed his eyes, and dreamt of a life of forever with the woman that slept in his arms. There was no wooden door. Just bliss, love, and happiness.

Nineteen

The next morning, James woke up with Sophie still asleep in his arms. A smile crossed his face instantly. The world was back as it should be, he decided. Yes, there was still the odd couple to deal with, along with anyone else that came at them, but they could conquer anything as long as they were together. As a family. He hoped Sophie saw it the same way. James vowed to himself right then and there to never be parted from her again. His heart couldn't take it. He would do whatever it took to keep her, even if it meant leaving his actual family behind, including Ben and Tina.

Sophie stirred underneath his arms and winced immediately after. "Easy," James whispered. "You're still pretty banged up," he said, with a hint of frustration.

Once fully awake, Sophie noticed she was still half naked and gasped in embarrassment. "Nope," James said, heading her off at the

THE KEY

pass, rolling on top of her and gently holding her arms against the pillows. "Just as I am all yours, these..." he said, looking at her wonderfully perky breasts before him, "are mine," he finished with a wicked smile. "Now, where did I leave off?"

"Oh, my gosh!" Sophie said, suddenly horrified. "I fell asleep!" Her face turned a deep red.

"You've been to hell and back," James reminded her. "You're bound to be a little tired. Now, where were we?" he asked, slowly lowering his mouth to gently kiss the top of each one of her breasts before putting one fully in his mouth. Sophie arched her back and sucked in a sharp breath, forgetting all the pain in her ribs as she bit her bottom lip and let out a soft moan.

James teased her nipple with his tongue and teeth before raising his head. "Now, Babe," he whispered softly. "As much as I love hearing your pleasure, you're going to have to keep it down so we don't get interrupted by Frick and Frack next door." She let out a giggle, and he immediately started growing hard against her. "God, I love that sound," he said dreamily as he let go of one of her hands to cup her other breast and put it all in his mouth to enjoy the life it had to give to him.

Sophie arched her back, quickly grabbed a pillow with her now free hand, and shoved it in her mouth to stifle her moan of pleasure. He grinned against her breast and mumbled, "That's my girl," while he continued to torture her with pleasure. "We can't have you lopsided after all," James said with a wicked smile, before moving to the middle and kissing her gently in the crevice of them both. He slowly worked his way down her stomach to her belly button, kissing her over her bandages.

Sophie began arching her back up and down while moaning with pleasure as he moved down her body, growing wet between her legs. He purred with pleasure against her belly, moving further and further down her bare skin. She no longer felt pain. Just heat and need coursed through her veins. Need for him. All of him.

James moved to the end of the bed, removing her shoes eagerly for her. He came back up to undo her pants and gently pull them off. Sophie wiggled with anticipation underneath his touch, which just made him want her more. He began to nibble and kiss her inner right thigh. Suddenly, realizing she hadn't exactly shaved her legs or prepared in any way for this magical occasion, Sophie went to sit up immediately. But anticipating her moves, James held her chest down with his hand, just strong enough to prevent her from sitting up and stopping him. "Nope," he teased. "I'm not done yet down here."

"But I haven't even shaved my legs!" Sophie whined. "Surely, you want me to shower first," she pleaded.

"Sssshhhh," James reminded her. "I have waited for days for you, Babe. I'm not waiting anymore," he said defiantly, and took to kissing and nibbling on her inner thigh once more. Sophie's head swirled, and she forgot the argument she had started. She shoved the pillow in her mouth again and moaned loudly with surrender as James started at her knee and worked his way up. He slowly ran his fingers between her belly and the waistband before he pulled down her panties and flung them to the floor. He started at her knee again, worked his way up, nestled his nose in her hair, and moved to the left side.

He was maddening! But the torture was nothing but complete pleasure. Sophie's back rose and fell with a need like she had never

THE KEY

known. She felt him lick the stickiness that rolled down her thighs. God, she wanted him! Unexpectedly, she felt something soft moving inside her. She gasped in the pillow she held over her mouth and began moving to the same rhythm as his tongue. Her body squirmed under his touch, as her need seemed to continue to grow, despite her thinking she had already reached her max. How could this be?! Sophie continued to groan louder and louder into the pillow, giving James the encouragement to keep going. She was so wet and sweet that her scent and taste intoxicated him. He finally came up for air and gently slid his fingers inside of her.

"Mmmmm," he moaned in pleasure. "Looks like you're enjoying this," he teased.

"Oh my God, yes!" he heard Sophie's muffled voice in the pillow and smiled with complete satisfaction. He wanted to make her feel him fully, but he didn't want to hurt her either. "Do you want me to keep going?" James asked with a hint of concern.

"There's more?!" he heard her gasp behind the pillow.

"Yes, Baby," he chuckled. "A lot more, but if this is too much I can stop."

"Please don't!" he heard Sophie plead desperately from behind the pillow. "I need you so badly!"

James smiled, knowing she needed him as much as he needed her. "Not yet," he said sheepishly and went down on her again. He massaged her breast as he worked his magic, feeling her grow hotter and hotter under his touch. "Not yet," he murmured against her skin.

"James, please!" Sophie begged as she squirmed under his touch.

"Not yet," he answered and came up for air. She heard the

drawer of the nightstand open up and close, and the rip of a wrapper being torn. His fingers kept rhythm inside of her as he worked on whatever he had gotten from the drawer. She felt herself ready to explode when he slowed down his movements and whispered, "not yet."

"James!" Sophie pleaded again. "I can't take it anymore!"

"I know, Baby," he whispered. "I'm coming." And with that, he pulled out his fingers. He leaned down by her ear and asked, "Ready?"

"Yes!" Sophie begged back, and out of nowhere, something much larger was inside of her. She gasped at the difference. He waited patiently for her to adjust around him before he started to slowly move up and down inside of her. "Whoa," he heard her gasp, and knew he needed to be gentle. She was so tight and hot around him.

James took his time as Sophie adjusted and found her rhythm matching his. "Oh!" he heard her moan. Her back arched higher, and she moaned louder and more frequently. It made him want her so much more. James never knew sex could be this intimate or passionate. He didn't know he could need someone this badly. It took all of his strength to keep the slower pace, despite his need to have her come. He knew this needed to be special for her, but it was as if it was his first time, too. At least, his first time with someone he actually loved.

James could feel her shaking beneath him. She was going to come soon, and so was he. He leaned down and removed the pillow from her face. "I need to see you," he said, looking deep into her eyes that had turned the deepest shade of blue he had ever seen. Sophie knew he was looking into her soul, and she didn't care. He had it. He had her. All of her. And together, they erupted around each other as he

THE KEY

crushed his mouth on hers to taste her and stifle the scream that escaped her lips. Their heads swirled with light-headedness as he gently pushed further and further inside of her. Sophie's body quaked underneath him. James rolled her on top of him, still desperately giving himself to her through his body and mouth. He felt her collapse against him and laid her head on his chest. They were sweaty and trying to catch their breath.

"Wow," Sophie breathed out after what felt like an eternity.

"I agree," James breathed, lifting her gently off of him, and removing the condom to toss it in the trash.

"I didn't know," she whispered.

"Me either," he whispered back, stroking her hair and lightly grazing her back.

"Really?" Sophie asked, lifting her head up to look him in the eyes.

"Why are you always surprised that you're so amazing?" James asked, brushing the hair that now stuck to her forehead.

"I mean, I think it's actually you, who is the amazing one," Sophie said shyly.

"It takes two, Babe," James said seriously. "I have only been with one other person, and it was nothing even remotely close to as amazing as it was with you, just now," he said, looking her straight in the eye, and immediately putting his finger to her lips. "And don't say 'really' as if you can't believe it," he added seriously. "It takes a lot to be intimate on this kind of level, and I don't take it lightly. But I have never had it as amazing as I just had it with you, and I think there's a reason for that. When you're meant to be with that person, it makes it much more powerful and rich. It's mind-blowing, and magical to give so much of yourself to one person but completely worth it. At least, I think so," he finished, looking away.

Sophie studied his face in the sunlight. He had already given so much to her, but now he had truly given everything he was to her, and let her enjoy the ride. She never imagined that this would be as special to him as it was to her, and it made her love him even more for it. "I agree," Sophie said confidently, for the first time since she had shared herself with him. "I just didn't realize that it would be half as special to you as it would be to me, and for that, I'm sorry," she said, turning his head to look deep into his eyes. "I'm glad you were my first. I'd be okay with you being my last, personally," Sophie added with an enormous smile.

"I'm sure we can work something out," James said, smiling with the biggest weight lifted off his shoulder. "Come," he said, rolling her to the side of him and helping her out of bed. "Let's clean up," he said, throwing the covers over the bed to hide the spot of blood. He didn't want Sophie to be horrified after such an amazing gift she had given him. James quickly led her to the bathroom.

"Shower together?" Sophie asked in a bit of shock.

"Baby, we're never doing anything apart again," James said, turning on the water, making sure it wasn't too hot.

"I like the sound of that," Sophie said, seeing his naked body fully for the first time, and taking it all in. James carefully took the wrap off from around her ribs. He tried very hard not to get angered by the bruising that showed bluntly against her moonlight pale skin, but he was thankful to see it already turning to a yellowish green. James opened the shower door and pulled her under the water with him. He kissed her as he gently washed the dirt, sweat, blood, and lovemaking

THE KEY

from her body.

Sophie was on cloud nine as James kissed her gently and wrapped the towel carefully around her naked body. "Dry off, and we'll have Ben check you out," James said softly in her ear.

"I think you've already got that covered," Sophie giggled. He smiled at that magical sound and loved the life that seemed to have been put back into her body. Sophie was glowing, and Tina would know immediately why, but he didn't care. His little sister would be happy for them both. It would be Ben, that would be the most pissed off at them.

"Let's get you dressed first," he said softly. Sophie went to grab her dirty clothes and put them back on. "I think we need to wash those first," James said, watching her in fascination.

"I don't have any other clothes," Sophie said, looking at the floor in embarrassment.

"Tina has them for you," James said, squeezing her hand to reassure her, and unlocked the adjoining door. "Hey, Ti," he asked quietly, not sure if they were awake yet.

"Yes," Tina said, opening the door with a smug grin.

"I need some of your assistance," James said in a low whisper. "We need some clothes."

"Oh!" she said excitedly, grabbed the backpack, and pushed through the door. Tina side-stepped James as he closed the door behind her. He wasn't ready to face Ben just yet. "Well, you're a sight for sore eyes," Tina said, relieved more than ever seeing Sophie stand in front of her, completely ignoring the fact she was naked under the towel wrapped around her.

"Hello, old friend," Sophie whispered and smiled at her. "I hear you have some clothes for me? It appears the ones I have with me require washing first," she said, making a face at James. Tina turned to see the dusty, sweaty, and bloody clothing James held up to rest his case with her.

"Or burn them," Tina added in disgust.

"They come in handy for fighting," Sophie pouted.

"Okay," Tina said, wrinkling her nose. "We'll get them washed," she said in defeat. "Come," Tina said, pushing Sophie by her shoulders into the bathroom. "We have a lot to get caught up on," Tina hollered over her shoulder. "But start with last night," she said in a hushed whisper in Sophie's ear, who blushed immediately before the door closed. James just smiled and shook his head.

"Girls," he said to himself, rolling his eyes.

"Hey," Ben said, interrupting his thoughts. "Where's my wife?"

"Fixing something in my bathroom," James stretched the truth. "How was your night?" he asked hastily, distracting his friend.

"Amazing, per usual," Ben said with a proud smile. "Thanks for the advice," he said, slugging his friend in the arm.

"Hold on to that thought," James said under his breath in a half prayer. "Ti, Ben's out here looking for you," he hollered, signaling the girls to hurry.

"How are you holding up?" Ben asked, looking at his friend full of concern.

"Last night was more than I could wish for," James said

THE KEY

honestly.

"Oh?" Ben asked, confused. "So, a night alone did you good?"

"Last night was perfect," James assured his friend, trying to keep the lying that he'd already been telling to a minimum. "Listen," James started, trying to ease the blow as much as possible. "Whatever happens, just remember that I did what I thought was best for all of us. For my family," James emphasized.

"Bro, we've been through this, and got past it," Ben said, putting his hands up and stepping back. "I get it. It still sucks, and it kills me we left her behind, but I do understand, even though I don't agree with it. I'm trying to get past it, so just let me," Ben added, looking at the ground.

"Well, I want you to hold on to that," James said as he heard Tina open the door behind him.

"Hey love!" she said cheerfully, trying to brighten up what appeared to be an already gloomy husband before her. "Did I tell you how amazing last night was?" Tina said with a gigantic grin, trying to ease the blow for herself for what was to come.

"Yes, you did," Ben grinned triumphantly. "Several times," he said, giving her a gentle kiss. "But you can keep telling me. I'm sure James doesn't mind," he winked at his friend, gloating.

"Not at all." James bowed and smiled back.

"Good," Tina said. "Because I don't want you to be mad at us..." she said, trailing off.

"What's going on?" Ben said suddenly on the defense.

"Hi, Ben," Sophie said softly, coming out from around the bathroom door.

"What the hell?!" Ben yelled, but it was Sophie that got to him first, and put her good hand over his mouth to stop him from yelling.

"I missed you too, my friend," Sophie said, gently kissing him on the side of the cheek. Ben squirmed underneath her, but her strength was impeccable. "I need you to not yell when I remove my hand," Sophie said in her motherly voice, and nodded to encourage him to follow suite.

Ben didn't know if he needed to be pissed off or grateful to see her. Sophie watched the flood of emotions cross his face. "If you're going to be mad at anyone," she added sternly, "you need to be mad at me. This was my plan," Sophie lied. James and Tina both started to protest, but the look on Sophie's face made them both go silent. She was going to take the fall, to save them both from the wrath that was about to come. They knew it, and they respected her for it, but the guilt grew in both of them knowing the truth.

"Now, we're still being followed, which is why I need you to stay calm," Sophie said more gently. "And know this hurt me a hell of a lot more than it hurt you, no matter what you feel in this moment," she said, with tears coming to her eyes. Ben slowly nodded, seeing firsthand that she meant it. Sophie nodded in agreement and removed her hand slowly from his mouth. "I've missed you so much," Sophie whispered, with her voice breaking as she threw her arms around him. Ben stood still, not moving at all, before giving into his own grief and returning the hug. It caused him to notice the ace bandage wrapped tightly around Sophie's ribs. He pulled her back instantly and looked at her with horror as he fully took in the bruising and splinted wrist.

"Sophie," Ben whispered in horror. "Sit down and let me look at you," he instructed.

"I was hoping you would," she said sweetly. Sophie let Ben

THE KEY

guide her to the bed behind them.

"I don't know where to start," Ben said beside himself.

"I tend to start at the top and work my way down," Sophie offered with a smile.

"Grab the first aid kit, and a flashlight," Ben ordered Tina, who left for the other room and quickly returned with the supplies. Ben shined the light in Sophie's eyes and began asking the typical concussion questions. She answered obediently as she patiently waited for him to work his way down. Thankfully, she had started to already heal, so he wouldn't see the full effects of the battle with Simon. Sophie knew Ben would suspect much more than James. She gave Ben extra care and attention as he examined her to let him know she was doing much better.

Ben felt the dried scabs on the back of her head, and the one just above her forehead. He looked at her with concern, but she just gave a slight shake of the head, telling him not to draw attention to every detail. Sophie was okay and already healing. Ben sighed heavily and continued working his way down.

"Well, you've definitely broken some ribs. Without a scan, it's hard to tell how many and where exactly. But luckily, we know they only last a couple of days," he winked at her, trying to lighten the mood for everyone, including himself. Sophie smiled and winked back, which made his anger with her soften. "You did a good job resetting your wrist," Ben said in amazement.

"Not my first rodeo," Sophie shrugged, as if it were no big deal. Ben looked at her tiresomely and rolled his eyes.

"Well, it looks like your wrist broke all the way through, so it might take longer, but it's hard to tell," Ben said, looking into her eyes.

The blank stare Sophie gave back verified that she didn't know what he knew, so Ben swiftly continued on. "You don't seem to have a concussion, but you will definitely have to take it easy for the next couple of days. Doctor's orders," Ben added, looking at Sophie sternly. He was trying to stay mad, but it was hard. She had become like a sister to him, and he could never stay mad at his family for very long.

"I can do that," Sophie said with a sigh as she let him re-wrap her ribs again.

"What the hell happened?" Ben asked, looking her in the eye. "And who the hell said you could leave us behind?" he said as the anger stirred deeper than he realized.

"Well," Sophie started slowly, "while James and I were fighting everyone outside, I was pretty sure I knew that creepy French guy that kept lurking around. I had a terrible feeling about him."

"I'm sorry I lost him," Tina whispered.

"Don't be," Sophie said, assuring her. "The guy was a trained assassin who I had crossed paths with a long time ago. I just didn't remember him at the time. All I knew about him was that he was extremely dangerous." The others pulled up chairs as James sat next to Sophie and put his arm around her.

"I knew he was still watching, so I told James privately that I would have to lure him away," Sophie lied, not skipping a beat. "I knew his voice. And even though I couldn't place it I knew he would kill all of you out of spite for me," she said, choking up as she spoke. James squeezed her tightly while Ben and Tina put their hands on her knees to give her added comfort. "If it didn't look like I had left you for good, then they would keep coming for you, and I couldn't live with myself if anything..." Sophie trailed off, her voice breaking.

THE KEY

She swallowed to regain her composure. "So, James made it look like he was kicking me out, because he knew I wouldn't be able to walk away from you guys. We needed it to be believable," she emphasized. "But your wife is too smart for her own good, and figured James out immediately," Sophie added, looking at Tina with a heart full of love. "Luckily, your reaction sold it," she said, looking at Ben with pure sisterly love. "They didn't believe James, and still don't, which is why that strange couple is still following you," Sophie said, looking at James to encourage him to stay silent. "They agreed to not tell you in my absence, knowing that's what I would ask them to do," Sophie added firmly.

"I ran until I was exhausted, and caught the train to New Hampshire," she pushed on. "I knew Simon would have to follow me, allowing you all to stay safe. While I rested on the train, I remembered Simon, and the true psychopath he was even back when we were teenagers in Paris."

"Paris?" Tina asked in confusion.

"Yeah, that part's still fuzzy," Sophie shrugged. "We were at some sort of school for martial arts. Simon had some sort of sick obsession with me and kept talking about how the weak needed to be replaced by the two of us." Sophie's eyes teared up at the thought of Giselle. "Simon killed my friend right before my eyes just to 'teach me a lesson'. He showed no empathy for life other than his own." She paused to swallow the lump in her throat. "They had to lock him up, but someone had obviously set him free, not knowing what a true cold-blooded killer he actually was. So, I had to lead him as far away from you as I could," Sophie said, urging Ben to understand where she was coming from. "I got a ride from a sweet old guy named Bill, to Vermont.

But that was a mistake, and I should have known better. I was just missing you guys so much. I didn't want to be alone, but instead I ended up taking Bill's life," Sophie said, as a tear ran down her cheek before she could catch it.

James wiped the tear away and kissed her cheek gently. The trio listened in agony as their hearts broke for her, knowing everything was much more traumatic than she was willing to share. It made it even worse for them to hear.

"I took a bus to New York," Sophie pushed on quickly. She knew she was losing it. Recapping the events just made it all come back to life. During all of it, Sophie was just focused on surviving. Reliving everything made it real, and that was even worse than experiencing it for the first time. "I got to Brooklyn and went to the old Jumping Jack Power Plant. I waited for Simon. But Simon had Bill for bait, and he killed him before I could do anything about it," Sophie sobbed. Tina and Ben jumped up and threw their arms around her.

"You didn't kill Bill," Tina said with anger, pulling away. "Freaking Simon did! There was nothing you could have done," she said, rubbing Sophie's arms and holding her good hand.

"I shouldn't have let him give me a ride," Sophie sobbed. "But I selfishly didn't want to be alone, and now his family is without him," she cried in their arms. "But I was just trying to keep you safe, because he would have killed you without a thought just to cause me pain, and I couldn't..." Sophie bawled, and truly grieved for the life she had cost for the first time since it had happened. Everyone waited patiently for her to let out the pain that she had been holding onto in their absence.

After a few moments of silence, Tina urged her to continue. "I knew no one would be protected as long as Simon still lived, so I did

THE KEY

what I had to in order to keep you safe," Sophie said, with determination and no other explanation. "Then, I called the cops so that Bill could be buried, and his family would know what happened. They could grieve him properly. Afterwards, I traveled east for a bit, eventually heading back to you," Sophie finished in a barely audible whisper. Although there were more questions to ask, no one dared to ask them. This was a journey none of them could go on with her, and that was the most painful fact of all. There was nothing they could do, but try to help her heal from what was clearly a devastating voyage she was forced to go on alone.

But Ben's fury grew silently and uncontrollably. It erupted before he even saw it coming. "Why would you do something so stupid?" Ben said in a low growl. "We could have helped," he said firmly.

"You would have died, and that was not a price I was willing to pay," Sophie growled back. She knew his pain and understood it. Sophie knew Ben would eventually see the whole picture. At least she hoped he would with enough time.

"That was not your choice to make," Ben said, as his eyes dilated and his anger spread through his body.

"It *WAS* my choice," Sophie said, with a warning tone. "My life costs other people theirs, and that is something I have to live with for the rest of my life," she said, losing her composure again. "Do you have any *IDEA* what that is like?" Sophie asked, as her own frustration rose. "I finally have a family for the first time since I was ten, and I was *NOT* willing to sacrifice it like my parents chose to sacrifice themselves for me," she yelled, building on the anger that brewed deep within. "If you die, then I have no purpose. If you die, every life taken was for N-O-T-

H-I-N-G. You may not like my choices, but they are to keep you safe. So you can have the kids with your loving wife that I never will get to have. I do it so you have NO sacrifices, because I make them for you. Your life means more to me than my own. And because it's my life on the freaking line, I will make choices that help me save yours, even when you don't like them," Sophie hissed through her clenched jaw as she glared at Ben with a beat red face and eyes so dilated you could barely see the blue that hid within them.

No one said a word. Ben scowled at her, then at James, then at his wife. "You knew, and you chose not to tell me," Ben said, turning his anger on his friend and his wife. "You knew I was hurting, and you CHOSE to keep me in the dark," he said, full of pain, glaring at his wife.

"It had to be believable," Tina said, begging for his forgiveness. "They didn't believe that James would actually leave her. When I saw we were being followed, I knew we had no choice but to stay silent. It was the hardest thing I have *EVER* done," Tina pleaded with him, and tried to grab his hand. Ben just yanked it away.

"You were checking for bugs in the hotel rooms," Ben said quietly, frowning at his wife.

"Yes," Tina said, looking at the floor, trying not to provoke him any further. She had honestly never seen him so mad before in her life. All she could do was pray that they would survive this. All of them.

"You washed the car every day," Ben said in a low voice.

"Making sure they did not bug the car," Tina whispered.

"And knowing that it wasn't, you thought it best to *LIE* to me, then to ask me to play along with you?" Ben hissed at her.

"We had to be sure," James interjected, but Ben just shot up his hand to silence him.

THE KEY

"Him, I understand, but you chose to break your vows, because you didn't think I was worth trusting?" Ben asked in a low growl, full of pain.

"We all made sacrifices," Sophie stepped in.

"Don't," Ben said suddenly, looking at Sophie with the same venom he showed currently towards his wife. "I have nothing more to say to you right now."

"That's fine," Sophie retorted. "But you needed to know the stakes that *WE* went through to keep you safe."

"I can't even look at you," Ben said, shaking his head. "Any of you," he said, scowling at his wife. He went to their room, grabbed a bag, and started shoving clothes into it.

"Where are you going?" Tina asked in full panic. "We need to stay together!" she pleaded.

"I can't be in the same room as you all," Ben said as he continued to throw stuff into a bag.

"Are you leaving me?" Tina asked in desperation. Ben only paused for a second, then continued to pack before throwing open the door.

"When will you be back?" Tina cried after him.

"I don't know," Ben said, over his shoulder and took off for the elevators. Tina fell to her knees and sobbed in the doorway. The odd couple tried not to look too interested as James came to collect her limp body from the floor. He kicked the door closed and gently laid her on the bed as she curled up into the fetal position. Tina howled from her broken heart. Both Sophie and James curled up around her and held Tina while she sobbed.

"He'll be back," James whispered.

233

"I don't know," Tina wept, uncertain of her future for the first time in her life.

"He just needs to cool off," Sophie said, moving the hair from her wet cheeks, but Tina wasn't so sure he was coming back. She suddenly felt completely empty, as the other half of her heart stormed out into the streets and left everything he knew behind him.

Twenty

"I think I should go look for him," James offered, staring out the window. The sun was about to go down, and Ben had been gone for over ten hours without a word.

"No," Tina said flatly. "But I do need some food."

"What do you want, Honey?" Sophie asked softly, brushing the hair from Tina's face. She continued to lie in the fetal position, with Sophie stretched out by her side. Neither had left her all day, and everyone's stomach was growling.

"You pick," Tina said, with no emotion.

Sophie looked at James desperately. He shrugged with obvious concern on his face. "Pizza?" he finally offered.

"And maybe some ice cream," Sophie added. That seemed to be the go to for all the chick flicks they had watched in the past.

"On it," James said, grabbing his wallet, and leaving the girls to survive on their own. He was furious with Ben, and not sure what he could do to make Tina feel any better. He was helpless, and all he wanted was for everyone to go back to getting along so they could deal with the actual problem at hand. The man with the cane. James shook his head as he left the hotel and took to the streets. The brunette appeared from behind, but he continued to ignore her. When Ben returned, well, if he returned, James was going to shake him senseless for breaking Tina so badly over nothing. He understood Ben was mad, but he was definitely blowing it out of proportion.

Sophie absent-mindedly stroked Tina's hair as she watched the streets from the bed. She didn't want to get too close to the window in case more were watching, but her eyes were like a hawk, casing the streets for any sign of Ben. Tina sighed heavily from beside her.

"You're never going to tell us the complete story, are you?" Tina asked flatly.

"Probably not," Sophie said honestly.

"I know this was James' idea," Tina confessed.

"I figured as much," Sophie said as she watched the streets and stroked Tina's hair.

"You didn't know either, did you?" Tina asked with no emotion.

"Not at first," Sophie replied.

"I didn't think so," Tina said flatly.

"That's because you're incredibly smart," Sophie said softly, as her heart broke for her friend. She knew exactly how she felt, and it was a horrible feeling knowing she couldn't take it away from her.

"Well, you did say there'd be sacrifices," Tina said bluntly.

Sophie stopped stroking her hair and looked at her friend. "I didn't mean this," Sophie said, full of guilt.

THE KEY

"I know," Tina said, squeezing her good hand. "I know."

Sophie went back to stroking her hair and looking out the window. "Do you want to watch a movie?" She asked Tina absent-mindedly.

"Yes, please," Tina replied flatly.

"Preference?" Sophie asked as she kept her eyes on the window but grabbed the remote.

"Anything but romance," Tina said bluntly. "Action?" she offered.

"Action it is," Sophie said, changing the channels to find Tina something to watch while she continued to scan the street.

"Thank you," Tina said after a few minutes.

"For what?" Sophie asked.

"For being the sister I always wanted and needed," Tina said, choking up. Sophie didn't know how to respond, so she just squeezed Tina's hand back, and continued to stroke her hair while she desperately tried to find her husband in the streets down below.

"That's a lot of food for one person," the brunette said, pressing her breasts up against James' back. She peered over his shoulder as he purchased the ice cream from a grocery store nearby.

"Probably because it's not," James responded flatly. This woman got on his nerves. Especially knowing Sophie was waiting for him to return to her.

"Oh?" she asked with curiosity in her fake Spanish accent. "A party?"

"No," James answered shortly, letting his frustration show.

"I'm sorry," she said, looking down at the floor. "My husband is away for business, and I'm just getting very lonely without him," she lied. James guessed his business was tracking Ben wherever the hell he had gone.

"Sorry to hear," James said, shoving the cash to the blonde clerk that clearly hated her job, and ignored them both. "Keep the change," he muttered, grabbing the pizza and ice cream, and walking as fast as he could away from her.

"Not that sorry," the brunette said in hot pursuit. "You seemed like such a gentleman," the brunette pouted, keeping in step with him.

"People are deceiving." James shrugged and continued his pace. Sophie would have lost her by now, he thought to himself as pride swelled in his chest.

"Well, if you're fine leaving a lonely lady all by herself, then I can't stop you," she pouted, sticking her fat bottom lip out.

"Listen," James said, suddenly coming to a halt. "My sister's in the fetal position, because her husband lost his mind. He left her for God knows how long. I can only handle one lonely lady at a time, and family beats strangers."

"We don't have to stay strangers," the brunette said as she batted her lashes and ran her finger down his flexed arm.

"Lady, I don't know how to be any more clearly," James said bluntly. "I'm not interested." He turned on his heels and continued walking. Even if she wasn't out to scout them, or kill them, or whatever her current job title was, Sophie was the only one that would ever have his heart. And when everything settled down, if it ever settled down, he would ask her to marry him. This much he knew. His pace suddenly quickened even more as he hurried back to the woman that held his heart and soul.

Tina automatically lifted her head when the door opened, but laid it back down the second she saw it was James. "You're going to have to sit up to eat, Ti," he encouraged, as he laid the food on the table. "Thought this would be a cookie dough kind of situation," James said, putting the ice cream into the fridge.

"You thought correctly," Tina said, blankly watching the TV "Per usual."

"Listen, Ti," James started, but Tina just held up her hand.

"We all made choices we thought were the best at the time," she said flatly, not removing her eyes from the TV. James looked at the floor for a second before serving everyone.

"I hope pepperoni is alright for everyone," he added gloomily.

"Did you have any trouble?" Sophie asked, not taking her eyes off the street.

"Nothing I couldn't handle," James shrugged. "The brunette tried to join us. Said she was lonely." He recapped their encounter while biting down on his greasy piece of pizza. Tina sat up for the first time since this morning, picked up her plate, and numbly ate what was in front of her.

"Lonely, huh?" Sophie said, with a hint of jealousy as she continued to watch outside.

"Yeah, but I turned her down flat. Had to get back to my girl," James said, smiling at her jealous tone. "Not in so many words, of course," he added, winking at her. They ate in silence and paid no real attention to what was on the TV. It was purely background noise. Tina ate most of the ice cream by herself, then slowly drifted off to sleep, feeling absolutely nothing.

Sophie continued to keep her hawk eyes on the street. "Can you really see from there?" James asked in awe.

"Yes," Sophie said, as she focused on an image she'd grown to know well. She turned to look at James with both relief and alarm in her eyes. James jumped out of bed and stood behind the door. It only took a few minutes for them both to hear the door being electronically unlocked by a key. James grabbed the extended arm as he jerked open the door and pulled the figure inside.

"What the hell!" Ben shouted as James held him in a headlock.

"What the hell is that it's after midnight, you've been gone all freaking day, and your wife was broken the whole time you were gone!" hissed James at his friend.

Tina sat up and rubbed her eyes. Once they focused and she saw Ben being held down by James, she jumped out of bed and towered over him. "Let him go," Tina ordered. Ben straightened up just in time to get the hardest slap across his face that he had ever received from a man or woman.

"Hey!" Ben whined, rubbing his cheek.

James stepped between them, and Sophie held Tina as she turned and buried her head into Sophie's shoulder. There were no more tears to cry at this point. "Now, if we're done pissing each other off, you could tell us where the hell you've been, and what you've been

THE KEY

doing while your wife mourned your loss," James said, frowning at his friend, emphasizing the words "wife" and "mourned" to Ben.

"I was collecting data," Ben mumbled.

"What?" Tina said, turning around with a look that would have sent Ben's body into flames if Tina had the power to. Ben took a couple of steps back.

"I was really hurt, so I went for a walk," Ben started while he stood slightly behind James in case any more attacks came. "I found myself at the library, when the short fat guy sat down, mumbling a couple of tables down from me. So, I figured if he was following me, I could use it to my advantage," he said, staring at the floor. "I caused a scene and left the library to go to Mario's for a drink," Ben said, smiling to himself. "Turns out the short one really talks once you get enough alcohol in him," Ben said with pride. "And I can act after all," he said, taking a cheap shot at Tina and James, but the look on Sophie's face had him stop dead in his tracks.

"Anyway," Ben continued. "Apparently, the short one is in love with the brunette, and he's upset because they're pulling them soon to go follow Sophie's fake trail. She was so convincing they don't think they need to stay on us right now. Which I found to be a bit odd, but the short one said they were running out of time to get the key."

"Why would they be running out of time?" Tina asked, spinning around, deep in thought. "It's not like it's something that expires."

"Maybe it does, though," Ben shrugged. "It's been at least ten years since they gave it to Sophie. That's a long time to try and get a hold of something."

"We need to find it first," Sophie said with authority. "Just in case."

"What I don't understand is why not destroy it to begin with?" Ben asked out loud. "Why give it to Sophie to hold all these years without her having a clue what it actually was?"

"Maybe she wasn't supposed to know, until now," James said, deep in thought. "Or they think she already has, and that's why time is running out."

"Either way, it's late," Sophie said. "And we need to sleep before we can solve another puzzle."

"We haven't solved one yet," Tina said, frustrated. "All we get is more questions."

"Doesn't mean we're not going to," Sophie winked at her. "Get some sleep," she said, kissing her friend on the forehead and leading her to bed.

Ben went to sleep next to her until she growled, "Doghouse."

"Yeah, well, you should be in the doghouse, too, but I have a big enough heart to forgive you," he whined as he grabbed a pillow and blanket to sleep on the floor.

"Good point," Tina said flatly, turning her back on him and shutting off the light next to her. Ben stared at her, not sure if that meant he was still supposed to sleep on the floor or not. Tina sighed. "Lie down, Nerd," she said, just before closing her eyes to sleep. Ben sulked into the sheets next to her and turned his back to her before turning off his light and going to sleep.

James grabbed Sophie's hand and pulled her into their own room. He closed the door softly. "Do you think they will be okay," Sophie asked in concern.

"With time," James assured, "all wounds heal." They quickly got into their pj's and snuggled under the covers as Sophie crawled into

THE KEY

James' open arms. They drifted into the darkness.

The wooden door appeared before her, but when Sophie went to open it, the dang thing wouldn't budge. "What the heck?" Sophie said out loud. The surrounding walls began to suddenly close in around her. "Hey!" she hollered, and started banging on the walls and door to escape.

"Stay quiet, Peanut," she heard her dad's voice warn her from the other side of the door. She heard his footsteps run around, and then the rapid firing of several guns. Sophie felt panic in the pit of her stomach, just like the first time she had experienced her parent's murder. Only, she wasn't a little girl this time. She remained her current self in the back hole of the closet. Sophie closed her eyes and covered her ears. Once was plenty to see this nightmare play all the way out. She didn't have the stomach to do it again.

Sophie waited for the man with the cane to come. He searched for her but never found her. Sophie then heard the lackey, again, from upstairs come and inform the man with the cane that she was M.I.A. She sensed his agitation as he tapped his cane and waited for them both to leave again. Sophie had seen all of this before and figured it out. Why show it to her again? For torture? Did they not understand how much she missed them? What she had lost? What they took from her without even asking? Anger grew within her as she sat with her arms around her knees, rocking as the time passed by.

Suddenly, she heard whatever blocked the door being moved,

and the door slowly opened. Light flooded the tiny black space. A shadowy figure was crouched down in front of her, but she still saw no face. "Hello, Peanut," said a familiar voice that she couldn't quite place.

"Hello," Sophie responded, just to see if that changed anything. The figure tilted his head and paused.

"I'm a friend of your parents. They sent me to come get you," he said, slower than she remembered.

"How do I know you're a friend?" Sophie dared to ask the shadowy figure. "How do I know you don't work for the man with the cane?"

The shadow chuckled. "Because you're still alive. You know you get past this part, and continue on," he said, with a hint of humor. "So, clearly, you made the right decision, and I was telling the truth," he added.

"How do I know you?" Sophie asked, crossing her arms.

"You didn't before," the shadow mimicked her and crossed his own arms.

"Then why go with you now?" she asked stubbornly.

"Stubborn like your mother," he laughed, shaking his head.

"But I know you," Sophie said, studying him closely.

"You do," he said, uncrossing his arms, and holding out his hand.

Sophie hesitated and then stuck her hand out towards the shadow. She felt his warmth immediately, but he remained a shadow. "Why can't I see you?" she asked, staring at the blackness.

"You have to want to," the shadow shrugged, and pulled her into the light with him.

"I know you," Sophie said, getting frustrated with herself.

THE KEY

"Better than most," he sighed.

"I want to see you," she said, annoyed.

"Then open your eyes," he offered.

"What? They are open!" Sophie exclaimed.

"Are they?" he asked softly.

"UGH!" Sophie yelled in annoyance, trying desperately to focus on the figure before her with no face.

"You won't see me if you don't allow yourself to," he said in a fatherly voice that rung through her head. Sophie closed her eyes, trying desperately to remember. She saw his hands as they aged with hers. His arms held her tight as a child when she woke up from a bad dream. She heard his laugh, and it warmed her heart. Pieces of him came to her as they swirled around her like a tornado.

"I need to see you," Sophie whispered to herself.

"And so you shall," he said softly as more of him slowly came into light. His image circled around her. Then suddenly everything went black again, and the silence was deafening. She slowly opened her eyes and found familiar dark hazel eyes staring back at her. "Hello, old friend," he said with the warmest smile. Sophie gasped and sat up immediately.

"Mario!" she whispered into the blackness.

"What?" James asked her sleepily.

"Nothing. Go back to sleep," Sophie said, lying back down next to him.

"It's not ideal to have your girl call out another man's name while she's in bed with you, you know," James mumbled as he gave her a quick squeeze and faded back to sleep.

"It's a name we needed, nothing more," Sophie said, mostly to herself as she quickly drifted off.

Twenty-One

Eddie couldn't remember exactly how he had gotten to where he was today. It had been so long since he last saw Sophie and her family. Sophie used to help him with the mean teachers and the bullies he encountered at school. Everyone picked on him. He was small and a misfit. He belonged to no one. Eddie lived with a foster family down the street from Sophie. He remembered the day that her father stepped in and kept him from being beaten by his foster dad for the millionth time...*Greg*.

Greg was a tall, skinny man who drank more than he made, and spent more time on his couch than he did at his job. He smelled constantly of booze and cigarettes. His leathery wrinkled tan skin matched his faded blonde buzz cut. He had a gut that stuck out enough to prevent his pants from staying up, even with a belt. Greg's favorite pass time was putting his cigarettes out on Eddie's skin, just because he could. The scars were still on Eddie's arms and chest. Greg cussed, and stumbled, and beat all the kids with his belt whenever the mood struck him. His wife, Milly, just stood back and watched. She would sneak the kids candy when Greg was gone, but otherwise told them to just stay out of his way as much as possible.

Their house was old and smelled of smoke and booze. Faded torn curtains hung on the rod for dear life to cover the small clouded windows. It was dark and musty. The only life that the house contained were of the fifteen various aged foster kids that brought the couple enough money from the state for them to not have to work much at all.

Eddie's clothes never fit him, and he made himself toys out of things like paperclips and paper. Books were not allowed in the house. Greg said they "didn't need to be getting smart on him. They were only a paycheck. Nothing more." But the state still required the kids to be sent to school. That's where Eddie met Sophie.

She was a beautiful, sassy redhead who was too smart for her own good. She always had her nose in a book and spent a lot of time smarting off to the teachers. They rarely punished her, because she was always proving them wrong. He was too nervous to talk to her directly, so Eddie spent all of his time watching her. She was magnificent.

They did not give Eddie lunch money. There was never any to spare. He sat in the corner of the lunchroom by himself, and just watched everyone around him. Eddie nibbled on a piece of bread that Milly had snuck a little peanut butter on for him. He liked Milly. She was nice. But one of the big six graders never believed Eddie when he told him he never had any lunch money to give him. He just picked up Eddie by his oversized t-shirt and socked him in the stomach while making fun of him for everyone to see.

THE KEY

One day was different, though. Sophie was in the lunch room instead of outside. She sat quietly in the corner with her nose in a book, as usual, while she nibbled on her own peanut butter and jelly sandwich. The bully came by and picked Eddie up by his shirt. He lifted Eddie all the way off the bench. "Where's my money, Rat?" he bellowed at Eddie.

"Milly doesn't give me money," Eddie stammered. "We don't get enough."

"Well, you better figure out how to get some, Troll," the bully rumbled. "You have to pay the toll."

"I'll pay it," Sophie said sweetly, standing right behind the bully.

"Go away, little girl," he laughed. "I'll come for you another day. I'm busy."

Sophie stood her ground with her hands crossed behind her back. "But I'm here to pay," she pouted, stuck out her bottom lip, and batted her long black lashes at him.

"Are you, now?" he asked, intrigued, and dropped Eddie on the table.

"But you have to promise not to pick on him anymore," Sophie said, tossing her head in Eddie's direction.

"You don't have enough for that," the bully laughed in her face.

"Who said I was giving you money?" Sophie said with a sly smile, and began swaying back and forth.

"No money, no paid toll," the bully said, crossing his arms.

"Says you," Sophie shrugged. The whole cafeteria was watching them, and they whooped and hollered every time Sophie snapped back. It fed her need to win even more.

"So, what are you going to give me that's worth me not pounding the both of you into the ground right now in front of everyone?" he demanded as his anger grew.

"A well-deserved butt kicking," Sophie said, crossing her arms and staring him down. The cafeteria went silent, and you could hear a pin drop.

"Sophie, no," Eddie begged. "He can beat me up, honestly. I'm used to it." Sophie ignored him.

"What do you say, Tucker? I kick your butt, and you never touch Edward again. You win, and I pay for both of us for the rest of our lives," Sophie said with determination.

"Ooooo," whispered all the kids in the lunch room.

"You're not supposed to hit a girl," his lackey said, pulling on the sleeve of his shirt.

"Sophie's no girl," Tucker laughed. "Besides, it's easy money for life. No first grader is going to beat me. Deal!" he said, shoving his hand in Sophie's face.

"Deal," she said, purposely lightly shaking his in return.

But Sophie did beat him that day. She even pulled his underwear over his head, causing him to yell so the entire school could hear him. They dragged Sophie to the principal's office, and Tucker never made eye contact with Eddie or Sophie again. Eddie listened carefully outside the door as the principal told Mr. Harris that Sophie's behavior was completely unacceptable. He said they should expel her. Eddie was thankful when Mr. Harris pointed out that had the school delt with its bullying problem, his daughter wouldn't have had to step in. They made Sophie promise out loud that she would never fight on school property again. Eddie ran and hid behind the stairs before they

THE KEY

opened the door to come out.

Mr. Harris stopped and looked at the stairs. "Is that him?" he asked his daughter, full of curiosity.

"Yes, father," Sophie replied bluntly.

"I see," Mr. Harris said, and put his hand on his daughter's back as they walked to the front door. "Man, your mom cooked so much food tonight, we won't be able to eat it all, just the three of us. Maybe you should have a friend over to help us eat it?" he said loudly so Eddie could hear him.

Sophie looked at him, confused. "I don't have any friends," she said bluntly.

"Are you sure?" Mr. Harris said, nodding toward the stairs.

Sophie frowned as she looked towards the stairs, but knew exactly what her father was implying. She sighed heavily before walking over to Eddie. "Do you want to come for dinner?" Sophie asked flatly.

"I don't think I can," said Eddie in horror at the thought of asking Greg to go over to Sophie's for dinner.

"I tried." Sophie shrugged and walked back to her dad. "He said he can't come," she said, shrugging to her father.

"Hhhmmm," her father said to himself as they walked to the car together.

That night, Mr. Harris showed up at Greg's door, just when he was attempting to beat Eddie within an inch of his life. He asked if Eddie could come over for dinner and play with Sophie. Greg told Mr. Harris to go to hell and spit in his face. Mr. Harris stuck his foot in the door to prevent Greg from slamming it shut.

"Let me put it another way," Mr. Harris said, smiling. "Eddie's coming over for dinner. In fact, Eddie's coming over whenever he wants to, and you will not lay a hand on him from here on out."

"Who the hell do you think you are?" shouted Greg, spitting in Mr. Harris' face again.

"The man that can break your nose, push the bones so far up your face that they will inject into your brain, and kill you instantly," Mr. Harris said with a straight face and a smile.

"Oh, yeah?" Greg shouted, stepping into Mr. Harris' face.

"Yeah," Mr. Harris smiled, and quickly shoved the base of his palm up Greg's nose, breaking it instantly, and causing blood to gush from it.

"Fucker!" Greg screamed, stumbling back.

"Next time, it will be further," Mr. Harris said bluntly. "Eddie, grab your coat. You're coming over for dinner." Eddie stood in complete shock in the middle of the living room. "Come Eddie," Mr. Harris said more softly. "Our food is getting cold." Eddie grabbed his coat and ran to the door where Mr. Harris escorted him out and walked him down the street. He put his hand on Eddie's back, just like he had with Sophie earlier. "Now, Eddie," Mr. Harris said, looking straight ahead. "Not a mention of this to anyone. It has to be our secret." Eddie looked up at him and nodded. "Good. My wife hates it when I fight." Mr. Harris winked and walked Eddie to their house.

Greg never touched Eddie again. No one did. Sophie kept him safe at school, and Mr. Harris kept him safe at home. He hated going back there, but Mr. Harris explained it would only make him stronger. He promised Eddie would always be safe from here on out. Eddie believed him. He spent a lot of time at Sophie's house. Mr. Harris played catch with him and taught him puzzles. Mrs. Harris always cooked enough food for Eddie to have for lunches the next day. Eddie felt the most wanted, for being a boy wanted by no one his whole life. Sophie taught him some tricks for staying safe, but made him promise not to tell her mother. They played games whenever he could get Sophie to put her book down.

Then one day, they were all gone. No goodbyes. No notice. The house just went dark one day. Eddie heard shots from afar, but there was no news of any wrongdoing in the neighborhood. And his friend was gone. He had no one to keep him safe anymore. Eddie cried every night before going to sleep, and he prayed to God to have them return safely. But after a couple of months, his tears dried up, and his prayers remained unanswered.

Greg went back to beating Eddie senselessly, and the kids tortured him at school. It wasn't until the day he turned sixteen that he was finally free.

Eddie started working under the table at an early age for a rundown auto shop. No one asked how old he was as long as he fixed their car for them. He hid the money from Greg and Milly. While other kids saved up for their first car, Eddie saved up for his escape. He would never get into college, anyway. He wasn't good with the book stuff like Sophie was. Eddie was much better with his hands. Numbers and people watching made him happy. Eddie knew people better than they knew themselves just by watching them.

On his sixteenth birthday, Eddie kissed Milly goodnight and hugged her extra-long while he thanked her for the little she had done for him. Then he went to bed. His bed was empty by morning.

Right or wrong, Eddie did what he had to in order to survive. He took random odd jobs here and there. He lived in places best suited for rats than people, but it was what he could afford. It turned out Eddie was good with computers, despite never going to college or graduating from high school. His people watching skills earned him some cash on the side.

Eddie helped catch countless women and men cheating in the City of Sin, among other things, and got paid for his surveillance. He never lived comfortably, but he survived. Eddie was already numb from what society had handed him since birth. He assumed he was destined for this line of work. Years passed, and he still found himself in a church, lighting a candle for Sophie every year on her birthday. Nothing less, nothing more.

It would be outside of the MGM Grand Hotel on a bench that he first come across Clarice. He was nineteen and could spot a mark from a mile away. She was much younger and prettier back then. Her heart seemed to even still beat occasionally. "Hello, Edward," she said coolly, after sitting down next to him. Clarice had on black high heels, black stockings that emphasized her athletic legs, a black short skirt, and a red silk short-sleeved blouse. It was unbutton far enough to show her perky breasts in a black lace bra underneath. She had long blonde hair that was curled just past her shoulders.

"I prefer, Eddie," he said flatly, watching the streets.

"Hello, Eddie," Clarice started again, calmly watching a man and woman hold hands as they crossed the street in front of them. They could hear "Hey Big Spender" playing for the fountain show in front of the Bellagio in the distance.

"I don't know who you are, but I'm not taking on new clients right now," Eddie said bluntly. The Strip was extra full tonight as people hurried to get the last feel of summer on this Labor Day weekend.

"I think you'll want this one," Clarice said, as the corner of her lips curled up into a smile. "We have a mutual friend, you and I," she said coolly. "A Sophie Harris to be exact."

Eddie's heart stopped at the name. It had been years since he had heard it, and it was a pain he didn't feel like reliving right now. "What do I care about that bitch for?" Eddie said, pretending to be pissed. Although he never quite could find himself truly mad at Sophie for some reason, despite her leaving him behind to hurt by himself.

"You don't know, do you?" Clarice said, faking sympathy. "She didn't leave you all those years ago. Someone who Jack worked for had him viciously murdered, and they kidnapped Sophie when she was just a child." Clarice watched the street, but kept her focus to watching Eddie out of the corner of her eye. She saw his face waver for a slight second in shock before recovering his composure. Clarice fought to let her pleasure show.

"It would have been on the news," Eddie shrugged, and continued to watch the people in front of him.

"Not if it was a contract killer," Clarice casually retorted back. Eddie continued to watch the surrounding people, but she knew he was hooked.

"Who killed them?" Eddie asked casually.

"Jack worked for a man that was trying to take over the world with his science projects. But Jack caught on, and he tried to leave. Unfortunately, for his family and him, that wasn't exactly an option. The man kidnapped Sophie and tortured her. He brain washed her into becoming an assassin. The man now keeps her locked away, and I want to help free her," Clarice said, cuing a tear to fall down her cheek.

Eddie knew it was a show, but what if what she was telling him was true? He had to see if he could get more information. "Why would you want to do that?" he asked with no emotion in his voice.

"Because Jess was the closest thing that I had to a sister. Sophie might as well be my niece. My father and I have been trying to track her down, and bring her in safely so we can help her get better. We want to help Sophie do the work her mother always wanted her to do. Save people," Clarice finished, pulling out a tissue from her pocket and dabbing her eyes with it.

"And how do you happen to know all of this?" Eddie asked flatly, with much doubt.

"Because he came for me, too," Clarice said, choking on the words. "Luckily, my father is very strong and powerful, and he could keep me safe. But, poor Sophie. She doesn't even know she's on the wrong side!" Clarice said with her voice breaking. Damn, she deserved an Oscar for this role.

"What do you want from me?" Eddie asked without being unable to hide his curiosity.

"You know Sophie better than anyone," Clarice said, laying it on thick. "She needs to be brought in by someone she trusts. A friend. And we've been watching you. Your work speaks for itself. If anyone can find her, it's you," she added, batting her blonde eyelashes at him.

Eddie's gut told him to walk away, and his gut was never wrong. But what if this woman was right? What if Sophie didn't leave him behind? What if she had been taken and had been searching for Eddie this whole time? She had saved his life countless times. What if Eddie could save hers just this once, to return the favor? "Let me think about it," Eddie mumbled, as he got off the bench and walked away.

THE KEY

Clarice wasn't worried for a second. She knew she had him. She knew he couldn't resist saving Sophie. Whether or not he knew it, that stupid kid had fallen in love with her so many years ago. He just couldn't admit it yet.

She waited patiently for him, outside The Queens Hotel on Fremont Street, standing outside of a limousine holding the door. Eddie had thrown most of his things into a duffle bag. It was a good thing, because he would never return to Vegas. He would never go anywhere. He would stay in the underground bunker, starring at computer screens, chasing a ghost from his past.

Eddie watched Sophie for almost two years, learning some of her habits. She always knew she was being watched, though, and changed her behavior often. He still came to know some of her routines, regardless.

Everyone had a routine, even if they tried not to. It's human nature. It is our biggest flaw. Sophie changed her hair occasionally, but she could never quite change her demeanor. She was just so much more graceful than most. Sophie was oddly quicker too. Whoever trained her definitely trained her well.

What didn't quite add up was how good a fighter she was, even as a kid. Although it got her in trouble often in the beginning of their friendship, Sophie was definitely more scared of her mother finding out than her father. Eddie never understood why. Mrs. Harris didn't have a single mean bone in her body. She was an amazing cook, who worked hard, and went on a lot of business trips, but otherwise, she was a remarkable homemaker.

Eddie wondered if Sophie would remember him. If they had wiped her mind, how did Clarice know if she remembered any of them? But Eddie learned quickly, this was a "just do it and don't ask questions" kind of environment.

Clarice watched over him often and became shorter with him as finding Sophie took longer and longer. She assured Eddie that the "teams" she sent were to bring in the trained killer Sophie had become. Clarice promised therapists would be standing by to help her adjust back to the girl that he loved so much. But everyone has a routine. Clarice didn't understand that Eddie would read her sooner than planned.

Things added up less and less as time went by. Eddie wasn't allowed to ask questions, but their behavior gave him almost all the answers he needed. Eddie was preparing to walk away, and go warn Sophie when he first met the old man with the cane. It would be the one and only time Eddie would ever see him in the full light. The thought made him shutter to his core. He closed his eyes and tried not to think about it, but the memory flooded his brain all the same.

One day, Eddie was asked to go to the main office. A place he had never been allowed to enter before. He walked timidly into the room to find a giant red leather chair with its back to him, sitting largely behind a desk that looked like the one that sat in the Oval office of the White House.

"Sit down, my boy," boomed a large elderly voice from the other side of the giant red chair.

"I'm good," said Eddie nervously.

"Sit down," the voice threatened, and Eddie quickly took a seat.

"I hear you're thinking about leaving us," the man said, remaining in the shadows.

Eddie had told no one, which meant someone had watched him

THE KEY

as well. "Well, I was just thinking about it," Eddie said, clearing his throat. "I'm not having much luck keeping up with Sophie, so I figured you wanted someone that could do better," he lied.

"Oh, quite the contrary," the deep voice said with a hint of excitement. "You keep up with her better than anyone I have ever seen." Eddie squirmed uncomfortably in the black leather chair he sat in just on the other side of the desk. "In fact, I KNOW you're the right person for the job," the man emphasized.

"I don't know about that," Eddie backpedaled.

"It's not about what you know, my boy. It's what I know. That's why I get to determine your fate," he said, smiling at the wall.

"My fate?" Eddie swallowed. "I was told I could go after I found her. I've found her. Now it's time to go," Eddie said as defiantly as possible.

"We're told so many things throughout our lives," the old man said with humor. "It is our choices that define us, and I believe you were told you would also need to help bring her in. She is not here; therefore, you remain."

"No one can bring her in!" Eddie said in protest. "Clarice sends teams constantly, and Sophie wipes them out every time!"

"Yes, she's a challenge," the old man said with a hint of pride. "But we need to bring her in. For her safety," he added hastily. Eddie knew otherwise. "She is destined for great things, and for her family's sake, we need to make sure that comes true. We owe them that much," the old man said, speaking more to himself than to Eddie. Then the red leather chair slowly turned around. Eddie took in a quick breath and held it.

The old man was disfigured. Someone had clearly burnt half his face off. A hole remained where his ear used to be. Half his mouth was missing lips. Eddie had seen a lot of horrific things in his life, but this real life horror movie made him swallow the vomit threatening to come out of his mouth. Grey, long, wavy hair covered the old man's shoulders. He wore a black suit and tie, and had the thickest gold ring with some sort of symbol etched in it.

The old man grabbed a gold topped cane when he stood up and walked towards Eddie to give him a closer look. Eddie saw why the cane was needed. His left leg dragged slightly behind him. The old man leaned on the desk behind him, just inches away from Eddie's face.

"You see," the old man continued. "Choices define us. They shape us into the greatness we're destined to become. You have a choice right now. You can stay and help Sophie, or you can leave and have her continue to suffer alone. Lost in this world, and taking lives without realizing it's for the wrong reason. The question is...what are you going to choose?"

But those weren't Eddie's choices at all, and he knew it. His choices were to bring Sophie in, and possibly live another day. Or leave now and never see the light of day again. At least staying meant Eddie could help save Sophie from this freak show, one that he would never survive. Those were Eddie's actual choices.

The old man was right, though. Choices define us. His continued bad choices put Eddie in a cemented hell, without ever seeing sunlight again, living amongst freaks and psychopaths. Eddie had to choose wisely, but was it going to be to save Sophie or simply save himself? He wasn't sure what he would choose. For the moment, Eddie chose to survive. He was no good to anyone dead.

"Excellent choice," the old man said without Eddie saying a

THE KEY

word. *Was his brain bugged?* He would have to proceed with caution from now on. "You may go," the old man said, and Eddie got up and left as quickly as possible.

The old man would never be seen in the light again. He would stick to the shadows, only showing his hands to the light. He would have Eddie watch as he had countless people killed, just as a reminder of his "choices". Eddie stayed quiet, and spent his time thinking, assessing behavior, and wondering if Sophie would ever come save him one last time.

Twenty-two

"So, do we stay and wait for our friends to leave? Or do we get the hell out of dodge?" James asked, when they were together again in Ben and Tina's room. They were figure-eighting, pacing to think. It looked like a choreographed dance, more than just a group of adults trying to figure out their next move.

"We can't leave without seeing Mario," Sophie said bluntly.

"Mario? What's he got to do with anything?" Tina asked, in total confusion.

"I don't know exactly," Sophie answered honestly. "All I know is that he's the one that helped get me out of the closet the day my parents were murdered. I think he's helped to raise me this whole time."

"Why didn't seeing him the first time jog your memory, I wonder?" asked Ben, out loud to no one.

THE KEY

"That explains his interest in why Sophie wasn't with us," Tina added, deep in thought.

"Why not say anything, though?" James asked, frustrated.

"He probably thought it was safer that way," Tina offered.

"Still should have said something," James muttered.

"How does one get to Mario without our friends seeing Sophie?" Ben asked, tapping his fingers on his chin.

Tina stopped suddenly, forcing the boys to run into her. "The same way she came in," she said with a coy smile. "And a date night for distraction," Tina added, winking at Ben.

"Thought I was in the doghouse," Ben mumbled, staring at the floor.

"Well, you got good data, and you need to work yourself out anyway," Tina said, sweetly kissing him on the cheek, making him smile and blush all at once. "So, Ben will take me out to make up for being an ass, and leaving me in the first place," Tina said, grinning at Ben. "And James will offer to stay behind. Sophie and James can then sneak out, and go see Mario to find out what the hell is going on!" Tina ended triumphantly.

"How did you get in, anyway?" James asked her curiously.

"Yeah, we're going to have to come up with a Plan B," Sophie said, giggling. James pouted, and she just shook her head and laughed. "Maybe Mario's answers can help us decide if we need to wait or not. We will not be able to stay here for much longer, though," Sophie warned. "They will catch on that it's a false trail, and come back for you guys. We need to be gone before then."

"Do you think my parents are alright?" James asked, out of the blue. Sophie rushed to his side and gave him a hug.

"I'm sure of it," Sophie whispered in his ear.

"Did you tell her about the bag?" Tina asked.

"What bag?" Sophie asked, looking into his pained eyes.

"Dad left this for us," James said, grabbing the backpack and dumping the contents onto the bed. Sophie saw the mini laptop, burner phones, passports with empty photos, and cash in various currencies. She was impressed.

"Why did he have this?" Sophie asked, out of pure curiosity.

"Said he learned from your dad," James shrugged.

"Makes you wonder if they knew we would all cross paths," Ben said, out of nowhere again. Sophie looked at James. Was fate on their side, or did her parents know this would happen all along? Or maybe a bit of both? She learned not to question when it came to people crossing her path. Everything happened for a reason. And her reason was the three people standing with her now.

"Well, we still have to get food in and out of the room without Frick and Frack noticing," Ben said with a frown. "Room service is too obvious, and we can't have Sophie starving to death if she's to be kicking ass from here on out," he said, putting his hands on his hips like his wife. James was right. Too much of Tina was merging into Ben, and he wasn't sure how good that was right now. Ben chuckled to himself at the thought of wearing an apron and baking while he waited for his wife to come home from work.

"Focus," Tina smirked. She wasn't sure where his head had gone, but it was clearly off course, as usual. She loved him for it, though.

"We should probably get supplies today, just in case," Tina said with authority. "It may be our last day here. What do we need?" she asked, turning to Sophie.

Sophie made a list based on the contents of the backpack, and the things James had already been collecting for Tina without her knowing. "I knew I kept you for a reason," Tina said, kissing his cheek. James shifted uncomfortably, although he knew Sophie wouldn't mind. Tina was the little sister James never had. Nothing more. "We'll have to split up. Whoever they don't follow will get the food," Tina ordered. They all nodded and agreed with the tasks at hand, while Sophie unintentionally pouted.

James bit her bottom lip lightly and kissed her mouth passionately. "No pouting," he breathed.

"It's just really hard to stay here and do nothing," Sophie whined.

"You will not be doing nothing, Babe," James assured her. "You'll be coming up with Plan B while we're gone," he winked at her. Sophie smiled and grew excited with her own secret mission. Climbing the side of the building was definitely out. It would still be too noticeable this early in the evening, and Sophie was unsure of James' scaling abilities. She chuckled at the thought of him hanging outside the window, and begging for her to reconsider. The trio left to grab the supplies, and Sophie got to planning.

Tina knew Ben would get sensible snacks to keep them fueled for the next couple of days. He was a doctor in training, after all. She also knew the odd couple couldn't pass up trying to figure out what she was looking for at the library. Tina needed to make one last stop there. The brunette would volunteer to follow her crush, James, and the short one would protest, because he couldn't stand the library. But Tina hadn't found what she was looking for yet. "Go on," she said to Ben and James. "I have to get something from the library before I forget." They exchanged curious looks, but the boys just shrugged and headed south. "I'm going to grab some snacks to keep in the room. I can only eat hotel food for so long," Ben said, showing his disgust. He really was a talented actor. James would have to remember to give him a lot more credit next time. He laughed at his friend and shook his head.

"I guess I'll just shop by myself," James pouted, knowing he would be stuck with the brunette. He wondered if he would have as much luck getting data as Ben had with the brunette's stout partner. Probably not. She was definitely harder to crack, but James might have to throw her a bone. Maybe he could let her buy him lunch. It didn't hurt to try…he thought with a smug smile on his face. James quickly got to work collecting things that didn't look like they mattered when put together but would make all the difference in the world.

After an hour, with his mission complete, James began to lazily browse the book section, looking for something that Sophie might like to read. Outside of *Anne of Green Gables*, he didn't really know what she liked, but he wanted to try all the same.

"Oh, a reader, are we?" the brunette asked in her thick, fake Spanish accent. She was clearly at least bilingual, but she was trying way too hard to make it obvious.

"Kind of," James said, not paying her much attention. He had Sophie on his mind. But then again, James always had Sophie on his

THE KEY

mind.

"Anything in particular?" she asked, batting her lashes at him.

"Not really. What do you suggest?" James asked, suddenly turning to her and throwing her off her game.

"What?" she said, more in an American accent than she intended to.

"I need a recommendation. What do you recommend?" James asked, giving her his best boyish smile. "That is, if your husband wouldn't mind," he said gently.

"Oh, um, of course not," she said, trying to regain her composure. "I'm more of a mystery kind of girl," she said, her accent sounding more authentic. "This one's not bad," she added, pulling one out for him. James skimmed the back cover, but thought Sophie had enough mystery and drama in her life. She didn't need to read about it too.

"What about a romantic comedy?" James asked, deep in thought. She stared blankly at him, unsure of what was happening. "Don't tell anyone, but I'm actually a hopeless romantic," he added for good measure. "I know I just got my heart severely broken, but I can't help but wonder if my Mrs. Right isn't waiting for me," James said smiling, as he thought of Sophie lying in bed, naked, waiting for him to come ravish her.

"Oh, well, I did like this one," she said, grabbing another one off the shelf. "It makes you laugh at the main character, because she's trying so hard to find Mr. Right. All this chaos happens to her, but the man that's perfect for her is right in front of her the entire time," she said with her actual accent, and getting lost in James' blue eyes.

"You know," James said with a smile, "I think I will try it," he said, making a mental note not to tell Sophie the brunette helped him pick it out. "You're much more attractive when you're not trying so hard," James said, as an afterthought, while he went to pay for the book. She blinked in shock, then quickly raced up beside him. "Your husband is a very lucky man," he added, winking at her.

"He's not really my husband," she confessed, and covered her mouth with her hand.

"Well, that makes it easier to buy your lunch then," James said smoothly. Apparently, he was a better actor than he thought. "Come on," James said with a smile. "You pick. Just not Mario's. I can't eat there again today," he said honestly. She smiled and asked for Mexican. So, they headed to Chevy's for lunch. He was just getting data, James told himself, although the guilt made his stomach too weak to eat anything.

Tina sat down and pulled out her notes. There was something missing. She just couldn't put her finger on it. Her notes were written in her own personal shorthand, so she knew it was safe to leave them out. Tina paced the aisles and fingered the dusty scientific books stacked around her. But the stout partner didn't take pictures of Tina's notes like she expected him to. Instead, he walked up to her and smiled. "Can you help me?" he asked politely in a thick Russian accent.

"Um," Tina said, completely thrown off. "I can try."

"I'm not much of a book person, myself, but I think I need help," he said with a depressed face. "My assignment is almost up, and I need

THE KEY

to do something special so my wife knows I love her."

"Have you tried telling her?" Tina asked, confused. Granted, the odd couple had already proven they weren't the brightest of the bunch, but she didn't quite see what the point of this game plan was.

"Me not so good with words," he said, looking down at the floor. "And I might not get another chance to tell her," he added, defeated.

"Wow," Tina said, surprised that her heart strings were being pulled for this stranger that had the job of spying on them. "You've loved her for a while, haven't you?" she asked softly.

"Yes, and talking to your husband last night made me realize if I don't tell her now, she will never know, but I'm afraid," he said, with his eyes tearing up.

If this was some back story, he definitely deserved an Oscar. Something told her he was being honest. "Well, I have some work to do of my own, today," Tina said, watching his face fall even more. She sighed, giving into her suddenly aching heart.

"Do you know the thing that always gets me about my husband?" she asked. The stout man looked up at her eagerly. "He may not always use the right words at the right times, but he always does a ton of little things throughout the day to make sure I know how much he cares," she offered honestly.

"Like what?" the man asked with full interest. "Flowers?"

"Not just flowers," Tina said with a smile. "One day, while I was at work, he bought Post-its and put love notes on them. He stuck them all around the house for me to find, like behind cabinet doors, the bathroom mirror, and the nightstand," she added for clarification. "He draws me bubble baths with candles and soft music after I've had a long hard day," Tina said, remembering all the times Ben was waiting for her to come home, even after he had a long day at the hospital. "But he does the simple things, like massaging my feet at the end of the day, cooking dinner, putting notes in my lunches, telling me to 'Have a Great Day', and things like that," Tina said, winking at him. She suddenly realized that Ben didn't deserve to be in the doghouse nearly as bad as she did and made a mental note to prove that to him for the next several months. No matter if they were on the run or not.

"What are you working on?" he asked suddenly, and she remembered that he still had a job to do, even if he was in love with his partner and she had no clue.

"A puzzle," Tina said vaguely.

"Are you close to solving it?" he asked cautiously.

"No," Tina said honestly. But she was going to, she promised herself.

"Well, you helped me. I can help you," he offered with a smile.

"Thank you, but I've got this," Tina said sweetly. "It's the challenge that makes it fun," she whispered, adding for good measure, before she went back to browsing the dusty books on both sides of her.

"Offer still stands," he smiled and nodded. Tina watched him ask the desk clerk for some paper and a pen. He chewed the end of the pen, deep in thought, and wrote himself some notes. Occasionally, he looked up to check on her, and smiled while giving her a thumbs up.

What an odd little man, Tina thought to herself. Then, unexpectedly, she was heartbroken, unsure of his fate with his current boss. Hopefully, his dream would come true before they killed him. Tina would send good thoughts his way all the same.

THE KEY

The trio returned to a relieved Sophie. Tina was extra chipper. "Had a good day?" Sophie laughed at her friend.

"Very," Tina smiled, and hummed as she surprised Ben with a passionate kiss out of nowhere.

"Wow," Ben breathed when she came up for air. "What was that for?" he asked cautiously.

"All the little things," Tina said, shrugging, and headed to the bathroom to get ready for their date.

"Well, she's in a good mood," James laughed.

"Sssshhh!" hissed Ben. "Don't jinx me, Bro!" he begged.

"I got what you asked for," James laughed, shaking his head as he dumped out the contents of his backpack. "And I got you this," he said, tossing the book to Sophie, who was sitting on Tina and Ben's bed.

"Oh?" Sophie said, with a raised eyebrow.

"You said you like books," James said, second-guessing himself. "I know you were cooped up alone today, but next time, you'll at least have something to read," he said, staring at the floor while regretting his decision.

Sophie jumped up and gave James his own passionate kiss, and James' knees went weak. "Thank you," she breathed, when she came up for air.

"I should have picked up two," James said, catching his breath.

Sophie giggled and his heart skipped a beat. For the first time in his life, since being left at the altar, he wanted to listen to that laugh forever. He wanted a ring to put on her finger.

"Where are you going to take Tina tonight?" Sophie asked Ben, breaking James' train of thought.

"Not Mario's," Ben laughed. "Ideas?"

"I saw a really fancy restaurant a block from Chevy's today at lunch," James offered.

"You went to Chevy's for lunch?" Ben asked with a raised eyebrow.

"Well, I couldn't shake the stupid brunette, so I took her to lunch instead," James said, annoyed that Ben had brought it up at all.

"The brunette, again?" Sophie asked, with a hint of jealousy in her voice. She couldn't help it.

"Just to collect data," James said firmly to assure her. "She's an agreeable person once she stops trying so hard, but my heart and soul is already taken," he added bluntly and staring into Sophie's eyes. Sophie knew she had no need to be jealous, but it didn't make her like the brunette any more.

"And what data did you collect," Sophie said, crossing her arms and taunting him.

James laughed and shook his head. "Nothing terribly useful," he said with frustration. "I guess you win the Oscar, Ben," he said in defeat.

"How long was lunch?" Sophie tried to sound casual.

"An hour or so," James said. "But it was hard to focus when I was thinking of you the whole time. Probably why I'm no good at getting data," he said with his boyish grin and walking towards her. "Can't keep my head in the game," he shrugged and kissed her passionately to return the favor.

THE KEY

"Still in the room," Ben said in disgust.

"Then go get ready for your date," James offered.

"You're in *MY* room," Ben pointed out.

"Shall we?" James said, holding his arm out for Sophie. She giggled and took it while they walked to their own room.

"So, seriously," Sophie continued, "what all did you talk about?" The curiosity was killing her. "She probably told you more than you think," she added for good measure. James quickly recapped his lunch for her, leaving out the fact that the brunette had picked out the book for him, of course. Sophie dissected the conversation in her head, but saw nothing clearly yet. It doesn't mean it wasn't useful. It just didn't fit quite yet. "It's going to be a late night, tonight," Sophie said, suddenly changing the subject. "We'll have to wait until after the bar closes," she said, deep in thought.

"Naptime then?" he asked, smiling coyly.

"Well, maybe not quite yet," Sophie said, as the heat and electricity brewed from her core.

"Good, cause I'm not sure I can sleep, just yet," James said, looking into her eyes with heat and desire.

"We'd better do something about that then, huh?" Sophie offered, as her chest rose and fell rapidly with anticipation.

"Probably," James said, getting up to lock the adjoining door. He pulled his shirt off as he walked to the bed, exposing his rock-hard muscles that were crying desperately to be freed. Sophie gulped and bit her bottom lip. "You're killing me, Smalls," James growled, as he jumped on the bed to take her mouth with his.

James set his alarm to make sure they didn't oversleep. It was 2 a.m. and the streets were almost a ghost town down below. "So how are we getting out of here?" James asked curiously.

"You're going through the front door," Sophie smiled reassuringly. "I'll meet you outside," she winked.

"And how are *you* getting out of here?" James asked with a chuckle, full of interest.

"If I told you, I'd have to kill you, and I'm kinda partial to you at the moment," Sophie said with her Cheshire smile.

"Remind me to stay on your good side," James laughed.

"Will do," Sophie winked, shoving him towards the door once he was dressed. "Now get going!" she hissed.

"Come find me," James said in a hushed tone, and kissed her gently.

"I always do," Sophie said, catching her breath as he parted from her. He gave her one last look and snuck out the front door quietly. Sophie put the backpack on the bed and removed the vent cover from the wall. She climbed in quietly, pulled the backpack inside with her, and replaced the vent cover using hooks on the inside. Anyone on the outside who might come in wouldn't suspect that someone had removed it at all. Sophie quietly made her way through the vent system to the alleyway. No one was waiting for her, so she dropped like a cat, landing gracefully on her feet. Sophie waited to make sure no one was tracking James. Apparently, the odd couple was taking the night off. Sophie kept her distance as she followed James to

THE KEY

the back door of Mario's.

The alleyway was pitch black, narrow, and smelled of a mixture of cigarette smoke and garbage. A couple of hunter green dumpsters laid just outside of the back door, overflowing with trash bags. Trash day was clearly coming up. A flickering street lamp did little for making one feel safe while being back there. It was the perfect cover to sneak in without being noticed by any passerby.

Mario had already locked the door in order to close up in peace. Sophie picked the lock quickly and opened the door. "Is there anything you can't do?" James asked in awe.

"We have a lifetime to figure out," Sophie said, winking at him and sliding inside first. James closed the door quietly behind him.

"Do you think he'll be mad we came?" James whispered.

"No," Mario replied. "He'll just kick your ass for it," he said, determined. Sophie immediately pushed James out of the way and blocked the fast swing that came from the end of Mario's fist. He continued to swing at the hooded black figure, but she blocked his every attempt. So, Mario ducked and did a spin kick on the floor, knocking the hooded figure back a few steps, but not fully down. "Game on," Mario said with a wicked smile. Sophie smiled under the hood that covered her face, took stance, and waved him to come for her.

It had been a while since Mario had been in a fight, but his body hadn't forgotten how. He came at the hooded figure swinging, kicking, and pushing any reachable objects at them as he forced them backwards up against the wall. The figure was oddly being cautious not to fight back. Mario wasn't sure why. Had they not come for him?

James watched in amazement at Sophie's control to block

everything Mario threw at her, without even giving a single punch back in return. He watched Sophie run up the beam next to her in order to get her back free from being pinned against the wall. Pride grew in James' chest until Mario grabbed a pipe within reach, and held it up like a weapon. "No!" James yelled, but Sophie held up her hand and signaled him to be quiet.

She continued to duck Mario's swings, and jumped the low blows, until she came across a pipe of her own. Sophie twirled it a few times, testing its weight. She held it in the air behind her, took stance, and waited for Mario's move.

Suddenly, it was like watching a sword fight with pipes, as each opponent swung at each other, occasionally hitting a supporting beam or wall when they missed. James knew Sophie was in control, but it didn't stop the fear and panic swelling from within his chest.

Mario had managed to knock the pipe from Sophie's hands. She didn't even look at it as it fell to the ground. She took a couple of steps backwards with her hands in the air. "Nice try," Mario said in triumph. But when he charged Sophie with the pipe, she simply grabbed onto it, swirled around, and had it pointing at Mario's chest with his body pinned to the wall. "Enough!" Sophie yelled, and took the hood off her head.

"Sophie?" Mario asked, unsure if it was really her.

"Hello, old friend," she said with her Cheshire smile.

Mario pushed the pipe away from his chest and pulled her into his arms. "What the hell?!" he exclaimed.

"I need your help," Sophie said, soaking in the familiar warmth and smell of whiskey and cigars.

Mario pulled back to study her thoroughly. She still had the

THE KEY

splint on her wrist, but her ribs were fully healed. "What happened?" he said disapprovingly, seeing the splint on Sophie's wrist.

"Simon," Sophie shrugged, and put the pipe down on the bar.

"He's going to pay," Mario sneered.

"He already has," Sophie assured, patting his shoulder and walking around to sit at the bar. James came out of the shadows, and sat down next to her.

"I wasn't sure what was going on when I saw you. You didn't give me much to work with," Mario said in a fatherly tone.

"Well, I kind of got hit by a van and forgot some stuff," Sophie said casually. Mario's body tensed up instantly. "I'm getting it back," she assured, "but I do still have some sizeable holes," Sophie whispered. Mario stood behind the bar and made a Malibu Rum and pineapple for Sophie, and cracked some beers for James and him. When he slid the drinks over to them, Sophie noticed a face that she had seen only in her dreams, looking back at her.

"Why do you have a picture of my mother on your wall?" Sophie asked, completely confused and forgetting her original questions.

Mario turned around and grinned fondly at the photo before turning back to Sophie. "Your mother and I go *WAY* back," he said with a smile. "Before your dad, of course," he quickly added, so she knew he hadn't betrayed her.

"You came and got me out of the closet," Sophie said in a daze.

"That I did," Mario said, with a troubled heart. "From the day you were born, I was the unofficial Godfather. Jess made me promise to always keep you safe, even if she couldn't," he said, staring at the floor. They could hear the heartbreak in his voice.

"What happened after that night?" Sophie asked softly.

"How much is missing?" Mario asked cautiously.

"Most of it, I'm afraid," Sophie said, frustrated.

"Well," Mario said, sitting down. "The instructions were to keep you moving, and have you trained by your mother's most favorite teachers," he sighed. "But there were no instructions once you turned eighteen. Just a letter left to you, from your parents, that you read by yourself. Then, you told me you would come back to me when it was safe. I haven't seen you since," Mario said, giving her a weak smile.

"We traveled the world," Sophie said slowly, as the images of various countries flew in front of her eyes. Each memory had Mario at her side.

"That, we did," Mario said, observing her.

"I learned all sorts of things," Sophie said as an afterthought, as visions of Sophie at various ages of training circled around her. So much training. From fighting, to books, to taking machinery and guns apart, only to put them back together again. Hot wiring cars, gymnastics, driving, computers, and anything else imaginable. Mario being horrified to buy Sophie her first tampons. He helped her cut and dye her hair over the years. He held her when she cried herself to sleep. He cooked her meals and taught her how to fend for herself in any environment. He took over the role of both mother and father as she went through her awkward teenage phase. He had kept her safe for so many years.

"That, you did," Mario said gently. "Although, you gave the Monks a run for their money when they taught you meditation," he laughed at a fond memory that Sophie couldn't see herself.

"And you don't know where the letter is?" Sophie asked,

THE KEY

confused.

"Ashes in a fire somewhere in Sweden, and long gone, I assume," Mario said, eyeing her.

"Well, that's not helpful," Sophie grunted in frustration.

"What are you looking for?" Mario asked, curiously.

"The key Dad gave me," Sophie said, looking at him with sudden hope. "Dad made some sort of key, and the man with the cane wants it. I have to find it first. Only I can't remember where I put it," Sophie said in a rush, and crossing her arms while looking at Mario for the answer.

"Sorry, Kid," Mario said with dismay. "I don't know about any key. You were my only objective. Your mother didn't tell me anything more." He noticed she had said "man with the cane" and nothing more. Sophie clearly had more remembering to do, but he kept it to himself.

"What did my mother do?" Sophie asked, putting her hands on the bar and leaning in with full curiosity.

"Special ops," Mario said, leaning back on the counter behind him and crossing his arms. "Mostly for the government," he said with a smile. "We met in Vietnam, long before you were ever a thought," Mario said, obviously seeing Jess in his mind. "It was our first job together."

"What happened?" Sophie asked, putting her elbows on the bar and holding her chin in her hands.

"Your dad," Mario chuckled. "One look at her, and he fell for her hook line and sinker, like everyone else she crossed paths with. But it was your dad who actually captured your mother's heart." Sophie smiled, and her heart warmed hearing about her parents. "I had already left the government. But for your dad, your mom wanted to give up everything, and be a homemaker for the wacky scientist who stole her heart," Mario said, smiling.

"So, she gave up everything for him?" Sophie asked in awe. James studied the picture behind them. Mario was 20 years younger and had his arm around a woman who could have passed for Sophie's twin. Neither of them had a job to give up, but James wondered if Sophie would choose him like her mother chose to be with her father.

"It was complicated," Mario frowned. "She was doing odd jobs out of obligation, but her boss wasn't ready to let her quit cold turkey."

"The man with the cane?" Sophie asked out of nowhere.

Mario nodded and hurried on. "He bought out the company your father was working for and started making Jack develop things that hurt others without his knowledge," he said in annoyance. "But then you were born, and everything changed," Mario said with a smile. "Your mother stopped cold turkey, your dad quit his job, and they were going to move away and live happily ever after," Mario said, as his smile faded. "The old man said if Jack did one more job, then they could go, but Jack found out that his work was hurting others and refused to continue. Your mother never said, but I'm pretty sure the old man threated to take your life if Jack didn't finish the work. But the man with the cane started to take too much interest in you, so Jack started working on another project instead…you."

James took his eyes off the photo and looked at Mario with concern. Sophie dropped her hands onto the bar. "Your mother started training you, and your father made arrangements in case something went wrong," Mario, again, continued on quickly. "Jack only told me what I was supposed to do until you turned eighteen. I think he believed your mother would still be with you, but your mother had

THE KEY

plans of her own," Mario said, looking at the floor and gulping away the lump in his throat. "She was busy contacting all of her old contacts to help us stay safe until you became an adult. Jess would never leave Jack to die alone," Mario said, as his eyes filled with tears.

"Jack left us the money and paperwork, and your mother left information on where to take you and when," he shrugged, turning away to grab another beer so Sophie wouldn't see his tears fighting to fall. "They instructed me to give you the sealed letter when you turned eighteen, and so I did," Mario said, opening the beer. "You never told me what it said. You just kissed me on the cheek and said goodbye. But you would come get me once it was safe. So, I was very confused to see you walking in with the Moore boy and his friends," Mario said, nodding in James' direction.

"How do you know me?" James asked suddenly.

"You were coming to my bar before you could walk properly with your dad," Mario chuckled. "I know all of my regulars," he said, winking at him.

"Well, it's still not safe, unfortunately," Sophie said in defeat. "And now I've lost whatever this key is supposed to be, so I can't stop the man with the cane," she said with frustration. "I'm sorry to give you false hope," Sophie said, suddenly looking at Mario with guilt.

"Don't worry about me, Kid," Mario winked at her. "What better way to hide an asset than in plain sight, as an old fuddy duddy bartender," Mario chuckled and sipped his beer. "I'm not worried," he shrugged with a smile. "But your mom's favorite phrase was, 'Home is where the heart is' if that helps," Mario said, nodding at the heart shaped necklace that hung around Sophie's neck.

Sophie looked down at the necklace and back at Mario. "So I've been told," she said sarcastically, knowing the necklace held the answer. She just needed to find out how.

"You need to get going," Mario warned. "The darkness has eyes too," he said, looking around.

Sophie nodded in understanding. "Stay safe, old friend," she whispered, as she got up and kissed Mario on the cheek, making him turn a rosy pink.

"You too, Kid," he said, as his eyes filled with water again, and he promptly blinked it away. "Take care of her," Mario whispered, as James passed him, in a fatherly concern.

"Trying my best, Sir," James said as he patted Mario on the shoulder, and left him standing alone to finish his beer. Mario stood in the empty bar remembering the greatest love he ever had who was lost to a wacky scientist he came to call his friend.

Twenty-three

"What did you find out?" Tina whispered in Sophie's ear, shaking her gently.

"That I need more sleep," Sophie mumbled, and pulled the covers over her head.

"But I've waited all night to hear!" Tina whined.

"And you were sleeping while you were waiting," Sophie growled.

"Let the girl sleep!" Ben hissed at Tina as he pulled her away from the bed.

"But it's almost 8 a.m.," Tina said, pouting.

"So, let's go get some breakfast, and let them tell us when they get up," Ben sighed as he tried pulling Tina out of their room.

James reached over and grabbed the notebook on the nightstand, and threw it at his friends, signaling them to leave. "Go!" he shouted.

"Fine," Tina grumbled, and stuck her tongue out at them both before stomping away.

"I'll buy you as much time as I can," Ben said apologetically as he left. James and Sophie snuggled into each other to grab some more sleep.

"I will never forget to lock that door, again," James teased as he sipped on his coffee and found his humor after having another hour of sleep.

"No one said you had to wait to come tell us," Tina retorted stubbornly.

"I did!" Ben said, rolling his eyes at his wife. Sophie walked around the room, rubbing the necklace between her fingers as she paced. James recapped their evening while Tina tapped her fingers impatiently on the desk she was sitting at.

"Of course, home is where the heart is!" Tina shouted, throwing her hands up into the air. "How is that helpful?" she grumbled, crossing her arms in frustration.

"Maybe the key isn't the necklace," Ben offered. "Maybe it's at her childhood home?"

"No," Sophie said with certainty. "The necklace is the key."

"Maybe the lock is at the old house?" Tina asked, sitting up with sudden inspiration.

"I don't think so," Sophie said, as she continued to rub the necklace. "That would be too easy to find."

THE KEY

"Not if they didn't know what the lock looked like," James suggested.

"That's true," Tina agreed. "Could explain why you never went back."

"So could the graphic murder of my parents," Sophie snorted, and continued walking around. She was missing something. She just didn't know what. Everyone else was staring at the floor. Sophie stopped, realizing that just because she had come to some sort of terms with her parent's death, it still made everyone else feel sorry for her. "I'm sorry," Sophie said. "I was just trying to lighten the mood," she said with guilt.

"What if it is at the house?" Ben asked, trying to get everyone back on track.

"They would watch the house, and expect me to return," Sophie said, as she started pacing the room again. Something was missing.

"Even after all of these years?" Ben asked, shocked.

"It would be the first place I would expect you to return to," Tina confirmed.

"My mother went to extensive measures to make sure that I was trained to take on anything thrown at me," Sophie thought out loud. "Which means she would expect me to keep it on me at all times to ensure its safety…" her voice trailed off as she took off the necklace. "What if home *was* where the heart was, and it's not the necklace that is the key, but it holds the key?" Sophie said, ending in a whisper, deep in thought.

"Like inside the heart?" Tina asked, standing up, and taking the necklace from Sophie to get a closer look. "But there's no kind of opening," Tina stated, as she turned it over repeatedly with her fingers.

"Maybe you have to make one," James said, standing behind Tina, and looking over her shoulder.

"We would have to be careful," Tina said, deep in thought. "If something is inside, then we don't want to damage it."

"But won't opening it, damage it?" Ben said, with something else weighing heavy on his heart.

"I think the key is a little more important, Babe," Tina said in dismay.

Ben grabbed her by the elbow and pulled Tina aside. "That's the last and only thing she has from her parents," Ben whispered, full of concern in Tina's ear.

"Oh," Tina stopped immediately. She had never lost anyone close to her, but Sophie had been on the run since she was ten. She has no photos, no family, and nothing to remember them by, besides the necklace Tina now held in her hand and intended to destroy. "We'll find another way," Tina said, handing the necklace back to her at once.

"What?" Sophie asked in confusion.

"Ben made an excellent point," Tina said slowly. "We shouldn't destroy the last thing your parents gave you until we know for sure it's worth destroying."

James assessed the situation, and straightaway understood what Tina meant. "Yeah, Babe," he added, putting his hand on Sophie's lower back. "We'll find another way," he assured.

"Maybe like a scan of some sort!" Ben interjected.

"No," Sophie said stubbornly. "We need to open it!"

"Sophie," James said, stepping in front of her, and brushing the hair from her face, "do you realize that this is the last thing you have to remember your parents by, and it will most likely get destroyed if we

THE KEY

try to open it?"

"I get that, but..." Sophie started.

"But your new family doesn't want to be responsible for taking the last memory of your original family from you," James said gently, before kissing her on the forehead. "We'll find another way," he added.

"What if we're not meant to destroy it?" Tina asked, looking at Sophie sideways.

"What do you mean?" James asked.

"Sophie's dad was a scientist," Tina said, walking towards Sophie. "What if the heart is just the case, and the key is actually inside, like Sophie said? What better way to hide the key if someone happened to get it from her?" Tina stated, deep in thought.

"Then what opens the case?" Sophie asked.

"If I wanted to keep it safe, I would make sure it wasn't something obvious, but still easily accessible," James offered with a shrug.

"So, what's something not obvious, but easily accessible?" Ben asked.

"Sophie..." Tina said in a whisper.

"What?" Sophie asked, staring at her.

"You. You're the something not obvious but easily accessible!" Tina exclaimed.

"I don't understand," Sophie said in confusion.

"You have to hold on to it, because you're the only one that can open it!" Tina said excitedly.

"But I don't know how," Sophie said in frustration.

"Voice activation?" James asked Tina.

"No, our voices can change as we age. It's too risky," Tina said, rubbing her chin with her thumb and index finger, deep in thought. "It would have to be something that would never change, no matter how old you got," she said, frowning.

"So, what doesn't change as you age?" James asked, getting frustrated.

"Fingerprints," Ben said, quietly to himself.

"What?" James asked, turning to his friend.

"Think about it," Ben said, taking Sophie's hand into his and showing off her fingers. "Your fingertips stay the same, from the time you're born to the time you die. They're durable and unique to the individual, which really means only Sophie could open it," he said with a triumphant smile.

"I knew I kept you around for a reason," Tina said, smiling and kissing him on the cheek.

"But I've rubbed it constantly without it opening," Sophie stated.

"That's because it's like taking a picture of a moving target," Ben said. "You would just have to find the right combination that your father used to set up the lock. It's like a touch-tone phone or keypad. It has to register however many points of recognition that your dad set up, and with fingerprints, it can be as little as three to as many as a million."

"Well, at least that's something that can be worked on whether we stay or go, which we need to decide to do sooner than later," James said.

"I vote go," Tina said.

"Yeah, I'm kinda maxed out, myself," added Ben. "Sophie found us, and I don't enjoy waiting here like sitting ducks."

THE KEY

"They're right," Sophie said bluntly. "The longer we stay, the sooner they will figure out that the trail is a fake and come back here. It's easier to travel at night," she added.

"Then make sure we have everything we need before we go," James said with authority. "We don't know when we will have an opportunity to shop again." Sophie began trying different patterns with her fingers as the rest determined what else they might need.

Ben and Tina went on a last run for supplies, and James stayed behind with Sophie. After several hours of trying, Sophie was maxed out on ideas and full of aggravation. She took the necklace and threw it across the room, but James caught it midair and put it back on her.

"Easy, Slugger," he said gently. "We still need this, I think."

"It does no good if I can't figure out how to open it!" Sophie grunted, while crossing her arms and sticking out her bottom lip.

"Don't pout," James said with his boyish grin, and bit her bottom lip before kissing her passionately. "It's too distracting," he added honestly. "I think we need a break."

"And what do you suggest?" Sophie said with a Cheshire smile.

"As much as I enjoy that, I think we need something a little more subtle," James laughed.

"I guess," Sophie sighed heavily.

"Come on," James laughed, pulling her into the bathroom. "Strip," he ordered.

"Didn't you just say we're not doing that?" Sophie asked, confused.

"Trust me," James smiled. "Strip," he repeated.

She undressed while James filled up the tub with warm water. He added some of the bubble bath provided by the hotel and dimmed the lights. Sophie stood naked, covering herself and watching him with curiosity. He went into the bedroom and grabbed his cellphone. After a few seconds, there was soothing music coming from the speaker. "Get in," James ordered. Sophie just stared at him with confusion. "Come on now," he said, lightly spanking her bottom. She giggled and climbed into the warm bath. James quickly got undressed, grabbed a washcloth, and climbed in behind her. "Close your eyes," he whispered. Sophie obeyed. She felt the warm, wet washcloth being lightly moved in a circular motion on her back. She relaxed immediately and laid her back against his smooth, warm chest.

"Helping?" James asked softly.

"Mmmmhmmm," was the only response Sophie had the energy to muster. James slowly washed her neck, moving slowly over her eager breasts and down her belly. Then he ever so softly traced her body with his fingertips. He felt her body melt completely against him.

"We may not have the ocean, but we can definitely improvise," James whispered against her ear.

"You just wanted me naked in a tub," Sophie grinned.

"Extra bonus," James chuckled. "Now, relax," he ordered. She took in a deep breath and let it out. Her chest rose and fell in time with his, as he continued to gently graze her with his fingertips. She fell deeper and deeper into the darkness until the wooden door appeared in front of her.

"Dad, I need you!" Sophie shouted into the darkness.

"Do you, now?" she heard the familiar voice call back.

"Yes, please!" Sophie begged.

"The door's always open for you, Peanut," he whispered in her ear. She reached out, turned the handle, and was flooded by light and

THE KEY

warmth. Sophie recognized her father's office immediately. Jack was sitting back in his black leather computer chair, humming, and tapping his fingers on the desk while staring at the screen before him.

"What's that song?" little Sophie asked, as she came skipping into the office, studying her father. She looked like she was about five.

"Oh, it's an old song, Peanut," Jack said with a smile on his face. "One of my favorites."

"How does it go?" Sophie asked, full of curiosity and wonder.

Her father smiled his own Cheshire grin, spun the chair around, and began to hum to her his favorite song. Jack stood up and started walking slowly towards her. Little Sophie giggled with anticipation. Jack held out his hand for her to take it. He stood still as little Sophie stepped onto the top of his feet. "So Sophie, will you save the last dance for me?..."

Jack continued to hum as he moved her around the room, dipped her, and then picked her up to spin her around in his arms. Little Sophie giggled with such glee, it made current Sophie laugh herself. Holding the last note longer than the rest, Jack finished with one knee on the ground and the little girl sitting on the other.

"I love this song!" the little girl exclaimed.

"Well," her father said gently, "if you promise to always save the last dance for me, it can be our song," Jack said with a wink.

"Just for us?" the little girl asked eagerly.

"Just for us," Jack assured her. The little girl leaned over and kissed him on the cheek before hopping down.

"How did you meet mom?" the little girl asked out of nowhere.

"Well," Jack said, pausing for effect. "If you ask her, she'll say it was at a convention when we were in college. But the truth of the matter is that we met when we were in high school. She just doesn't remember," Jack said, holding his finger to his lips, showing it was a secret.

He got up and sat back in his computer chair, and the little girl eagerly climbed into his lap to hear his story. "I went to a different school than your mother," Jack started, smiling as he reflected on his memory. "Your mother was very popular, and I was more of a geek," he said, pushing his glasses up his nose for effect. "I played trumpet in the band, and my school visited her school for a competition."

"You play the trumpet?" the little girl asked, sounding doubtful.

Jack just smiled and nodded to the black instrument case in the corner of his office. "I was going to be a musician when I grew up," he chuckled.

"Why didn't you?" the little girl asked.

"I knew if I was ever to get a woman like your mother to fall in love with me, that I needed to be sure I could provide her with everything she would ever want. A musician doesn't make any money," Jack added to her confused facial expression. "And I was really good in science," he shrugged.

"Do you regret it?" the little girl asked, surprising him with how mature she was for her age.

"Nope," Jack said, setting her down. "But I do have to get back to work, Peanut, so go on and play," he said, gently kissing her on the forehead and patting her behind. Little Sophie jumped and giggled as she ran away.

Jack got out of the chair and walked directly over to Sophie. "May I have this dance?" he asked gently, as he bowed before her. A

THE KEY

tear ran down Sophie's cheek as she bowed in return, and once again stepped on the top of her father's feet as she took his hand. It wasn't often she was allowed to actually interact with them in her dreams. Jack held her close as he hummed their song and swayed with her. "You need to get to work, Peanut," he whispered in her ear.

"Just a little bit longer," Sophie begged, as silent tears ran down her cheeks. "I need more time."

"Unfortunately, we don't have it," Jack said, pulling away and wiping her tears from her cheeks. "Come now," he said, gently kissing her on the forehead. "It's time," Jack whispered as he lifted her off his feet and backed away.

"Why is time running out?" Sophie asked in desperation.

"Because he's lost his patience, and he's coming," her dad said with a distraught look on his face.

"They're always coming!" Sophie yelled. "What makes this any different?" But her dad just kept backing away without a word, and Sophie was being pulled out the wooden door.

"Why won't you answer me!" Sophie screamed at him.

"I can't," Jack said, before the door slammed in her face. She jerked her eyes open, and sat up so quickly, water spilled over the sides of the tub.

"Whoa!" James said, grabbing her by the waist and pulling her into his arms. "Easy," he said gently in her ear, while combing her hair with his fingers. Sophie was hyperventilating without even realizing it. She worked to get her breathing back to normal.

"Everything alright?" James asked cautiously.

"I know how to open it," Sophie said, pulling away, splashing water everywhere, and grabbing a towel. James scrambled to follow.

Twenty-four

Sophie quickly dried off and put a bathrobe on. James followed suite. "Gonna give me a hint?" he asked, in full curiosity.

"Not until I know I'm right," Sophie said with a weak smile. James heard Tina and Ben return on the other side of the door.

"You might want to come in here," James said, opening the door for them.

"Eeeewww, we don't need to be *that* kind of couples," Tina said, wrinkling her face in disgust.

"Yeah, Bro," Ben said in horror. "I think the bedroom should definitely be the one thing we keep separate," he said in hesitation.

"Oh stop, Nerds," James said, rolling his eyes. "We were in the bath trying to relax, and Sophie has an idea for opening the necklace," he said, annoyed.

"OH!" Tina exclaimed, and rushed into the room. Sophie had

THE KEY

her eyes closed, trying to focus. She began humming.

"What's she doing?" Ben asked.

"Ssshhh!" Sophie hissed and went back to closing her eyes and humming. Slowly, she started using her thumb on one side and danced her first three fingers to match the rhythm that she was humming. It sounded like a chorus of a song, but no one else could place it. Sophie held the last note a bit longer than the rest, and the necklace began to glow.

"Look!" Tina exclaimed.

Sophie opened her eyes and looked down. The smallest heart on the necklace suddenly had a seam all around it, and the front part separated as if the necklace was suddenly a locket. Within the heart rested a 15 x 11 millimeter black SD card.

"What is that?" Tina asked, coming in for a closer look.

"The key to everything," Sophie whispered, popping it out and handing it to her friend. "Your turn," she said with a smile.

Tina grasped the card and inspected it thoroughly. "Another puzzle," she giggled with glee.

"Only you would find all of this fun," James said, rolling his eyes.

Tina stuck her tongue out at James and turned to Sophie. "Challenge accepted!"

"We will need to be careful where we load it," Sophie warned. "We don't know who's watching what."

Tina laughed, "Not my first rodeo, my friend. Laptop," she said, holding out her hand to James, who looked at her with confusion. "The one your dad gave you," Tina coached.

"Oh," James said puzzled, and went to grab the mini laptop out of the backpack.

"Pretty sure that's why we have this," Tina said, to help everyone with their confusion. She took the laptop into her room and set it on the desk before digging into her own backpack for her secure adaptor.

"Perks of work," Tina smiled, holding it up in the air. She attached the adapter and pushed the SD card in. A couple of black boxes with racing code popped up. Tina began typing away immediately. "Nice try," she said with a wicked smile. They did not know what she was doing, but she was typing like a madwoman in a race to beat the scrolling, rapid coding that was running in front of her. After a few minutes, the screen went completely black.

"Um, Ti," Ben said slowly.

Tina just held up her hand to silence them. "Wait for it..." she whispered. Within seconds, the screen came to life. It was a picture of the Sophie she had seen so many times in her dreams. Then it asked for a password.

Tina turned and looked at Sophie. "Any ideas?"

"Based on the picture, maybe me?" Sophie guessed, but it rejected it.

"Try her mom," James offered, but it also got rejected.

"I'm not sure how many tries we get before we will get locked out. Typically, things are set to three, so we should try to make this one count," Tina warned.

Sophie closed her eyes and saw her dad smiling and nodding in encouragement. "Peanut," she whispered.

Everyone looked at her. "Are you sure?" Tina asked.

"Yes," Sophie said, full of doubt.

THE KEY

"You're the boss," Tina said, turning around to type the word "Peanut" into the computer. Once again, the screen went black.

"What does that mean?" Ben asked, confused and concerned all at once.

"I'm not sure," Tina said with hesitation. It remained black for another minute or two, and they suspected the worst. Then, out of nowhere, the computer jumped to life, window after window popping up.

"What the hell?" James asked, but the windows continued to pop open. Each had various information on it. From reports, to notes, to sketches, to mechanical plans. It took a full twenty minutes before the computer stopped opening multiple windows.

"I think this is going to take us a while," Tina said with a hint of sarcasm.

"We don't have awhile," Sophie reminded them. "And we need to move."

"No problem," Tina said, taking out the SD card and giving it back to Sophie. "I do my best work remotely," she said, winking at Sophie, and started packing up. "We've got this," Tina assured.

"If anyone can do it, it's Ti," James whispered in Sophie's ear.

"Oh, I'm not worried," Sophie laughed. "The man with the cane should, though." She turned around and packed her things as well. Everyone collected their stuff, and Sophie marked out their next moves. She gave a quick lesson on how to move around without being detected. It was important that they kept the upper hand. They waited until the early morning hours before sneaking out of the hotel room and heading for the bus station. Taking the car was too risky. James sold it earlier to the valet attendant with no questions asked, and the four of them raced against time to catch the last bus leaving. No one sat together. Sophie took the seat at the very back of the bus alone. She knew it bothered James having to be by himself, but four people traveling together was a lot more obvious than four people traveling alone. Sophie watched each of them carefully as they rested up on the ride.

    Sophie never expected to have the life she was living. She definitely never expected to be living it with others. Each of them had volunteered to give up their life for her. They had sacrificed everything to help her with a mission she didn't even understand.

    Sophie found her first and only true love and soulmate and gained a brother and a sister she had never had before. Now, she had to do everything in her power to keep them safe from the man with the cane. Their sacrifices couldn't be for nothing.

    Sophie wanted to say goodbye to Mario, but she knew it was way too risky. They had an open-ended relationship, and she would keep her original promise…return once it was safe. Sophie knew they had a four-hour journey, and she would need her rest. She closed her eyes and found darkness. No wooden door, no loving parents, no James and friends. Just a set of elderly hands with a golden ring that tapped impatiently on the end of a gold topped cane….

THE KEY

Did you enjoy this book?

Your feedback helps me provide the best quality books and helps other readers like you discover great books. Please be sure to leave a review.

If you want early access to future books be sure to subscribe to my newsletter at:
https://chasingstormllc.beehiiv.com/

The Sophie Lee Saga

The Key: Book One of the Sophie Lee Saga
The Protector: Book Two of the Sophie Lee Saga
Dead Draw: Book Three of the Sophie Lee Saga
Birth of the Legend: Book Four of the Sophie Lee Saga
Reign of the Raven: Book Five of the Sophie Lee Saga

The Fate vs Foe Novella Series

Fate vs Foe
Family of Blood
Family of Love
Family of Fate

Other Books by Stormi Lewis

Deck the Ex (2026)

The Protector
Book Two of the Sophie Lee Saga

The Protector

"I can't believe you lost her, AGAIN!" screamed Clarice, holding Eddie by his shirt and preventing his feet from touching the ground. For an anorexic looking thing, she had some serious strength in her.

"Stand down!" she heard her father yell from the shadows.

"Edward, here, has lost your 'pet', AGAIN!" Clarice said, through her clenched jaw.

"Stand down," the old man gave a final warning from the shadows. Clarice resentfully put Eddie down.

"Maybe if you stopped sending incompetent people in to get her, we'd have her by now," Eddie growled, while massaging his chest.

"You think you can do better?" Clarice hissed, glaring down over him.

"Edward is correct," the old man said, annoyed. "You really must find better help."

"You always take his side!" Clarice shouted at the darkness.

"Watch your tone, Child," the old man threatened. "And if you didn't let him always be right, I wouldn't have to point it out constantly."

"UGH!" she screamed and stormed off to her quarters. Clarice slammed the door shut behind her. "Little twerp!" she screamed to no one, as she bent down, grabbed the knife hiding on the outside of her ankle, and threw it at the door behind her. It landed square in the middle of Sophie's head. It was a picture of Sophie with her parents at her fifth birthday party. Right before Clarice tried to drown Sophie in the pool.

"You're no better," she muttered to the figure with a knife sticking out of her forehead. Clarice sighed heavily before going to the door and retrieving her knife. She paused to look at Sophie's mother before stomping over to her bed and lying down. She stared at the ceiling and thought about the first time she had met Jess.

Clarice hadn't minded her in the beginning. She even thought they could be friends one day. Jess was kind to everyone, but her heart would be her greatest downfall. Clarice's father made a point to show more interest in Jess, even back then, and made sure Clarice knew her work never could measure up. He always said healthy competition was good for the soul, but it would forever be one-sided with Clarice on the losing end every time. She grunted and rolled on her side.

Clarice remembered the day Jess came in on cloud nine. She was going on and on about some nerd scientist she had met, and declared in front of everyone that she was "in love." Clarice made the same face of disgust that she had made the day she found out. She never understood what Jess saw in Jack, but it made her father furious, and for that, she was glad.

Things grew even worse once Sophie was born and Jess demanded to quit. It was music to Clarice's ears, but her father wouldn't stand for it. He even ordered Clarice to kill the little girl on

THE KEY

her fifth birthday. The sooner the better. Clarice was excited to accept the challenge. Sophie was too smart for her own good, and Clarice was tired of being second best. But Jess had interfered before she could take the child's last breath, forcing her father to re-evaluate. If Jess wasn't willing to be his number one team member, then her daughter would take her place. Clarice would never cross his mind. She never had, so why start now?

A tear rolled down her cheek as she remembered the day she, herself, had announced she was walking away from his business. Clarice gathered the courage to enter his office unannounced. He laughed in her face as if she were a clown performing for the king. "Who would take you?" the old man sneered at her.

"Some people find my skills plenty helpful," Clarice said, putting her hands on her hips in defiance as he sat in his large red leather chair behind his redwood desk.

"Your mother thought the same thing, and look where that got her?" he gave a hard laugh, rolling his eyes, and going back to writing whatever he had been working on.

The image of her father strangling her mother up against the kitchen wall, simply because for the first time in her life, Clarice's mother demanded that he be a father to his children, played clearly in her head. The old man held her high as her feet dangled beneath her, and her hands desperately clawed at the hand that held her neck so tightly. Her eyes were wide and full of fear. They turned red. Her lips swelled up, and she gasped for air. "Got something to say, Child," the old man growled at Clarice, as she stood in the living room at the age of nine, watching the life of her mother leave right before her eyes.

"No, Sir," Clarice responded, knowing if she did, she would be next. Then her mother jerked convulsively before going limp under her father's out-stretched arm. He let go, letting the body slide down the kitchen wall, falling face first onto the hard tile floor. Her eyes still open, but no life left in them. Clarice swallowed, waiting to see if she would be next, but her father just stepped over the dead body and got a beer from the fridge. He eyed Clarice with suspicion, but continued to sip his beer. She stared at her mother's blank expression. Clarice tilted her head to study it, before mimicking it and walking away.

Her father always brought up her mother as a reminder of what he was capable of, but Clarice was already well aware. She had killed, tortured, and hunted for him with the hope to one day be accepted. But that would never be the result. Clarice knew that at twenty-one, and she wanted to be free and find the love that Jess had claimed existed for everyone...even Clarice.

"So, go then," the old man said flatly. "It's not like you're any good here," he shrugged.

Clarice sighed heavily in defeat and turned to leave the office.

"Of course..." the old man teased. Clarice froze immediately.

"Of course, what?" she regrettably asked.

"Of course, someone will have to train the child properly," he said, tapping the pen on his chin.

"Isn't that what your 'pet' is for?" Clarice snide, keeping her back dangerously, facing her father.

"If Jess wants out, I will give her an out," the old man shrugged, but Clarice knew that meant he was going to murder Jess. "But her daughter can take her place, and who better to teach her than you," he provoked.

Clarice knew it was bait. She knew if she didn't leave now, she would never have a life to call her own. This opportunity would never exist again. But her desperate need for her father's approval took over, and Clarice gave him her heart to crush, yet again. It was her sole mission to bring the child in, and make Sophie into the soldier her father desired. Jess had other plans, though, and the mission was becoming more of a pain than Clarice thought it was worth. However, her father would never accept the reality of the situation. His obsession grew with each team's failure. The girl was already in her early twenties, and Clarice was tired and over it. No one was worth chasing for over ten years. Not even this brat.

Sophie evaded every team Clarice ever sent, and she did it with a sickening smile. Although she couldn't blame the girl. Clarice would be doing the same if she was on the winning side of the fight, too. But Sophie wasn't the average girl, either. You didn't need a big fancy doctor degree to notice she was faster than a typical human, genius level intelligence, and God knows whatever else they hadn't uncovered yet. The girl was trouble with a capital T, and she would be her father's downfall. Clarice wondered if there would be a side to choose, which side she would take. She sighed heavily and rolled back onto her back.

Her father never gave her an opportunity to dream of what she wanted to be when she grew up. Only that it would be by his side, like a loyal dog, constantly seeking her master's approval. Her mother had been murdered. Her brother's neck snapped like a twig, with no sign of remorse because he became too "difficult". A dog that was kicked to death, because it barked too loud one day. A sister, gone, for simply wanting something different. Clarice gave her father everything he demanded, but he still couldn't give her any respect or something remotely copying love. But someone like Jess had a husband who adored her and died for her. A daughter that was her world, and would survive it all, while Clarice had no one at all.

Her own father still had a soft spot for Jess after she demanded to be set free. Blood meant nothing to him, especially if Clarice's was spilled in the process of achieving his plans. She closed her eyes and tried to get some rest, but all she found was darkness and a heart that desperately wanted to be loved.

THE KEY

Acknowledgements

The Sophie Lee Saga would never have existed if it hadn't been for several people in my life. My mother, for putting the original seed of writing a fiction book into my crazy head. It was her comment that I later mentioned to Shyera McCollough when I was so desperate to find balance in a world that was quickly spiraling out of control due to the Covid-19 pandemic.

When discussing possible writing topics, I mentioned a story that had been started and never finished in middle school. I laughed, telling her that my mother mentioned that my writing draws people in and I could be like Nora Roberts with a fiction novel. She was immediately invested and insisting that this story needed to be told.

Once a few pages were written, I shared it with my friend, Mario. He insisted it needed to be a saga. I couldn't believe he thought it was going to last that long when it wasn't even a full chapter yet! However, the thought intrigued me way too much to pass it up.

I found myself leaving "Easter Eggs" for what I envisioned to come as Sophie continued her journey. Writing *The Key* allowed me to have another thing to bond over with my father. He was the first to read the rough draft of *The Key* with my mother a close second. Before I knew it, my mother was offering ideas to wrap up the Saga with *The Key* not even being completed yet! Thus, my parents quickly became my creative writing team.

When it was time to get started on *The Protector,* we sat around the dining room table and tossed around ideas and what I was stuck on. It is truly a blessing to have such a supportive team for my current journey. I love that my father is still sending me text messages of their ideas that never stop flowing!

You, my readers, also keep me going. I wasn't sure if you were going to love the story as much as I did, but you eagerly proved me wrong! At first, your excitement was a little overwhelming. It made me want to write an even better second book. I hope you enjoy it as much as I enjoyed writing it.

This story took an unexpected turn, as usual when the story is writing itself. I found myself diving deeper into the world that Jack and Jess remain to keep Sophie safe. The world Algos wants to crumble in order to gain total control of Sophie and her abilities. This new inspiration is thanks to the OG Storm Chaser.

It is a difficult journey to be on when the person who supported you the most is slipping before your very eyes. The woman that never hesitated to tell me how proud of me she was and how much she loved me now has a time clock that seems to be running out quicker and quicker as the days pass. I strongly believe that loved ones never truly leave us when they pass on to another plane, but I wasn't quite ready to be done hearing her stories or praises.

Thus, the dream realm unintentionally grew. Rules became more defined as you meet the Counsel of Death, and learn the ultimate punishment for breaking the rules of this sacred place. Although it has become another battle ground to face off Algos, it was inspired by the beloved OG Storm Chaser. The woman that will always hold my heart, and never be far away, even when the clock runs out. She may never fully understand how much she has inspired this story to grow, but I will always be grateful for everything she is and more.

About the Author

Stormi Lewis writes books—lucky for you, inconvenient for her characters. She's best known for her paranormal fantasy thrillers, **THE SOPHIE LEE SAGA** and the **FATE VS FOE** series, where folklore and bad decisions rarely survive unpunished.

She pleads the fifth on any BookTokers who don't make it out alive, but giving her milk chocolate could save your life. When she's not committing fictional crimes, Stormi advocates for mental-health awareness and lives with chronic migraines.

Stalk her for a change at https://linktr.ee/chasingstormi.

www.ingramcontent.com/pod-product-compliance
Lightning Source LLC
LaVergne TN
LVHW030240250326
834688LV00047B/1737